This is a work of fiction. Names, characters, places
and incidents either are a product of the author's
imagination or are used fictitiously.
Any resemblance to actual persons; living
or dead, businesses, companies, locales,
or events are entirely coincidental.

Cover Design by Alyson Conway

ISBN:0692641475
ISBN-13:9780692641477

1462

South Broadway

KC Decker

Sometimes what you are most afraid of doing is the very thing that will set you free.

Robert Tew

CHAPTER ONE

Broken

How long does it take to break a heart? Moments? Days? Some would argue it takes years to build a love before it could end in heartbreak. Do you factor in the time it takes you to drag your feet, hesitating even after your decision has been made? How about the long silence that follows the shattered heart? Is it your responsibility to help pick up the pieces? How about the amount of time it takes the broken hearted to move on? Does your sense of relief mitigate the depth of love felt by the other person? How about the wasted time spent stalling, resisting that final blow? It leaves the breakup hanging like a guillotine. Should you sugar coat your let-down? Just leave the disillusion to hide the carnage beneath your saccharine words?

All of these questions I ponder while absently staring at the ceiling. I'm lying limply beneath my grunting, thrusting, staggeringly disappointing boyfriend, William. It's a shame really, so handsome and so capable in life, yet so wrong for me.

It's been wrong for months. His tugging down the back of my shirt when I sat forward, lest anyone snatch a glimpse of

1

my exposed skin. He felt this particular act was charming. I thought it possessive and needy.

He also tended to start fights with the men whose gaze lingered on me just a beat too long. He is jealous and wrong for me, yet he's handsome.

I've fallen into that trap many times before; you know the one about judging a book by its cover? In fact, his looks probably bought him an extra few months. Well… that, and my superior avoidance tactics.

However, at this particular moment, he is decidedly less handsome. His overgrown black hair, wet with sweat, is swinging wildly back and forth into and out of his vision.

His breath is tinged with the burnt, sweet smell of last night's whiskey drinks, mingled with sour morning breath. It huffs explosively into my face while I hold my own breath and fight the urge to offer him a toothbrush.

His sweat is dripping on my chest. It beads up along his hairline then streaks his temples in muggy channels. His face contorts, gelling into and out of ecstasy.

He brings his hand away from the bed sheet and takes hold of my nipple; gently, carefully between finger and thumb. This I barely notice, except to register it as annoying.

Sighing, I return to my pondering, as his impending heartbreak looms in the air like a damp mist--a greasy aura.

I hear the front door, not exactly slam, but shut with authority. Once I know William is gone I throw on a t-shirt and some raggedy cutoff sweats.

Admittedly my timing was off, waiting until after the boring, lifeless sex to break up. In my defense, I had lain awake most of the night knowing I needed to end it, but not sure how, or what explanation I should give. It certainly couldn't have been the truth; the way he always smelled like curry or tended to accumulate a sticky film in the corners of his mouth. It also couldn't be the unsure, timid way he touched me, leaving me bored, disengaged and ultimately stymied by his lack of skill.

It couldn't be one of many truths, so I decided it needed to be vague, so as to not hurt his feelings. *I need to focus on work right now*, or, *My life is really complicated*, or, my old standby, *I really just need time to myself for a while; I'm too selfish for a relationship right now*. That one seemed to evoke the fewest questions, and left the guys with a built in reason to be angry or to move on. I was just a selfish person. There. Done. Not super clean, but done.

The authenticity of the statement did, however, settle a little too neatly, like a thrown pebble to the bottom of a murky lake. The selfish label acknowledged, then efficiently swept under the rug, rather than letting it marinate for too long, or wearing it like a badge.

As I strip the sheets from the bed, I feel a genuine sense of relief. Then I carry them like leper's rags out of my room.

I proceed to the kitchen, where the stackable washer and dryer sit aptly behind bi-fold doors.

I walk straight past the Inquisition, and only acknowledge their presence once I have poured a cup of coffee.

"Good morning," I announce, as two sets of eyes follow me from the kitchen. I'm feeling light, with an extra spring in my step--almost peppy, like I don't have a care in the world.

"Is it?" asks my roommate Devin. He sits with a bowl of cereal held before him, spoon suspended in mid-air. The look on his face is perplexed and skeptical of my announcement, having just witnessed Hurricane William blow by him.

"Yes, it is!" I say, triumphantly dropping into the oversized suede chair that sits adjacent to the couch. My thick hair looks as though I've been tumbled in the dryer cycle and I can feel their gazes get heavier and heavier, like wet towels thrown over the shower rod until it begins to sag.

"What's wrong with this one?" Devin's boyfriend Corey asks, and I detect a faint eye roll. Corey is a Marine, with short cropped brown hair, sharp angular features--a warrior bathed in a handsome facade. Between the two of them, he is the voice of reason, the calm behind the storm that is Devin.

Devin, on the other hand, is a free spirit; I've known him since we were kids. At first glance you wouldn't guess either of them gay; they are such rugged, manly guys. They can fix anything, lift anything, program anything; they are just like any other red-blooded American man, well *almost*.

Though Corey looks physically dangerous, he has the kindest, softest soul. Whereas Devin appears sweet, but he is the thinly veiled viper you don't necessarily see coming. He has a heart of gold, but he has been broken in ways that don't scar and don't completely heal either.

Devin has a creative force driving him to greatness. He is a lighting designer. His work is peppered throughout the city, from high society women to restaurateurs and nightclub owners. His client list is lengthy and impressive.

"It's not that anything is *wrong* with him as a person. He's just not for me," I finish lamely, knowing exactly how it sounds. Like I'm some black widow whore, who chews men up and spits them out just because I can.

When the truth is, I am aching for something. Some sort of awakening from my dull relationships maybe. There has to be more out there. My body has simply grown bored and cold. I'm tired of bland men. I need some inspiration. Or a challenge. Or *something*.

"Jessie, you are so predictable. You are so fickle, yet you always choose the same type of guy," Devin says. He knows me better than anyone, so I should listen to him instead of picking at my split ends, but I'm just not in the mood to be called fickle or predictable this morning.

"That's not true," I counter weakly, loving the feel of rich, delicious coffee ebbing down my throat; warm and comforting, not at all naggy or persistent.

Corey, trying to rein in Devin's harshness says, "You *seem* to be attracted to stable, comfortable--"

"Vanilla," Devin coughs out, interrupting Corey. Then sits back with his eyes widened, daring me to object to his appraisal of my trail of ex-boyfriends.

"As I was saying," he gives Devin a pointed glance, then continues, "You need to be challenged by a man, or you start to see him as weak. Then you lose respect for him and grow bored." His eyes are beseeching though he would never push, not like Devin.

"No. She dates boring men, who do boring things and lead boring lives. We have seen it time and time again--"

"Devin stop. Jessie, you can't keep doing the same thing and expect a different outcome," Corey says, sipping his own coffee while resting his hand on Devin's knee to soften his interruption.

"How very cliché of you, and just how do you propose I change my approach?" I challenge, squaring my jaw in anticipation of at least a few rounds, toe to toe before work.

"You need to stop seeking comfort. Step outside your usual boundaries, take some chances," Corey says. His enthusiasm is palpable, and he has a wildly animated expression, urging me to listen.

"Do something crazy," Devin states, as he sets his cereal bowl down on the coffee table then stands up. His cargo shorts are hanging loosely. He hitches them up one hip then stalks off, disappearing into his room.

Lounging back on the couch and rubbing the back of his neck, Corey ventures, "Was William really all that terrible?" He says this as though there wasn't a single thing wrong with William, but mountains of stuff wrong with me for thinking so. He is speaking with a sigh and a patronizing tone one should save for talking to obnoxious children.

"There was no passion, no excitement, no--"

"Fireworks?" Devin interrupts, as he returns with a marketing postcard and slaps it down on the table in front of me. "There are your fireworks!" He sits down heavy, filled with satisfaction then casually drapes his arm across Corey's thigh, as if it were his own personal armrest.

"Listen, Jessie," Corey says, "Passion is nice but it's not sustainable--look at me and Devin. We led our lives before each other seeking passion and excitement instead of *connection*. It was exciting and glutinous, but after a while, the lust fades, and you start to feel empty. You start to seek someone to share your life with. You start to care about their political and religious views instead of how many times they make you cum. Look at us, we aren't swinging from the ceiling fans, in a sexual frenzy all the time."

"Uh, yeah we are," smirks Devin.

"What I'm saying, is that sometimes you need to look beyond what you *think* you want and consider what you don't know you need." He pauses to let that sink in, but Devin quickly derails the point.

"Nope. That is a lovely sentiment, but Jessie needs to be wild and gluttonous. She first needs to experience sexual frenzy

6

and passion before she discounts it." He says this like it makes all the sense in the world and should be obvious to anyone.

"I'm not saying discount passion, I'm saying give it time to grow. I would much rather have the connection you and I share now, rather than all the years of crazed, unbridled, inexhaustible sex. I'm glad my club days are behind me," Corey says, punctuating it with a pointed look at Devin the incorrigible one.

"Me too," Devin says, "But right now she *needs* raw and unbridled--before she finds Mr. Right. She needs fireworks," Devin surmises, nodding to the forgotten postcard before me.

I reach down and pluck it from the coffee table. "1462? Isn't that when Columbus sailed the ocean blue?" I ask, ruffling my brows trying to remember the exact saying. Whispering to myself, as I glance up at the ceiling... *In fourteen hundred sixty-two, Columbus sailed the ocean blue, he had three ships, and left from Spain--*

"It's an address, Jessie! Besides 1492 is when Columbus sailed," Devin says with a disquieted grunt. "Did you learn nothing about that monster in history class?" He says this while tugging on his work boots and swiping the loose hair out of his eyes with an exasperated flick of his hand.

"Wait, are we talking about rape and pillaging? Or an address?" Corey asks, trying to bring a little levity to the situation. He is so good at balancing Devin. I'm not really sure how I managed Devin's grittiness before Corey, but I'm thankful for his intercessions now.

"1462 South Broadway." He stands, feeling proud of himself as if he could solve all of the world's problems if only everyone would listen to him.

"Are we still talking about my love life? I'm confused," I say, trying to steer the conversation back on course. Abandoning my split ends, I reach again for my bulky, stoneware coffee mug.

"Yes," Devin says, smiling broadly, "This is just what you need. You have to push your boundaries--stretch your comfort level." He yells this over his shoulder as he walks into the kitchen to place his bowl and coffee mug in the sink.

"What's there? What's at that address?" I ask, as I take a slow, cautious sip of my coffee. I'm feeling uneasy, like I somehow have been led into a trap.

"It's a … a club," Devin explains, obviously leaving out some important, glaring details as he stands before me, arms folded across his chest.

My eyes widen expectantly, waiting for him to continue. Corey starts laughing then brings his fist in front of his mouth in an attempt to hide his outburst, but I don't miss the derisiveness of the action or the glistening in his eyes.

"A BDSM club!?" he asks incredulously, over-blinking to clear the glee from his eyes.

"Fireworks," Devin winks, then gives me an insightful nod of his head. His hip is cocked as if he has already decided for me.

"Uh, the fireworks I was thinking about are more like sparklers. BDSM is on the atomic level," I say, but all the while I'm put-off that Corey had laughed at the thought, and that Devin thinks me too stodgy and boring to actually go.

"First of all, I'm a professional woman," I say, gearing up to present a litany of reasons why I couldn't possibly go to a BDSM club.

"Most people in the scene are too," Devin counters, and I'm derailed. I look at him with my mouth open, suddenly unable to list my objections.

"I heard they are super selective," Corey says as he rises, all but dismissing the idea. He heads into the kitchen, no doubt to put his and Devin's dishes into the dishwasher.

8

Devin looks at me with a seldom seen, serious look on his face. "Jessie, don't go just to prove us wrong. You need this, so do it for you. Take some risks in life. I personally don't think you will be happy with any man until you discover a little adventure within yourself. You are looking for these guys to excite you, to fulfill something *you* are missing inside. The thing is, no one can do that *for* you. You have to find it on your own," he says as he stands, hitching his shorts up again. "I've got to get to my shop but just think about what I said."

Devin's words follow me around all day like a curse or a looming shadow. They match me step for step, leering--taunting me. Is Devin right? Am I looking for something in a man that I should be discovering within myself? Do the proverbial fireworks need to come from me?

A BDSM club is a mile outside of my comfort zone, but I can't stop re-playing this morning's conversation in my head. It buzzes like a pesky mosquito, incessantly all morning, while I wade through land contracts at work.

By the time my afternoon meetings roll around, the buzz has turned into a palpable feeling. It feels as though I have a weight on my shoulders, like a child is sitting on them to view a parade.

Back at my desk, where I sit staring at the blinking light on my phone that reminds me I have voicemails, it hits me. An epiphany--like a bucket of ice water... *It's not them, it's me. I'm boring. I'm vanilla.* If I want more excitement out of life and my relationships, I need to find it within myself.

9

I've decided my woefully unexciting boyfriends are not the cause of, but rather a symptom of my own tedium. I'm a sapless tree, bored into the earth for a century of dusty existence, to wither away parched and stale.

I tap out a quick text to Devin, "I'm not saying I am, but if I *were* considering 1462, I'd need a lot more information."

CHAPTER TWO
Club

Teetering on my murderously high heels, I approach the address 1462 S. Broadway. I'm surprised to find it in a historical district and marvel at the urban revitalization. All around me is the very definition of metamorphosis. All the battered old warehouses have turned into modern new lofts and trendy restaurants. Boutiques and art galleries are peppered in with the offices and store fronts. The whole vibe is very chic and sophisticated, so the paradox of a looming BDSM dungeon confuses me.

My destination is an old brick building that at one time was an imposing warehouse. Based on the ancient chipping paint, it was once home to the *Fisher Mercantile Co.*

The loft style windows are new, but still have the look of old leaded glass frames, and they stand nearly floor to ceiling. The exterior of the building is a stylish display of urban reinvestment, but the interior remains to be seen. I figure it's probably a dark forsaken underworld, masked by a pretty exterior.

I'm so taken by the chic feel of the neighborhood and the massive pots on the sidewalk that spill over with bright flowers

11

and flowing vines, that I almost walk right past the entrance. The glass door flaunts the address 1462 in white crackling paint.

As I push the heavy door open, I'm met with a gust of air conditioning. The cool air contrasts deeply with the balmy evening, so I am quickly reminded of just how bare my legs are. My short, navy, pleated skirt offers little in the way of coverage.

Devin had carefully orchestrated my outfit to be demure yet undeniably hot. Sober--in a sexy way, from the long coiled strands of pearls around my neck to the 4-inch heels on my cramped feet.

The lobby smells crisply of eucalyptus and is nothing like I expected. It looks more like a lawyer's executive waiting room. There is gallery sized impressionist art adorning the exposed brick walls and elegant leather chairs. It is a dichotomy of worlds; dapper sophistication vs. seedy sex lair.

"Good evening Miss..." A velvety voice greets me, bringing me back to the fact that I am, indeed at a BDSM club and it has yet to be determined if I actually belong here--with or without Devin's coaching.

"Uh, Hayes. Jessie Hayes," I hastily reply, caught off guard, and then silently chide myself for using my real name. She will no doubt recognize me an amateur, rattling off my real name at the first hint of a challenge.

"Wonderful! Miss. Hayes my name is Mrs. Delacroix. How may I help you?" Mrs. Delacroix is an older woman, I'm guessing in her 60's though she is well maintained, to say the least. She is perfectly restored to her earlier years with flawless surgical precision. Her alert brown eyes and smooth forehead speak to her almost certain brow lift. Her eyes are kind and beautifully made up, displaying a voluminous set of false eyelashes. Her mouth is perfectly painted and turned into a warm smile. She's wearing a black pencil skirt and a high-necked yellow silk blouse. I like her immediately, her friendly countenance puts me at ease.

"Well," I say, looking around, "I know I'm at the right address, but I'm not sure I'm at the right plaaaaace," I say, dragging out the last word and giving her a knowing look. This seems like the understatement of the century, but I am determined to step outside of my comfort zone. I need to liven up my mundane life. I'm especially committed to proving to Devin and Corey that I *can* do this. I'm no shrinking violet, I have conquered much harder challenges than this. I have supported myself since I was seventeen and earned a petroleum engineering degree for goodness sake.

Her smile broadens, "Of course you are," she says, "Let's just fill out a bit of tiresome paperwork, shall we?" She walks behind a hulking mahogany desk then returns with a clipboard. She directs me to take a seat in one of the tufted leather chairs then asks, "May I get you a cappuccino?"

"No thank you," I say. I'm way too nervous already to add caffeine to the mix of anxiety and raw determination. I take the clipboard from her and settle into the chair, the cold leather promptly fusing to my bare legs.

"Ok then, I'll just be right here if you have any questions," she says as she settles herself behind the desk, first palming then plumping her sleek dark hair.

The paperwork, after welcoming me to 1462 begins with some glossary style definitions and "Common Principals Guiding the Relationships and Activities at 1462." The first is "ALGOLAGNIA" which is described as achieving sexual pleasure from pain. *Huh,* I think, and then continue. Next is "SAC" it reads, "The scene" can be classified as *Safe, Sane and Consensual.*" Further describing it as coined by David Stein, "To distinguish the kind of S/M he wanted to do, from the criminally abusive or neurotically self-destructive behavior popularly associated with the term *Sadomasochism*."

Subjective as it seems to me, I still drop my initials on the line next to the definition. I figure one can cast a pretty wide net around the terms "Safe" and "Sane" however the "Consensual" part is easier to wrap my head around.

The next definition is "RACK" which stands for "Risk Aware Consensual Kink." This feels a little more authentic to me when describing BDSM, but it still puts an extra gallop in my heartbeat. The definition includes words like "Edgeplay," "Alternative Sex," and "Riskier Behaviors." It closes with the philosophy that risk aware behaviors are not necessarily *Safe*…only *Safer.*

My earlobes start to heat up, and I shift uncomfortably in my chair, peeling my thighs away from the leather and re-crossing them before reading further. The next term is "Consensual, Non-Consent" defined as punishment or rape scenarios.

The next batch of initials follows the *Prohibited Edgeplay* section, which apparently, are the frowned-upon behaviors. "Erotic Asphyxiation or Breath Play," *No problem, Check.* "Fire play" *Check.* "Blood Play" *Check.* "Gun Play" *Check.* "Bestiality" *Gasp, Check.* "Scat" *Check.* And finally "Urolagnia" *Check.* There is an asterisk next to blood play and fire play indicating that they are allowed with prior permission and proper supervision. Yikes.

Feeling equal parts stunned and confused why anyone would want to engage in those acts, I set my pen down to re-evaluate my presence here. I was anticipating fetish wear, nudity and public sex--not cutting, burning and crapping on someone.

I must have radiated my hesitation, because Mrs. Delacroix, with her hands clasped neatly in her lap, says softly, "I would have worried if that section didn't cause you pause Dear."

She nods solemnly as if addressing the more depraved acts as crude and barbaric or unseemly.

I give a nervous laugh and say, "I'm just new to all this, and I'm a little unsure of what to expect." My earlobes are on fire now, so I adjust my hair to obscure them and pray the heated flush doesn't travel to my cheeks where it would be impossible to hide.

"Naturally Dear, however Bishop always takes care of his guests and will certainly insist on your safety." She says this as if Bishop were an upstanding citizen, running for mayor, her support for him unyielding.

"Bishop?" I ask as images of Catholic mass and the profession of faith come trickling into my consciousness, inappropriately timed for sure.

"Yes, he is…well, a bit of a gatekeeper. He controls access to the club. You see, here at 1462 our members are held to much higher standards. That way we can offer more of a…" she pauses, "Premier experience," she finishes then sits back to cross her ankles modestly. You would think she was speaking of Cotillion or a debutante ball--not a BDSM club. I smile at the image.

"Oh," I say lamely, then hurry to add, "So some people don't get in?" My curiosity is piqued; I'll never live it down if I get turned away. *See, you're too vanilla.*

"Oh…no," she says conspiratorially. "Maybe 30% or so actually become members. This is an elite establishment, not a raunchy bordello. Most of our guests confuse the two." She says this in a low voice, then stands, smooth's her skirt and backs away from the desk, just as the front door is opening.

"Good evening Darling, back so soon?" she pours on what seems to me like false hospitality. A thick gravy of southern charm disguising an acidic contempt.

The woman, meek as a kitten, comes in loosening her trench coat and plods toward a coat rack in the corner.

I ruffle my brow, wondering why she would be wearing a jacket in this heat. When the answer materializes as she eases the jacket off her shoulders. She reveals a wickedly cinched black latex corset, with zippers cutting across each breast. She wears black latex hot pants with a similar zipper savagely arching up from between her legs. At odds with her black, plastic looking outfit she wears knee-high socks and clunky Mary Jane shoes. The choice of shoes adds a childish element to the latex that I can't quite get on board with. Her face is marred with acne scars and reads plainly her discomfort.

"Yes, Mrs. Delacroix," she says timidly, "I am back, this is very important to me," her voice is stoic, yet determined.

Before she can take a seat, Mrs. Delacroix hurries to her side and guides her to an inconspicuous door at the back of the room. "Indeed it is. I believe Bishop is ready for you," Mrs. Delacroix says as she deposits her cleanly through the door.

She turns, walking back toward her desk shaking her head and tisking her disapproval. She seems relieved the little sub is no longer in the waiting room and looks at me with apologetic eyes.

"Wow!" I say, my voice thick with sarcasm. "I believe I've overdressed." Using humor at inappropriate times seems to be my hallmark, but suddenly I'm very aware of my--sober by comparison--choice of clothes. My stiletto heels have the right idea, but I suddenly feel dowdy in my pleated, navy skirt and my neatly pressed white button-down shirt. The fact that I'm braless and wearing incredibly skimpy panties had felt so salacious and daring moments ago. Now, it feels quite reserved.

Mrs. Delacroix, while sitting at her desk re-applies her red lipstick then stands and walks to the corner to retrieve the wayward girls' trench.

As if on cue, the back office door opens and out stomps the Mary Jane's, no longer playing the part of a meek sub. She snatches her jacket and huffs out the door.

"Do you still feel overdressed Dear?" Mrs. Delacroix hums, raising her perfectly composed eyebrows as if to say, "See, that is not what we are looking for."

I say, a bit more at ease now, "I suppose she didn't know the password?" Then cringe at yet another snarky remark. They are rolling so effortlessly off my tongue. *What was it my dad used to say? "Loose lips sinks ships?"*

"Certainly not," she huffs, aggrieved I might have thought so in the first place, and stricken by the thought. She recomposes herself, fluffing at her collar and smoothing her skirt again.

Turning my attention back to the paperwork at hand, I continue reading. The next section asks me to describe my "Hard Limits." I draw a decisive arrow to the "Prohibited Edgeplay" section then shiver with revulsion.

The next section is, "House Rules." In bold capital letters is the word "RUMPELSTILTSKIN" it's identified as the club safeword. Ok, yes, finally something familiar--no problem. It goes on further to describe the use of the terms yellow and red as caution and stop, respectively.

I unwittingly begin to chew on the end of my pen before I freeze, realizing the potential for all sorts of wily bacteria on it. I scrape my tongue under my teeth a few times and move on to the next rule. "You may not touch Bishop in any way." *OK, so club entrance is based on charm?... Oh crap, what if there are interview questions?*

"Excuse me, Mrs. Delacroix?" I clear my throat. She is sitting at her desk, legs crossed primly. "I'm new to this, so I'm just going to cut to the chase. What exactly is Bishop looking for?" I fidget a bit and fling my auburn hair over my shoulder ready to face the music.

She purses her lips, whether unnerved by my candor or appreciative of it, I'm not sure. She ponders my question for a long minute before answering. "I believe he is looking for a particular type of person, and seeking to weed out other types," she says, widening her eyes at the mention of *other types,* as if to nudge me into understanding.

"I don't understand, wasn't she the type?" I ask, gesturing to the door; meaning latex-ed and willing. To me, type is a strong word, what if you were the type in some regards but not others? I don't mind being naked, but I probably wouldn't like being flogged...I like men... but strangers? That would depend on a lot of factors--too many to list. I could dress up in fetish wear all day long but wouldn't want to crawl around on a leash. So type is a very abstract word for me.

"Maybe type is the wrong word. What I should have said is that he is looking for a certain *mentality.*" She nods her head, happy with the modification. Then she pulls some reading glasses out of her desk and rests them precariously on the tip of her nose. She leans into her computer monitor, suddenly interested in something that had caught her eye.

"You mean Dominant or submissive?" I ask while inwardly wondering which I was, though my timing in such matters is atrocious.

"Not necessarily, we have subs come in by the droves, most are denied access. They think all it takes is to come in, sit back on their heels, legs spread, eyes down. But really, there is more to it," she finishes.

I wonder if she has pegged me as a sub. I couldn't possibly be--I'm too assertive. But then, I'm no Dominant either. Devin is right, I walk all over weak men--and not in a good way; I end up resenting the hell out of them because of it. Do I have to be one or the other? Maybe just a good solid mix of the two, though you wouldn't think they would go together--like chicken and waffles.

"So I should be bolder?" I ask, but already a plan is forming in my head. I reach down fiddling with my breast pocket. They are still there, the little silver rings Devin couldn't convince me to wear.

"Bold is not always good either. Last night a guest stripped naked as a jaybird and did a handstand--with her legs wide open. She held the pose until Bishop left the room! I had to show her out," she says affronted, fanning herself with her hand.

I wonder how this sweet older woman ended up working here, she seems so prim and proper--so aghast by the racy antics. Then I imagine her in a corset with a whip and it comes together, much like picturing your parents having sex--delete.delete.delete.

"Ok, note to self, no yoga master stuff either," I say, heavy on the sarcastic humor that resonates so well with me lately--especially here for some reason. I decide to keep the tap dance and violin solo remarks to myself, though they sit heavy on my tongue.

"Hon, there are parts of the club that are very intense. Now, I'm not trying to scare or deter you, I just think people don't always know what they are agreeing to," she explains, while imploring with her eyes. "Bishop wants to make sure they can handle it. Most of the folks turned away lack the constitution for a place like this. It is no place for curious looky-loos, or for broken souls. Now, once you are allowed access, you will be expected to attend a club orientation. You know, to get familiar with the intricacies of 1462. The orientation will clear up any of your questions or hesitations."

Satisfied with her explanation, I continue flipping through the pages I have left, when a man walks in. He is dressed in black jeans, black cowboy boots, and a tight black t-shirt. His long blond hair is pulled back into a low, tight ponytail. His dark sunglasses hide his expression, but I guess it to be one of trepidation based on the fact that he is wearing them at all.

"Good Evenin' Mam," he politely nods to Mrs. Delacroix and flatly ignores me, though I'm the only other person in the room.

I turn my attention back to the clipboard determined to hurry through the rest of the paperwork. The actual contract is titled, "Temporary Contract of Consent." I (insert name) agree to hold 1462 harmless. Blah. Witnessing sexual activities and nudity. Blah. And will in no way hold the club liable for exposure to STD's...Yeah-dy, yeah-dy, blah. I want to get out of this waiting room before more people come in, so I finish the paperwork and sign the contract with a quick, erratic scrawl; more determined than ever to get in.

My plan to get past this All Mighty Bishop is beginning to emerge and solidify in my head. I sincerely hope he doesn't ask me questions. He would know straight away I'm not part of "the scene." Plus, I know my answers would be tinged with Devin's experiences and stories of his club days--and Bishop would hardly ask me about parachutes and testicle cuffs.

I stand to give my clipboard to Mrs. Delacroix as a newcomer swings the heavy door open, holding it for a coarse looking woman as she strides through the door. His eyes are cast on the floor, and between the two, he's clearly the submissive. He is collared around the neck with a thick leather strap and displays his deference to the woman in her every move.

She is dressed in thigh high boots and a black, tube top dress. She is impressive. Her inky hair looks like an oil spill down her stern back, complete with bluish tones on the surface that disperse and change as she moves.

With a heartfelt smile, Mrs. Delacroix places my paperwork on her desk and a hand on my lower back, directing me toward the mysterious door. I tap the trinkets in my pocket to make sure they are still there then take a deep breath.

I enter the room confident in my ability to woo men but when I see him, the confidence drains out of me like grain from a silo; slowly at first and then all at once. The door shuts behind me, and I feel the reverberations in my bones like rickets.

The stillness of the room is only broken by the flickering of the dozens of candles simmering behind Bishop. The wall of backlighting only adds to the ominous presence of him.

I stand rooted like an old banyan tree, unable to move my feet. My heart is pounding so hard it feels like it's trying to force the blood to forge new pathways through my veins. I'm more intimidated than I thought I would be, but I refuse to be sent home. So I focus my thoughts and quiet my racing mind.

"What can I do for you?" he asks in a sonorous tone that breaks the spell, allowing me to take a step closer. He is younger than I expected for someone running a BDSM club, but he is still older than me. He is handsome, meticulously disheveled and wearing a designer suit.

My mind swirls with answers to his question, because I'm afraid there is quite a lot I would like him to do for me. I smile and take another step toward him, meeting his gaze haughtily with my chin held high. The determination is set in the square of my jaw.

He returns my gaze with something that resembles cocky amusement. He is sitting in a brown leather Chesterfield chair,

21

one ankle resting on his other knee. He is slouched in a relaxed manner.

The chair curves around him at shoulder blade level, allowing him to rest his rocks glass casually on the arm of it. He holds the glass tipped at an angle, as if mere drops remain of his scotch.

The room is a large windowless space, devoid of furniture save for his chair. Behind him are dozens of glass votive candles, checker boarding the wall in countless rows and columns of flickering lights. The candles are emitting the same fresh eucalyptus scent that permeates the lobby.

Bishop takes a slow sip from his glass, eying me over the rim and looking nothing short of predatory. His dusty brown hair is tousled, just enough to be sexy as opposed to sloppy.

He is waiting for my answer, as I cock my head and take another few steps closer.

"I'm going to need your help with these," I say, as I reach into my breast pocket and retrieve the rings. I hold them clasped in my hand, hovering just above his lap.

Curiosity wins over skepticism, and he extends his palm, holding it beneath my closed fist. I open my hand, and the nipple rings clang together as they fall neatly into his palm.

For the first time since laying eyes on him, I see him falter, and then a slow, almost imperceptible smirk flickers across his face.

Unhurried, he sits up a bit so he can set his glass down on the floor. He drops the rings into the inside pocket of his designer suit jacket. Then he turns his carnal stare back to me, his eyes dark blue, stormy and brooding.

"Alright," he says, "Turn around."

I do as he bids. However, the feeling of having gained the upper hand sputters and then falls away completely when he says,

"Keep your feet together and bend over, legs straight, hands around your ankles."

I hold his gaze for a long moment before I slowly turn around. Newly sparked nervous energy is buzzing through me like honeybees in a jar. I bend over wondering if he is going to spank me or if he's just testing me to see if I can follow directions.

As if in answer to my unspoken question, he flips my skirt up. It rests on the small of my back, exposing me precariously to his sexy gaze.

Now I'm bent over in front of a stranger, all bluster and rapidly draining self-respect, with nothing covering my most intimate self but a lacy thong.

I feel his decisive hands on my hips then worry he intends to remove my protective shield of lace. He hooks two fingers under the flimsy material by each hip, then slowly drags my panties down. He works deliberately slow as if he is waiting for me to stop him, but I am too shocked to utter a sound.

I feel the thong catch between my legs. It hesitates in a final attempt to resist full disclosure. Then it releases and slides the rest of the way down, pooling at the hands dutifully clasped around my ankles.

The coolness of the air against my astonished, completely bare and totally exposed vagina is both shocking and exhilarating. I squeeze my eyes shut tight against the sudden shame of this unexpected overexposure. I am also startlingly aware of his gaze, as his eyes grope my most private parts. Perhaps because my legs are still together, I feel the tiniest modicum of decency, but overwhelmingly the rawness of the act is indescribably dirty.

Hyper-aware of his fixed stare, I can do nothing but suck in slow, deep, breaths. Breathing in the sharpness of the leather, blanketed by the warm, peaceful scent of the candles, does little to ease my mortification. As I'm wondering if he is going to touch me, I'm struck by an uncomfortable thought. *Would it be considered rape in a place like this?*

"Stand and hand me your panties," he says finally, with complete composure. I do as he directs, relieved to no longer be showcasing my nakedness, as my skirt drops back into place.

Finally, I feel some relief, as the blood that had been pooling in my engorged head begins to flow freely through my body again. It surges in heavy pulses like flood gates opening only to be slammed shut again.

In an attempt to regain some of my own composure, I turn and lock eyes with the enigmatic stranger. I'm silently challenging him to decide that I don't take direction.

Even though he is uncomfortably familiar with my body, he gives no indication as to the effect I might be having on him. Is he excited? Is my shocking exposure a turn on? His little show of dominance must be what they mean in BDSM circles by power exchange. I bet it's necessary for membership. Although there is no way of knowing what he is thinking, his poise is unflappable.

After scandalously enduring his show of dominance during the little peep show, I find I am more determined than ever to be granted access. The thrill is beckoning to me, *Come forth and be liberated.* So, while holding his smoldering gaze, I reach out and drop my panties in his lap. *Checkmate.*

"Turn around," he says, his voice is low and rumbling like distant thunder, then he stands up. "Hands behind your back." His quiet display of nonchalance is something you would expect to see at a Texas Hold Em table—calm and unreadable.

I can hear him rip my panties as I am complying with his request to turn around. Next, and with the steely grace of an undertaker, he gradually moves my elbows closer together behind my back. My sternum is straining against the pressure as he shifts my arms closer together. I'm surprised when he uses my torn panties to tie my arms behind my back.

He cinches a knot snugly below my elbows, with the lace aggressively biting into my forearms. The position thrusts my breasts prominently forward as they strain tightly against my shirt.

He takes his seat with quiet stealth, then says, "Now, come to me. Place your knees beside me here…and here," he gestures to either side of his thighs. "Kneel, do not sit." He is commanding but not threatening so I stubbornly continue to hold his gaze.

He looks like he should be on a billboard for scotch on the rocks, all bristly and brooding in his fine suit--not in a BDSM club. Cigar lounge maybe, sex lair--no way.

I feel strangely unbalanced with my arms drawn back like the rudder of a boat. Nevertheless, I climb awkwardly up to kneel precariously above his lap, placing my knees carefully next to each of his thighs.

The top two buttons of his shirt are unbuttoned, and I can see the pulse in his neck, as well as the tight ripple in his throat as he swallows hard.

My breasts are shamelessly straining against my blouse, the buttons hardly able to hold the carefully ironed fabric shut.

I have relied on my breasts since high school, capable as they are of captivating even the most discerning guys. In a way, I had even relied on them to get me into the club. I was confident that by bending the rules *and having him touch me*, instead of the forbidden other way around, the doors would swing wide open and I would march right through. Having proven my boldness and consequently my club credibility--however shaky it may be. I wanted to play my coyness with burning conviction. Like a college student demurely raising her skirt during class, opening her legs and flirting with her young professor, abashed yet undeniably assertive.

I naively thought I could waltz in, wave my breasts in his face and he would be powerless to resist their magnetism. I thought he would be drawn in like a moth to a flame, but ever the mystery, Bishop has managed to completely retain the upper hand. He has taken control and wielded it like a sword. It appears I have found a formidable opponent in this Bishop character.

In the past, my breasts have afforded me unchecked power over men. I wore my nipples like jewelry and used them as weapons.

The summer after finishing high school, I worked as a bartender in a rustic, peanut shells on the floor, barbecue joint. One day after changing the keg taps in the walk-in refrigerator, I returned to my post at the bar where a group of young businessmen had just arrived. Wiping my hands on the bar rag I used to twist off bottle tops all night; I had asked what I could get for them.

They had all stared at me dumbfounded, with their mouths gaping open and eyes fixed on my chest. Once I realized they were gawking at my hard nipples, I leaned in, feeling scandalous, and said in a low voice, "You think they look good? You ought to taste them." With a wicked smile, I had just walked away to help another patron, leaving them to dangle on their ropes.

Now here, having made up my mind to get into the club, I had counted on it being relatively easy. But in this moment, facing this handsome man; who apparently is not used to giving up control, I'm not so sure anymore. My straining nipples are inches from his face, yet he remains unflappable.

As the moment drags on, the stillness hangs in the air like a tethered bird of prey. I'm not sure how he will react. I caught him off guard by asking for his help, but whether or not he will actually affix the rings—remains to be seen.

As time passes I'm feeling more helpless, it's like I'm lingering in a soulless void. There is no backup plan if this doesn't work, just disgrace and loss of dignity while I try to gather my self-respect on my way out.

I am actually startled when he finally reacts. He reaches up to release the top straining button of my shirt with a graze of his finger. It isn't a hurried graze; it's more of a calm, steadfast caress of his super adept finger. Then the starched fabric pops open.

The strain of fabric against my chest is immediately and irrevocably released as my full breasts relax into the open fit of the shirt. I'm still partially covered up--though not at all concealed.

He is dutifully unfazed by my lack of bra as my breasts all but tumble out. He glances up into my eyes as he releases the next button, then the next, opening my shirt all the way and showcasing my breasts completely. Now my naked breasts are only inches from the chiseled jaw, dappled with evening stubble.

I can smell him now, warm skin and a faint sexy smell like next day cologne, it's soft and enchanting. His proximity coupled with his indecent stare makes me warm from the inside out.

However, my sudden heat is tempered by the biting lace that is wrenching my arms behind me like a vice. The position is causing a deep ache in my nearly displaced shoulders. My fingers, now as cold as corpse's from the firmly tied panties, repeatedly clench and unclench as I try to restore some precious blood flow to my fingers.

Stoically, I hold my awkward posture. He seems fond of long pauses, while his hard stare burns through me. So I just stare right back, daring him to do something--either untie me or twist on the nipple rings.

It's a game of wills about who will be the first to flinch, like playing bloody knuckles as a kid. My will is as strong as iron, but I can feel his breath against my breasts, warm and sanguine. It causes an ache to build deep in my abdomen.

Suddenly, without breaking eye contact, he leans in and licks my exposed nipple. It's not a lapping kind of lick, but more of a…a *flick*. It makes my insides clench together with a familiar urgency as a gasp gets wedged in my throat.

He witnesses the effect that small gesture has on me. It's only a breath catching in my throat--a millisecond of surprise, but it's enough to bring a mischievous, smirky grin to his face.

Sensing the crack in my self-assurance, he proceeds to clamp my nipple gently between his teeth and tug. The intensity of this deliberately drawn out act makes the pressure between my legs increase. The tension within now sits like a hot lead brick inside my pelvis. His eyes, now cobalt with indecency, twinkle in the flickering candlelight.

Never has such a singular act had this kind of effect on me. This strange new pretense of foreplay is cranking up my desire to an unfamiliar place. Never have I been so turned on by such a simple act, entirely devoid of any other stimulation.

I'm trying to conceal my clipped breaths, worried they sound more like panting. I watch as he slowly tugs then releases my nipple. He gives it another little flick with his tongue as he casually reaches into his jacket pocket. His crooked smile is in place as he withdraws a coiled ring.

These particular nipple rings can be made larger or smaller depending on the twist of the coil. They are made in a double braided style, so the coil is rather thick. When he slips the ring over my nipple, he drags the edge of the coil heavily across the tip before lowering it around the base and securing it firmly in place.

The erotic tension in my body is pulsing. The pain in my arms is making me crave the pleasure of his touch. He appraises his work like a lion that just brought down a pronghorn and is ready to dive into all the warm meaty spots.

His face softens, but his eyes have a treacherous glint to them that both worries and excites me. He leans forward nudging my shirt aside with his nose and simultaneously sucks my right nipple into his wet mouth. He only sucks for a moment, as if to simply dampen the hard peak, before releasing it with a snap.

With a languid motion, he begins to push my nipple first to one side and then the other with his firm tongue. Clearly he knows how to drive a woman wild because he continues even slower baaaack and forth, up and down. My nipple springs back to attention after each assertive flick.

I can no longer look into his darkening gaze. My head lolls back, and a quiet moan escapes my lips. My tortured lament breaks the spell, quick, like the crack of a lion tamers' whip.

Then he quickly slides on the other ring, twists it snugly into place and says simply, "You're ready."

1462 South Broadway

CHAPTER THREE
Threshold

In stark contrast to the dimly lit room where Bishop held court, the corridor is a wide, bright hallway with a door at the far end. I'm squinting my eyes against the light after having grown accustomed to the dimness.

I straighten myself as much as I can, hastily buttoning my shirt closed and smoothing down my skirt. My nipples are still held firmly by the stiff coil of the rings, my panties, of course, unaccounted for.

An enormous crystal chandelier hangs from an intricate ceiling medallion. The bright bulbs and the endless refracted light cast by the crystals only add to the brightness of the space. It multiplies it by ten thousand. The walls and ceiling are blindingly white, with lavish Board and Batten Wainscoting covering the walls.

The luxe, Hollywood Regency design style lends itself more to an extravagant gala or an opulent Dorothy Draper home. The stately dark wood floors are gleaming with a dazzling shine.

With some definite trepidation, I take one step and then another. I somehow thought once I made it past the all-powerful gatekeeper, I would be in the club--but this...this is nothing like I thought it would be.

My spiked heels click against the aristocratic floors, creating an echo and deepening the sense of lonely rapture created by the space. I sense my slow heedful breaths more than I can feel them, noting the gentle rise and fall of my chest.

I feel an eerie sensory void; it's making me cautious and hyper aware; it's almost a deafening *absence* of sound. This is what insignificance must sound like.

I cautiously keep my eyes fixed on the far door. The oval fluted door knob is my liberator it seems. I wonder what mysteries and secrets lay beyond it. Exactly what does the white paneled door conceal? There can certainly be no dungeon, no depraved sex den.

Granted, my understanding of BDSM is a bit shrouded in the mystique of Devin's homosexual playgrounds but the thought of smother boxes and humblers hiding obscured beyond the door makes me hesitate, and then stop altogether.

The unknowing coupled with the absolute stillness of the corridor pounds in my head. Time seems transfixed in space, like an ancient Grandfather clock whose pendulum has long since ground to a halt. Here, time and space seem a purely epistemological creation of my mind.

I continue walking even though an eerie sense of foreboding follows along behind me. I flatly refuse to turn back. No matter what lies beyond that door, I will face it. I flatly refuse to return to the foyer and face Bishop's smug face.

Despite letting me pass, I could still divine from his tentative eyes, that Bishop wasn't convinced I truly belonged. Or perhaps that was my own inner monologue ringing in my ears.

Now, having surpassed the Sphinx, I need to return with stories that will finally elevate me beyond the eye rolling accusations of being too prim, too sweet.....too predictable.

Decisively, I close the gap between myself and the thickly lacquered door. Then, with a sniper's focus and precision, I reach for the crystal knob.

Nothing. Not a wiggle, not a twitch. My heart sinks. It's like finally taking that first step out of a plane to skydive but being yanked back. Instead of the free fall and rushing air you expect, you're met with the hot, stifling air in the belly of the plane, smelling of fear and resignation.

The disappointment is paralyzing. Maybe, I had not been granted access after all. The handsome Oracle had not found me worthy after all. Turning around in a motion of coerced surrender, something catches my eye.

I see a beacon of flesh in an otherwise startlingly white universe. Puzzled, I narrow my eyes and walk toward the swath of skin. Right in the middle of a raised panel of Wainscoting is a hole.

Temperately and proudly through that hole, is a shockingly erect penis. Puzzled as I am by this mast of veiny skin, I'm also strangely relieved. Maybe I won't have to walk out in shame. The disappointment would have been worse than facing this new stranger behind the wall.

How very trusting he must be, this anonymous, mostly concealed man. In a BDSM playroom, which surely this is, he can have no way of knowing if I will hurt or punish him. In this parallel world, a stranger would be just as likely to flog him, as suck him. The unknowing must make him feel terribly vulnerable. The situation is decidedly precarious--the jolt of a violet wand vs. a hand job, Saint or sinner opposite you? Heaven or hell?

A shudder passes through me as I picture myself stepping up to my own glory hole and with total trust or complete psychosis, displaying my breasts through a wide cut out, trusting them to the unknown.

Just imagining the total vulnerability sends a warm cascade of warmth up my spine. It crawls to my cheeks forcing a flush. Would someone tickle my nipples with the caress of a feather? Or would they clamp or twist them mercilessly? Would it be the gentle, sweet touch of a lover or a wicked lash from a Dom?

A small bob of the man's penis brings me back to my very unnatural reality. Does he know I'm here? What if I know him? This particular thought sends my imagination into overdrive. I start thinking about my super-hot accountant behind the wall and am suddenly shy, nervous. *Now, I'll just need your W-2, and we can get started.*

I blow a wisp of hair out of my eyes and adjust my shirt with a new sense of resolve. Clearly, my entrance test is not over. Determined as I am to add some spice to my mundane, tedious life I will not be denied access. I want this too badly. I need it.

I take a step toward the glory hole, feeling a creepy prickle on my neck as if I'm being watched. I settle myself and try to picture my hot CPA behind the wall. The image gives me courage as I slowly reach out to touch it. It's nothing salacious, just a touch. I drag my fingernail gently from base to tip, a swipe really; up the satiny flesh.

This incremental touch elicits a quiet groan from behind the wall as a glossy drop of desire oozes out, clear and glistening.

He must be perched on the edge of letting go from the anticipation alone because the swipe was almost nothing--a precursor, a cautious step out onto the ledge.

I start to wonder if Bishop himself is watching, testing to see what I will do. Surely he has access, right?

It's crazy how I am reminded over and over that I am not the one in charge. Does that make me a sub? Maybe a reluctant one, I'm the one used to being in control. However, every time I think I gain the upper hand, I'm somehow knocked back. This has to be a test--will I take control or will I submit? Well, submission is not really in my DNA.

Does Bishop expect me to drop to my knees, eager to prove my place on the sexual fringe of society, naive yet desperate to fit in? Like the band girl, losing her virginity to the star quarterback behind the school bleachers.

I am certain my reaction is the key to unlocking the door. So I'm determined to at least appear unruffled to anyone who might be observing--and I am positive that someone is.

Filled with the certainty that Bishop is watching and inexplicably excited by the notion, I quickly make my decision. Smiling an inward smile, I realize I can be cunning and unexpected too.

I summon my long-slumbering inner vixen and reach up to the clasp of my pearl necklace. With deft hands I release the latch, letting go of one side of the necklace as the first of several loops drops down and dangles between my breasts. The swipe of the pearls against my skin brings an extra jolt of electricity to my ringed nipples, reminding me of my highly eroticized state. I carefully unwind the rest of the coils from around my neck.

I spare a thought for what lies beyond the locked door, what mysteries may lurk beyond the rabbit hole I will soon be careening down. My limited experience with 1462 is shrouded in mystery. Even the richly appointed foyer was so steeped in phantom desires and murky intentions, I was left feeling hazy and exalted all at once.

Now there is this glamorous corridor, an inception into a dewy unknown. It's an initiation of sorts, smacking of a gang "jump in" and feels just as rueful.

In my wildest dreams, I never would have expected such an assault on basic propriety. When I think BDSM club, I picture thumping music, dim, seedy rooms and bathroom stalls corralling groups of people. I imagine the damp sweat, hanging in the air like a fog of humidity; clinging to me, plastering my hair to my face and neck. I picture subs shackled to walls, as their Dom's muse about just the right form of corporal punishment--a whip, perhaps a cane?

I figured there would be leather, chains and ball gags, leashes and zip up masks. I expected to be punched in the face with the smell of sex. I expected to see the men, sticky with their own juices and the women, raw and writhing with desire. I expected group sex--tucked away or on every couch or pile of cushions.

In my mind, I had heard ecstatic moans of pleasure and sharp cries of pain. Nakedness everywhere, saggy breasts and flabby beer bellies, with body hair plastered against pasty, hairy asses.

My assumptions and wayward notions are being challenged by what I have seen, and by Bishop himself. Beyond the velvet rope, I have seen nothing seedy, deranged or drug seeking about it. Of course, my preconceived notions were ignorant, because nothing about that man bespoke of a slack-jawed clientele.

My vision of pallid, doughy skin slapping against ungroomed genitals just doesn't seem to fit anymore. It is becoming luminously clear, from the pristine lobby to the scrupulous selection process, I know nothing about BDSM clubs and even less about 1462 and the "Premier Experience" Mrs.

Delacroix had talked about. There were surprises around every corner; every time I thought I had the answer, this world turned me on my ear.

Now it's my honor and obligation; my prison and absolution to prove myself worthy. I withdraw the pearls from my body, feeling each silky bead drag across my warm skin.

My eyes have stilled, they are no longer darting around looking for the peeper's hole I'm certain exists. I focus on the riddle before me, the baluster of flesh seeming to promise membership with impunity. I step forward decisively now, dangling the strand of pearls above the stranger's stiff penis.

Once so sophisticated, the pearls now sway precariously back and forth across the very tip of this man, dangling like a very delicate pendulum and barely touching his skin. The incessant, redundancy of the flutter makes the man suck in his breath, and further engorges the deep vein on the underside of his penis and forcing his shaft to stand more stiffly at attention.

The penis pulses with what can only be described as a tormenting inward struggle. The struggle is to maintain a pragmatic sobriety within the lusty, carnal leaden chamber hidden behind the wall.

I maintain a steady careening with the necklace, causing the head of the penis to deepen in color and a low groan to seep through the wall. With a boost of satisfaction, I begin to coil the strand of smooth, cool beads around and around his rigid penis, base to tip. I encase the smooth skin in a sophisticated sleeve, just to the thick ridge of the glans.

Wrapping my hand around the beaded encasement, I begin to slowly coax it up his shaft. Working the beads assiduously slow, up and down, the edge of the pearls battering against the ridge of his tip. His muffled moans goad me on, up and down, uuup and doowwwwn, over and over.

His groans become haggard when I pick up the tempo and tighten my grip. The beads, rolling against my palm, repeatedly catch the lip of his penis, turning his vocalizations feral.

With his release growing near, I decide to wait until *just* before he lets go before I quickly free him from his pearly white chains. Not to mention, before he further fouls my necklace with his heady mix of endorphins and contrition.

Deliberating my move a moment too long, I misjudge the timing of his orgasm. As well as, any semblance of purity my pearls had managed to retain. He lurches and spurts violently, emptying his soul with a crashing eruption and anguished grunts. A bit to my horror, he oozes his warmth all over my stilled hand and deflowered pearls.

As I hold one end of the necklace, the pearls begin to slowly unwind themselves from the softening penis, while dripping thickly with disgust.

He slowly withdraws himself from the hole and slides a cover into place, very much like a camera shutter closing. And just like that, the mirage is gone. With nothing to speak to its existence except the rapidly cooling essence left on my hand.

I straighten up, with an air of having conquered the dragon. Then I square my shoulders and take an entitled step toward the crystal fluted door knob.

CHAPTER FOUR
Tricks

"What do you mean the fucking door was locked!?" shouted Devin, with indignance rolling off his tongue. He stands in angry protest, with his arms folded like a vice across his bare chest. Corey stands next to him shaking his head piteously.

"What do you want me to say? It was locked. Done. Bishop didn't let me in. I can't do anything about it now," I say defensively, filling my stem-less wine glass past what is usually considered acceptable.

I'm seated on the kitchen counter while Devin and Corey lean against the cabinets across from me. They have disregarded their dinner preparations, having been struck dumb by my retelling of the previous night's disaster

Devin reaches for the wine and takes a swig straight from the bottle before continuing. "See, you're too vanilla, you never would have lasted. I bet he could smell it on you."

"What part of my behavior was too vanilla Devin? When I bent over in front of him with no panties on? Or when he tied me up and put nipple rings on me? Ok, maybe you're right, the pearls were amateur. I should have just backed right up into his cock! Right?" I am shaking now, with my embarrassment showing itself as anger. I am overwhelmed with emotions, but I can't seem to decide how I feel about my dalliances with kink.

I am furious that I wasn't let in, I'm humiliated I performed like a trained monkey and I'm sad that Bishop had his way; in the end demonstrating what it really is to be a Dom or sub. But I'm mostly devastated that he didn't find me *worthy*; it's a huge hit to my self-esteem.

Once I grew out of my awkward, gangly childhood, my auburn hair, green eyes, and fair skin became exotic and beautiful instead of detrimental. People noticed me; men rubbernecked when I walked by, women folded into themselves. It has literally been years since I have felt not good enough. However, now the long silent, inner voice of a ruthlessly teased little girl is starting to speak up. That insecure, inner voice is starting to fracture my bold confidence. It's like water freezing in a rock fissure and causing the whole thing to break apart.

Devin doesn't answer my question; he just looks at me smugly, while judging. So I go on, "And just what would you have done Big Man? Wait. Let me guess, you would have dropped to your knees and sucked him off. Right?"

Devin takes a slow inhale while looking to Corey for help with the nearly hysterical woman across from him. Corey just smiles in a *you fed the bear, now you deal with it* kind of way. He raises his eyebrows while waiting for Devin to answer my question-- genuinely curious as to what Devin would have done if put in that situation.

"Well, in my heyday I might have," he looks to Corey as if to reiterate that his 'heyday' is in the past. "Or I might have backed up and taken it."

"No!" I gasp.

"I would have put a Jimmy on him first," he adds as if using a condom would alleviate my shock. Corey's shoulders rumble with a chuckle as he slowly shakes his head.

Corey is able to recognize the fundamental difference between my sex and gay men sex. But Devin doesn't understand what it might be like to not have two times the testosterone in a sexual relationship. So my shock baffles and unnerves him.

"What? It's hot. Imagine making eye contact with the guy behind the deli counter, and wondering if it was his fat cock--"

"Stop," I say raising my palm aggressively.

"Jessie, I've only just begun. What about the hot bank teller? The coffee barista? The quiet professor down the hall? It's very, very hot. It's a fantasy; it's whoever you want it to be." Devin finishes by raking his fingers through his already combative hair.

"But, what if it was someone nasty? Someone with rotten teeth? Or scabs all over? Then what?" I challenge as the wine in my stomach starts to turn sour.

"You can fantasize about those guys; I will fantasize about hot, sexy..." he buries his face in Corey's neck, eliciting a laughing groan as I hop off the counter and turn to leave the kitchen.

Corey calls out, "Are you going back?"

"Absolutely not! I'm all out of tricks," I grumble. I was hoping they would make me feel better, but this bitter pill I will have to swallow alone.

"Quitter!" Devin calls out, laughing as he comes up for air, then dissolves back into Corey while I stomp through our condo to my room.

1462 South Broadway

CHAPTER FIVE
Traitor

Cursing my wretched grocery cart as it pulls to the right, balking at my every attempt to align its path while I slog through the store. I toss in a bag of pre-washed, cut and ready to eat lettuce wondering when I became so lazy that I couldn't wash or chop my own lettuce. I suppose this is the age of convenience, pay three times as much merely to afford yourself the luxury of complacency.

As I further assess my own laziness, I realize I have just come from the gym, where I drove myself so I could run on the treadmill. My apathetic stupor is all around me. However, I do feel proud and self-righteous when I steer my cart past the conveniently cut up fruit and head to the full, un-assaulted dome of cantaloupes.

I haven't bothered to shower at the gym, preferring instead to carry my bad mood with me in the form of dried sweat and soggy gym clothes. My hair is a frazzled revolt to the ponytail, and my makeup has long since melted off. I can smell myself too, not quite ripe enough to present as BO, but funky just the same.

It keeps me company, my odor, reminding me of the punishing workouts I need these days just to circulate some endorphins so I can feel better. It's already been over a week since my walk of shame, punctuated by my rejection from 1462. But I still can't seem to shake off the bitter stonewall.

I'm not equipped to deal with failure. It has been so long since I failed at something. The inadequacy sits like a whiskey barrel on my chest.

Somewhere in the midst of my ruminations, I see him. Bishop, that arrogant prick is casually going about his grocery shopping, as if he were just an ordinary person, placing a bag of grapes into his cart. He is dressed simply, in trendy jeans and a basic t-shirt. He's all rumpled and sexy, that bastard.

My heart pumps fast and hard, my throat goes as dry as a Texas sidewalk, and my eyes squeeze into a haughty glare. All this, the instant I recognize him.

I attempt to drag a bit of moisture into my throat, but it only makes me start coughing. I quickly turn around to avoid being seen, as I choke and hack into my arm. Once I recover, I feign interest in first one cantaloupe and then another. *Damn it! Really? Gym clothes, mopped off makeup and hair all sweaty and now, NOW I have to run into him?*

I have been plotting and scheming for days about what I would say if I ever saw him again. I've been completely distracted by my need to regain my dignity and self-respect. Not to mention, I'm beyond angry he took them from me in the first place. Now of all times, of all the possibilities, here he is, in the produce department.

I wheel my traitorous cart right straight up to him before losing my nerve, and force out, "Oh, it's you. Hi." My face is a mask of secret contempt, but I manage a smile--or maybe a grimace, I'm not sure how it reads.

He has taken something extremely valuable from me, and I want it back.

"Have we met?" he asks, almost aloof but not totally. His perfectly mussed hair and charming smile are alight with amusement.

"Um. Yea, you could say that," I volley back, swallowing heavily as I hone in on his full lips. Then I glance timidly into his midnight colored eyes--so intimately acquainted with my body.

"Sorry, you must have me confused with someone else," he says, as he starts to push his cart past me.

I stop him with my hand on his cart. "No, No, it was pretty memorable. I'm not likely to forget those teeth," I press. I'm not allowing him an easy out, but the memory of his perfect teeth tugging on my nipple makes me wince. I want to gauge his discomfort, so I mention his teeth in hopes of making him squirm a little with the memory.

To his credit, he doesn't waver. "Sorry, wrong guy."

Twenty minutes later, as I swipe my debit card in the self-checkout lane, I feel utterly defeated. I could never go back to 1462 now; it would be way too pathetic. I would feel like a jilted teenager who couldn't accept that her boyfriend had broken up with her.

I will have to stay remanded to the throngs of polite, complacent society. I'll be shackled to those who will never walk on the wild side, never be able to shed the prude designation.

As I am walking out of the grocery store, my obligatory reusable bags clutched in my hands, I notice the smug bastard.

He is sitting righteously outside the grocery cafe, sipping coffee at a small bistro table.

Stubbornly not willing to give up my fight, I stalk over and pointedly drop into the chair across from him. My sudden decisive movement jostles his coffee as I sit.

He sits with one ankle propped on his other knee, settled back with an arrogant smile. He raises his sunglasses to the top of his head; his inquisitive eyes are now blazingly blue in the sun. He stares at me without a word, but underneath his cocky armor, I sense a playful lit to his demeanor.

"I took you for a juicer," I say. I offer no request to join him, as I zip up my hooded sweatshirt to spare him from my soggy sports bra, bathed in sweat.

"I'm sorry?" his swagger falters for a moment before he raises his cardboard sleeve covered, paper cup to his mouth for a slow, squinty-eyed sip.

"You know, someone who juices their meals," I offer in explanation, while cocking my head to the side.

"Why would I juice all my meals?" he asks with a mischievous smile.

"Not all of them, I guess you probably drink protein shakes too," I say, then add, "You know *Mr. Discipline*, *Mr. My Body is a Temple*. You just seem like that sort of guy. I've got to be honest though, I'm a little disappointed that you're sullying the whole image by drinking coffee." I deliver my statements like daggers; I mean them to cut. I want to shove him right off his high horse.

He smiles now, warmly this time, in sharp contrast to his vile, little smirk in the produce section. "What's your name?" he asks.

"Jessie," I answer, uncrossing my arms and relaxing a little.

"Well Jessie, you seem to make a lot of assumptions about me," he says, almost hurt but not quite.

"You just strike me as someone who likes to have total control," I press, knowing his penchant for commanding a situation.

He laughs, extends his hand and says, "My name is Silas."

I take his offered hand and firmly shake it. Instead of releasing my grip after an acceptable amount of time, he holds it securely. His grip lasts well beyond what etiquette deems polite, and he seems unapologetic for it.

"I'm sorry, were you born in 1930?" I say playfully. "Silas, huh? That's not at all what I expected."

"What did you expect?" he asks.

"Maybe Judas or Manson. Oh, wait. Wait...Attila," I say, jabbing further. I would be so pissed if someone talked down to me like this, but it feels good to take him down a notch.

"Such loathsome names Jessie, I'm almost sorry to disappoint you." He leans in a little, a challenge maybe? "I'm not sure how you think you know me so well, but you're wrong. Well, except the name, it is an old man's name," he smiles genuinely and becomes dangerously sexy. It's unnerving.

"Ok Jessie, now I'm going to make some assumptions about you," he says.

"Ok," I say, all but daring him to continue.

"Guys fall all over themselves for you, but you are still insecure because you grew up the ugly duckling. You stood out as different with your red hair, and we both know what different means to kids. You don't trust easily and expect to be let down by most people, therefore you only have a close set of a few good friends. You place everyone else in an acquaintance category, which subsequently casts you as a snob. Men find you striking, yet unapproachable. And finally, those captivating green eyes

47

have bewitched more than a few, leaving a trail of broken hearts behind you," he says, and then adds with triumph, "Am I close?"

"No. You…Silas, are wrong…" *cough*, "I am not a snob at all," I say lightly--too quickly, while inwardly choking on the bile in my throat. He is a little too accurate for my liking.

"Ha!" he laughs, then swallows hard on his coffee. He slowly moves both feet to the ground, saying, "Well, it was nice to meet you, Jessie." He places a little too much emphasis on the *meet you* part.

As we both stand, he adds, "Maybe I'll see you again soon."

He leans in, I think to kiss my cheek, but instead he clamps my earlobe between his teeth, slowly tugging as he backs up. He leaves an indecent trail of goose bumps down the back of my neck and arms.

Stunned, I can only gape at him as he winks and then walks away. I want to yell, *I knew it! I told you so!* But I'm too breathless from his touch. The effect it has on me is unnerving and very animalistic.

While standing rooted in place like a spouting garden gnome, I know with absolute certainty, I'm going back to 1462.

CHAPTER SIX
Access

There is no hesitation entering 1462 the second time. I barely spare a glance toward the paperwork I had previously agonized over. Then I scrawl my name at the bottom, with maybe a little extra flourish. Feeling almost arrogant I hand my paperwork back to Mrs. Delacroix, who looks genuinely happy to see me. Her perfect stacked wedge cut is flawlessly coiffed. Her warm brown eyes twinkle with a knowing gaze as she accepts my clipboard and says, "Bishop will see you shortly."

As I wait, excitement crackles off me like the snapping of static electricity, Bishop all but invited me back. *Maybe I'll see you again soon.* I look around, smiling at the fact that if someone wandered in off the street and didn't know better, they would think 1462 an ostentatious law firm. Mrs. Delacroix's desk is magnificent in all its regal glory. The rich mahogany and hand carved details lend an air of sophistication to the...uh, executive space.

I stand as Mrs. Delacroix approaches with a broad grin illuminating her face. She takes my arm, hugging it into her lithe frame and says, "I believe he is ready for you." She smells soft and pleasant like warm cashmere, and she snuggles me into her side like I'm the prodigal daughter, finally returning home. It comforts me, makes me feel like I belong.

"Hello Silas," I say, as he drinks in my black leather shorts and smooth, agile runners legs. My strappy, high heeled booties are only amplifying the tone in my legs--no small thanks to him. I have intensified my workouts by a thousand following his rejection, so this feels like a little bit of poetic justice.

He crooks an eyebrow and cracks a faint smile indicating his approval, but he says nothing.

"How do I get into the club…*Bishop*?" I ask, while closing the space between us, knowing I've captivated his interest.

"Perhaps the better question is *why* do you want to get into the club?" he asks, low and rumbling.

In my head, I'm screaming *because I need to free myself from always having to be so responsible and so virtuous. I want someone to take the reins, to relieve me of having to be in control, to lift the weight off my shoulders for once.* But of course, I can't say that, so instead, I say, "I like to feel powerful too." My eyes glint as I say this, knowing I have his full attention and wanting to sound mysterious.

"Powerful?" he says, while barely concealing his smirk. Then he stands up. "Ok then, come here."

My pulse starts to hammer in my wrists as I remember the last time he invited me to approach him. I start walking to him, more smoothly than I thought I could, but less than I had hoped for. I meet his gaze, there is a hurricane behind the murky blue depths, and I wonder what he is thinking.

"You want to feel powerful? Show me something powerful about yourself, and perhaps I will let you skip the orientation and send you to Declan instead."

I smile coyly and step even closer, a hair's width separating us. I can feel his warm breath as I look up into his stormy eyes. With my own crooked smile, I slowly withdraw a single strand of pearls from the pocket of my wispy shirt.

Betraying his indifference, a muscle in his jaw twitches and his nostrils flare ever so slightly. I read his response as a certain familiarity with the pearls. I'm now positive he had watched me use the necklace on the stranger, and that knowledge is liberating.

"Jessie," he says, using my name for the first time since I arrived.

"Yes," I say, and it sounds almost breathy.

"All you had to do was...knock."

CHAPTER SEVEN
Declan

As the door shuts behind me, I need a minute for my eyes to adjust to the gloomy, dim light. My senses are heightened, and I can smell dirt in the air, like after a windstorm. I take a few cautious steps down a short, darkened hallway as my heels sink into a packed dirt floor. This rings truer to the dungeon aspect I had expected. That is, before my assumptions were overshadowed by all the glamour and sophistication.

I can see the flicker of candlelight around the corner from where the short hallway stops in a dead end, so I move toward it. Turning the corner, I see a long dirt passageway lit with wall torches every twenty or so feet. As I'm making my way down the dirt corridor, I hear a deep voice.

"Thas it lass," comes a man's deep, rumbling Scottish accent. "Jest a bit fairther."

I walk toward the voice, my nerves beginning to hum. At the end of the passageway, a giant room opens up into what looks like the bowels of an old castle. I am stunned by the legitimacy of the room, I truly feel like I'm in another time, another place.

53

Standing before me is a massive Scotsman, well over six feet tall and hulking. The rugged man is dressed in a battered, red tartan kilt and dingy white shirt with billowing sleeves. The shirt is unlaced to the middle of his chest, revealing the chest of a linebacker. A rough plaid is slung over his left shoulder, while battered leather boots cling to his shins with thick leather ties.

He looks every bit a Scottish warrior, streaked with dirt and sweat. His burnished, coppery brown hair hangs in thick clumps nearly to his shoulders. His sharp gaze is the color of a winter sky, not quite gray but not blue either.

I'm afraid to look away; his seductive presence warms my blood and piques my interest. Devin is right, this is without a doubt what I need, but I feel like I should check myself at the door and become someone else. I need to forget about all my issues with relationships and buy into this fantasy.

He stands almost casually with his arms crossed. The raw, sexy, ferocity rolls off him in waves. He patiently waits as I take in the whole scene, watching me with an amused twinkle in his steely eyes.

Nervous to break the silence I venture, "Are you Declan?"

"Aye," he answers but doesn't expand.

Without moving my head, I hazard a quick look around, eyes darting about like a cornered animal. Strange medieval-looking devices are scattered throughout the huge room.

"What's that?" I ask, as unconcealed trepidation seeps into my voice.

"Thas a very old St. Andrew's Cross," he answers calmly. The cross is battered and deteriorated and has huge thick planks of railroad ties, crossing into the shape of an X. It has rusty metal shackles hanging from the two top points and two similar shackles resting on the ground at the base of each beam. There is a thick, peeling leather strap, hanging old and decrepit from the apex of the X. The whole archaic structure makes me shiver, but not entirely with fear. There is a bit of titillation mixed in, just imagining myself strapped to it.

Declan steps closer and says. "St. Andrew was a disciple of Christ, and the patron Saint of Scotland. He was crucifiet' and martert', but at his own request, on a diagonal cross, due tae his unwarthiness tae be crucifiet on the same type of cross as Jaesus." He speaks evenly and smoothly, his thick accent rhythmic and intoxicating.

My eyes have already moved to the rack against the stone wall. Various whips, canes, floggers, crops, belts, and switches line the structure. Not a single one strikes me as sexy or playful. Instead, they seem raw and vicious. They appear to lure me in, at the same time as warning me to stay away—almost humming a quiet malevolence all their own.

It feels like seventeenth century Scotland, and I'm the prisoner of a sexy Scottish Laird. My heart thumps, and alarms sound in my head because this is not just some lame role-play. In fact, I don't think Declan is playing at all and this room most certainly is not.

Declan must notice the dueling terror and provocation in my eyes because he says, "Dinna fash yerself lass." He places a strong hand firmly on my lower back, "Come with me." His touch makes my veins trill with anticipation, as he leads me away from the wall of medieval punishment.

He walks me toward what looks like an old pommel horse, covered in ancient, cracking leather. The sturdy wooden legs have big O-rings with leather straps attached.

He removes his hand from my low back gently grazing his warrior's calloused hands up my arms, causing goose bumps to flare up the tracks of his touch. He is gentle, his caress kind, as his winter gaze bores through me. He continues his adoring touch, reaching up to delicately hold the side of my face.

A timeless longing stirs within me and calms my nerves, as he runs his thumb tenderly across my cheekbone. I close my eyes, giving in to the fantasy and waiting for his kiss.

He leans in, brushing his lips across my ear and whispers, "Don't be scairt."

I nod my head as he drops his hands to my waist, then kisses me sweetly. I lean into him, craving and embracing the lurid fantasy.

His hands slide up my sides under my shirt, holding me by the rib cage. His rough hands are commanding, his lips firm. His scratchy stubble rasps against my skin as his kiss grows in need.

Assertively, he wisps my shirt over my head, forcing our lips to part as the silky fabric separates our lusty kiss.

I stand before him in four-inch strappy booties, short leather shorts and a black and pink, lace balconette style bra, my breasts displayed on a lacy stage.

Declan's stormy eyes lock on my breasts, hungry and insistent. He abruptly grabs my waist, swiftly hoisting me to his hips. I instinctively wrap my legs around his muscular body, clasping my high heel clad ankles just below his wool-covered ass.

He grabs a fistful of my hair, yanking my neck back as he drags his lips and his stubble over my neck and shoulders, heating me from the inside out. He crushes me into him, sliding his huge cracked palms up my smooth back, inciting a riot in my nerve endings with the simultaneous scratch and tickle.

Suffused with heat and desire, I'm completely entranced in this powerful role play. Raw sex appeal seethes from Declan like honey from a comb. His muscles shift and heave as his heart pounds against my chest. My forearms are wrapped tightly behind his neck, legs clamped soundly around his torso.

A trickle of sweat creeps down between my breasts just as I feel a gust of chilled air and hear the hard iron clang of a heavy door closing.

"Thas enoof Declan," says the glowering voice of a man.

I slowly pull my face away from Declan's, sucking his bottom lip into my mouth until it releases with an audible pop.

Declan grins at me, saying in a shallow voice, "Ah, yer a wicked hen."

We both turn to see who has entered the room and see a burlap cowled figure standing in the torchlight. He stands back by the stone wall with his face almost completely shrouded. He looks like a seventeenth-century monk but edgy, more menacing.

"Time tae see tae the skelpin," he grinds out, stepping deeper into the torchlight. He is big and imposing, almost like an omnipotent life force.

I look widely into Declan's eyes; suddenly I'm terrified of the whips and floggers. He gives me an almost imperceptible shake of his head and whispers, "Dinna fash," without moving his lips.

Declan takes my hand, leading me to the medieval pommel horse. He directs me to place the backs of my hands against it and lean forward, into my palms with my hips. My elbows are left jutting out from my sides.

I find I am nervous but willing, because in the short time with him, I have somehow come to trust Declan. He is so reassuring, it's like he wants to ease me through the experience like an unbroken horse.

The one consolation of being bent over and spanked across this bench is, at least I still have on my cute leather shorts. A little show of submission with a leather clad booty won't be so bad. I actually used to think being spanked would be degrading but to be honest, the thought of Declan continuing to touch me is incredibly exciting.

I feel calm as Declan draws the thick leather strap across my lower back, tightening it snuggly through two D-rings and causing the air to rush out of me in a whoosh.

I'm immobile now, tightly held to the leather bench with my hands pinned against my hips and body bent forward.

Declan grazes his palm across my back, soothing me with his calloused tickle again. As he strokes my back, he gradually skims his hand over my rear. Although I can no longer feel his rough touch through the leather, I can still feel the heat of his palm. Soothing, calming.

His roaming palm squeezes between my pelvis and the cracked leather of the bench, rendering me unable to breathe with the added tightening of the strap.

With a pop I can't hear, only feel, the button of my shorts is released, followed by a slow zzzzip. I feel my shorts loosen, then I suck in my breath. I'm suddenly very, very nervous.

"Shh. Thas a guid lassie," Declan soothes, as he begins to peel my shorts down my thighs. "Shh, thas right," he coos.

The heat and sweat have built up beneath the non-breathable fabric of my leather shorts, so when the cool air hits moist skin, it heightens my awareness of being stripped.

Declan drops to one knee, partially bending my right leg and slipping the stiff leather shorts over my strappy bootie. Then he moves my leg to the side, cinching a strap around my ankle from the base of the pommel horse. After tugging the shorts off my other foot, he proceeds to spread my legs widely apart. Then he swiftly fastens the other leather strap around my left ankle.

After divesting me of my shorts and securing my ankles tightly to the legs of the pommel horse, Declan, while still on one knee, places his palms on my calves then slowly runs his hands up my legs, only stopping once his hands reach the summit of my ass.

Now, my bent over booty is only partially concealed by the same black and pink lace as my bra. My panties are the racy, tanga style, where the lace sits high up but leaves my lower cheeks shamelessly exposed. This particular ass exposure is further magnified due to my bent over stance.

My heart is racing, as I consider what's to follow. I'm strangely turned on, and not just a little surprised by my carnal reaction. The anticipation alone is delicious, and posed as I am, I feel intensely erotic.

Declan groans as he admires the cheeky panties and my kinky, bound stance. My calves are taut from being pitched forward by my high heels, and my legs are held wide apart. He murmurs his praise making me feel supremely sexy and completely powerful despite my captive status.

Knowing the effect I'm having on Declan is heady, as I begin to realize the sexual power I have over him; without a single touch.

I had completely forgotten about the cowled man, who had thus far remained in the shadows, until he barks in his own gritty Scottish accent, "Get oon with it man!"

The shout snaps me out of my sexy haze and causes Declan to step to my side. I can feel the rough wool of his kilt brush against my protruding elbow. Then his rough palm begins to stroke my lacy backside, and I close my eyes relishing his attention.

All at once, I feel a sharp slap that causes my ass cheek to shudder in protest. Before I can register my surprise, another slap lands, this one harder than the first, then another. I can feel the heat rising from my skin, gradually becoming more of a prickle.

Redness rushes to the surface in response to the brusque spanking, matched only by the flare of embarrassment across my face. Then Declan stops spanking and begins to caress my heated, tender skin. While caressing, his fingers work their way under my panties, causing a flutter of anticipation deep within my belly.

He then yanks on the fabric, tearing the crotch of the panties ruthlessly away from the scrap of lace around my hips. The lace bites into my skin as Declan, in a show of brute force, tears the remaining bit away from my astonished body.

Shocked, I can do little more than raise my chest up from the pommel. When words fail me, Declan says, "Shh, it isn't sae bad lass." This time when his palm smacks down, he slowly drags his hand to the side, slightly spreading my ass cheeks.

The shrouded stranger who by his voice is much closer now, murmurs, "Aye, thas it." His voice is pleased, evidently liking the spreading of my pink cheeks.

With each slap, Declan continues to expose me to the stranger, who is now very close behind me. Slap, drrrrag, harder slap, drrrrag. He reveals me to the stranger more assertively with each smack. My mortification grows by the second, and I have to remind myself that this is a test.

After a while, Declan stops and walks behind me to admire his work while standing next to the stranger. I can feel myself flush with their attentive stares. They are so close, so focused on my spread-open and bent-over core.

The sheer embarrassment I'm feeling starts to mingle with a raunchy, erotic tension that is building steadily. The effect on my body is a crazy, cyclical reaction, one moment I feel like I will die of shame, the next, I'm completely turned on and aching for more.

Declan moves back to my side. I'm still intolerably spread out and exposed to the stranger; so I squeeze my eyes shut even tighter as the most recent wave of shame crashes over me.

I feel the crack of Declan's palm, then the feather touch of his fingers as they lightly glide over my bare vagina. This time an undeniable arousal begins to percolate deep in my body. Is it the erotic touches Declan steals, as he takes his hand away? Or is it the incontestable, unobstructed exposure of my most delicate parts? I can't be sure, but I know I want Declan's fingers to linger. In fact, I find myself eager for the slap just to feel his soothing fingers graze over my sex after.

I am embarrassingly aware of myself becoming slick and wet, as Declan continues. I grind my teeth together to fight against the morbid humiliation of my aroused state.

My ass cheeks are on fire, burning with a tingling sensation, so I find I am relieved when the spanking stops.

I feel Declan's hand, hot from exertion, caress my back. A moment later, my strapless bra springs free and drops to the floor beneath my bound torso. Now I am totally naked and completely vulnerable to these two men. My heart is pounding so fast, I can feel it rocking in my chest.

Even though Declan has been the only one to touch me, I feel the stranger's transfixed gaze every bit as much as a physical caress. I also believe, without a doubt, the stranger is the one in charge.

Next Declan grips my ass cheeks, gently squeezing them. He slowly moves them apart, spreading me open even wider for the stranger. I am supremely uncomfortable with the exposure, so I'm almost relieved when he drops his hands lower.

Declan then proceeds to fondle my presented flesh, spreading my lips apart and opening my soul to the stranger.

Declan continues to spread me open with the fingers of one hand, while reaching his other one around to cup my breast. He palms it before capturing my nipple between two of his knuckles. He gently squeezes, then less gently... tugs. As he continues to roll and pinch my hard nipple, I can feel sparks shooting to my exposed core.

The sexual ministrations and the display of my body have a treasonous effect on my otherwise rational brain. The yearning is beginning to take over, and the shame is dissolving away.

As my sexual desire rises, I arch my back and writhe against the intense craving, never realizing it could be summoned in this way. I press my full breast into Declan's palm, longing for more.

He continues rolling my nipple between his thumb and finger while his other hand finds my slippery vanity. He glides the edge of his palm, along my wetness, while his thumb grazes against my ass crack.

He parts my tender lips with the full length of his palm. Then finally, he slides his fingers forward enough to find my clit with the tip of his finger.

I'm perched so precariously on the side of his palm I can hardly take a breath. He slowly slides the edge of his hand back and forth between my folds, bumping my clitoris with each forward slide and making me gasp each time.

I'm shaking now, trembling, I can't stop myself. Inexplicably, I ache for his fingers to penetrate me, so I arch my back in invitation, changing the angle of his solicitous caress.

Declan's fingers begin to strum my nipple, faster and faster as I fall deeper into the fray. I can hear his ragged breathing while my own need continues to build.

Now my body is so sensitized to touch, that everything feels startlingly magnified.

The cracked leather across my hands and belly is crimping into my skin. I can feel each, tiny fracture in the worn leather. The lifting edges of the cracks, pinch and rake my skin.

I can also feel the roughness of the wool kilt scraping against my jutting elbow, as well as Declan's hardness, which periodically bumps into, or presses against my arm.

He mercilessly continues his nipple strumming with one hand, while the other slides and rocks between moist folds of skin. He pauses on the forward slide to press against my pulsing clit, and my eyes flutter closed.

I am so intensely aroused. I can't remember a time when I've been this wound up. No one has ever brought me to this level of stimulation before.

I start to pant while writhing against the scratchy bench and the solid strap pinning me to it. Soon, the pants turn to moans as my orgasm builds--climbing up and up, higher and higher. I'm almost…there, but not quite at the edge. Then, right before my release, Declan drops both hands to his sides and backs away from me.

I shoot him an acrimonious look, wondering why he stopped so suddenly. I'm confused and profoundly disappointed.

He looks back at me, smiling a wicked smile. Then raises two glistening fingers to his lips. He sucks them deeply into his mouth, then, ever so slowly, he drags them back out. Then… the traitor winks at me.

I see him glance at the cowled man behind me, then he steps forward again with his erection bobbing beneath his kilt. He stands facing my side, but he turns his shoulders toward the dark stranger. He leans over me, grasping both lower ass cheeks then spreads me open for the stranger again.   This most recent view of my vagina is far raunchier than any my shackled legs had previously afforded. Nothing's hidden from these men, my entire world is on explicit display, just for them.

"Aye, she's verra wet," the stranger growls as he steps forward, reaching between Declan's fingers and placing one finger firmly against my clit. Boldly, he taps it three times, causing intense jolts to zing through my body with each tap. The stranger drags his fingertip away from my clit, back through spread petals, and continues his brazen journey up to rest his wet finger against my anus.

"No," I breathe out, barely audible, afraid.

Declan chuckles deep in his chest, a low rumble. They stand there menacingly, with the silent threat of anal penetration an ever-looming threat.

I hold my breath, frozen in time. I'm praying the stranger won't cross that line but know he easily could. I had agreed to RACK, and all of a sudden the risk aware consensual kink seems *intensely* subjective.

The irony of the situation is that I had wanted Declan's fingers inside me, but he had refrained. It would be such a cruel twist to enter me now, in this way.

I have the word "Rumpelstiltskin" primed and ready to fall from my lips. Before I can utter the club safeword, both men step back as if sensing my boundary. I exhale a long, slow gust of gratitude, thankful to have dodged that bullet.

Now I feel desperate to close my legs, so I struggle against the ankle straps. They shake, but that's about all. It's like being caught in an inappropriate bear hug from a weird uncle, all wiggle but no give.

I hear the stranger mumble, "Guid Evenin." His voice is followed by the deep clang of the heavy iron door as it closes behind him.

In a series of jerky motions, Declan tugs and then releases the heavy strap across my back. My hands prickle to life with their freedom. He grabs the wool plaid from across his shoulder, frees it from his belt, then slings it over me; still warm from his body heat. He then sinks to one knee, deftly unbinding both my ankles.

I don't move my legs together right away, they feel like an old hinge that has rusted shut, but in my case rusted open. My hips are heavy, crotchety and cumbersome, so I just stay flopped across the spanking bench.

My head hangs limply, my neck having given up the fight. I feel wrung out, emotionally and physically, I have nothing left.

Declan places one hand lightly on my back, the other on my shoulder and helps me to stand. He adjusts his plaid around my shoulders and tenderly takes my hand into his, massaging the feeling back into it. My hands are as cold as ice and uncomfortably stiff from being pinned beneath me.

After massaging life back into my hands, he sweeps my hair behind my shoulders, lightly grazing my neck with the backs of his fingernails.

He draws me into him, pushing the wool back a bit from my neck and drops a careful kiss on my shoulder. He kisses his way slowly up my neck. I feel his touch start to warm me again, after having gone cold and limp. I feel weak and unsteady in his arms, but his tenderness helps me to regain some semblance of self.

Scooping me up like a small sleeping child, he carries me to a tall chair with straps and buckles 3/4 of the way up the back legs. There is a wooden claw-like opening jutting out from below the seat.

I can picture a person facing the chair with their wrists shackled to the back legs and their neck held in the claw device; bound against the crotch of the person sitting in the chair.

Declan is unfazed by the device, he simply raises one rugged boot and pushes the neck-clamp back under the seat of the chair. He sits down, and gathers me into him like a delicate bird.

His plaid feels scratchy against my bare skin, but I melt into him. He is so kind, rocking me and cooing in my ear, "I'm jest going tae hauld ye," and, "Sech a bonnie lass," and, "Thas guid, Shhhhh."

Sleepily, I close my eyes. I feel so taken care of. I no longer feel dirty or shameful, but what I'm surprised to feel is …cherished.

CHAPTER EIGHT
Work

Sitting at my computer, eyes glazed over by the contracts glaring back at me, I cannot get my mind to quiet. I desperately need to focus on work. I'm smack in the middle of negotiations for a twenty million dollar acquisition of mineral rights, so my mind drifting to 1462 is highly inappropriate. Given my circumstances, I doubt the oil and gas company I work for would approve of my mind wandering away from exploration and drill sites, only to daydream about sexy men.

Even if these men are capable of driving a woman insane, literally--straight to the nut house insane. I can't get my mind off how intoxicating a sexually capable man is; it's absolutely new to me.

Declan was phenomenal, but more and more I find myself thinking about Bishop, or Silas, whoever he is. I shake my head in an attempt to clear my mind, like you would with an old Etch-a-Sketch, but it doesn't work at all.

I need to navigate this contract, cure some title defects and approve a drill site lease, all before my afternoon meetings.

My land technician, Salinger, pokes his head in my office, "I'm going to grab lunch, are we good for 3:00?" He is referring to the 3:00 meeting with our cost analyst.

Instead of telling him, I would be ready if I could just get my mind off of S&M, I nod and smile. In my head I imagine a chime ringing, as a twinkle flashes on my tooth. My smile is that automatic, that fake. I sigh, and then put my nose to the grindstone.

Once Salinger is gone, I wonder if his biceps have always strained his shirt like that. I know more than a few women in our building have noticed because they tend to swoon a bit when he is near. Or they linger in the office lounge if he is refilling his coffee.

My phone beeps and from the speaker comes the receptionist's voice, "I have Devin on line two for you."

"Thank you Adelaide," I say, as I grab the receiver and cradle it to my shoulder. "Hey Devin."

"Wassup sexy bitch?" he asks, but it's not really a question, it's more of a Devin statement..

I laugh in spite of my foul mood. "Nothing's up, I'm just dying a slow painful death at work"

"Well, aren't you just full of sunshine and rainbows. What's wrong?" he asks, though I know he's not the slightest bit interested.

I sent three of his calls to my cell phone directly to voicemail earlier today, so the fact he is calling me at my desk means he has an ulterior motive.

"I can't concentrate on this acquisition, Salinger is waiting on me for the contract, but there are title defects, and I'm still waiting on figures--" I ramble on with hardly a breath before Devin interrupts me.

"Blah, Blah, Blah. You know I don't speak that language, Jessie," he says in a mock reprimand.

"Ok Dev, what do you want?" I ask, pushing myself away from the desk with both hands and lolling my head back.

"Well, you know I love your corporate fancy mouth," he says in a rush, "But right now, I need to talk about my needs."

"What needs?" I challenge, through a grin.

"Chicken Philly needs."

I laugh because his tone is so serious, but I should have known better. Devin is never serious. Everything is always presented as a red alert, a five-alarm fire, or a dire emergency-- and maybe it is to him, but to me, lunch does not necessitate three calls and a 911 text. The fact that I didn't even respond to his emergency text should indicate how badly he abuses it—truly. He epitomizes the boy who cried wolf.

"Give me until 1:00 and I'll meet you at Bruno's," I say, then hang up before he can re-negotiate.

I pull my chair back to the edge of my desk, where my computer casts an artificial glare across my glassy eyes and disengaged face. I cross my eyes at the blinking cursor, annoyed by its nagging, then turn my attention to the title commitment.

I need to ignore my new hyper-sexualized state. I mean, *of course* Salinger has always been good looking… and the security guard on the first floor, by the elevators. Right?

Walking into Bruno's Cheesesteak, I spot Devin right away. He's wearing loose cargo shorts that hang low on his hips and a tank top that clings to his muscled chest. He has accessorized with a canvas belt, which is usually all the effort he will put in when going to work. Devin is the kind of guy that always looks ready for the runway. Whether he has just rolled out of bed or is meeting with a wealthy client, he always looks perfect. Turbulent, but perfect.

He has a natural charisma that can win over the stuffiest executive, down to the lowliest street rat. Devin is ridiculously handsome; he turns the heads of both men and women in equal parts. Although his love of women is really more of an admiration for them, they have absolutely no sexual pull over him. Men on the other hand, flock to him and he bats them away like pesky fruit flies.

He didn't always bat them away, mind you. Devin is a reformed w-h-o-r-e. His sexual escapades would make your ears bleed. Ever since Corey though, Devin is content to settle down, retire his alley cat ways and be a responsible, doting boyfriend. He now prefers the intoxicating lure of falling deeply in love to rabid, casual sex.

"Hi beautiful," he says, as I take my seat at our freakishly small table. "Ah, I've missed this face," he adds, grabbing my head and pulling me forward for a peck on the lips.

"Dev, we had coffee this morning...in our kitchen," I remind him with a smile.

"Right. It's been hours," he winks, just as the waitress arrives.

"Two chicken Philly's, iced tea hold the lemon and a Coke," she says, with the voice of a two pack a day smoker. She is probably six months from cancer, ten from her stoma. Her face is puckered like she ate something sour but it could just be the rotting of her mouth from the inside out. She sets our lunch down and hurries off.

I love how Devin knows me so well, down to the lemon-less iced tea. Or is he right about my predictability?

"I know you have a ton of work, so I want to do my part in the interest of efficiency," he says, as if an explanation is necessary. "And, I'm buying, because I need a favor."

"Devin. Last time you needed a favor from me, you had a padlock around your balls," I say through a giggle.

"Uh. No. Like I'm going to let that happen again," he says pointedly, a smile creeping across his face with the memory.

"Well then, let me explain again. I love you, but I'm not into pegging, so stop asking," I'm laughing full on now. I can't resist teasing him, and his sardonic smirk only emboldens me.

He takes a hearty bite of his sandwich then sits back, arms crossed over his chest as if waiting for me to finish prodding.

"Listen you little hellcat, it's not that kind of favor," he says, laughing in spite of himself.

"Ok, what?" I ask, pinching my lips together trying to steady my face.

"I want you to come with me to a *Young Professionals* cocktail party," he keeps his eyes down as he takes another man bite of his sandwich. Only then does he look up begrudgingly after I've let the request hang in the air for a bit.

"Why? That's not my clientele, and the last thing you need is more business. Don't you have a waiting list for finished product?"

"Therein lies the problem. I need fabricators."

Suddenly it's clear to me why he wants me to go. He is afraid his homosexual persuasion will scare away potential fabricators, as if he could force his gayness on them or something. I groan at the thought, me, in the oil and gas industry, having to defend fracking for three hours.

"I'm a Landman Devin. That's not really a crowd-pleaser." I swallow a bite that feels like wet sand in my throat because I already know I will do him this favor.

"I'm not asking you to go drum up oil and gas business. I need you to help me find fabricators that might be, uh, uncomfortable with me at first," he explains before draining half his coke in a few unrestrained gulps.

His plan is clear but no less tempting. "I think I have a thing that night," I say only half joking, stirring my tea with the straw.

Devin raises his eyebrows. "I didn't say which night you little minx."

With a resigned sigh I concede what I knew all along, "Alright, I'll go."

Two nights after being railroaded by Devin, I find myself in a crowded bar full of *Young Professionals*, drinking a dirty martini and glaring at Devin across the room. I am stuck having a conversation with a stodgy, moth-eaten metal fabricator. "He is a lighting designer, I'm sure you have seen his work--very industrial or rustic as well as chic and sophisticated," I explain.

"Well, I'm not much for chic, but industrial is in my wheelhouse," he says, as he puffs up his chest. "You look like you could do some damage with an acetylene torch," he says, his breath humid and tinged green.

"Yeah, but I try to keep my acetylene torching to an absolute minimum--So here is Devin's card. I'm sure he will be very interested in your portfolio of work," I say, fast like I've had a gallon of caffeine and then turn on my heel hustling off toward the bar.

"Dirty martini please," I almost beg the handsome bartender.

A smile splits his emerging goatee and his mossy eyes twinkle, "How dirty? Playboy...or Penthouse?"

"I would say Hustler," says a deep, throaty voice behind me.

I spin around to face the presumptuous eavesdropper, already having filled my maximum quota of annoyance for the evening. But my crusty glare softens into a prom queen's stiff smile when I see Silas standing behind me.

"Dirty indeed," he says, his jaw so square, lips so perfect and his smiling eyes always one step ahead of me.

Silas takes the Martini from the bartender, handing him cash like the transaction were a drug deal, then passes me the glass. "Erik, thanks buddy. Are you coming this weekend? It should be quite an event," Silas says to the bartender, apparently knowing him.

"Trust me Silas, I wouldn't miss it," the bartender says, as he pours richly colored scotch into a glass then hands it to Silas.

"What are you doing here? Drumming up BDSM memberships?" I ask playfully.

"Not exactly," he says with a wry smile, then hands me his business card.

"Commercial real estate?" I choke then notice the name on the card. "Silas Bishop? That's why they call you Bishop?"

"Actually, my nickname has been Bishop ever since they put it on my hockey jersey as a kid; it's not a professional designation Jessie."

"And, lest we forget, commercial real estate developer has a nicer ring to it than S&M Dungeon Master," I say, teasing him.

"That may be true, but at young professionals meetings I do get some eyes glazing over with commercial real estate that I

73

surely wouldn't if I led with S&M," he says, amused with the direction of our conversation. "Would you like to sit down?"

"Love to," I say, thankful to have someone more exciting to talk to.

He guides me to a thickly lacquered bar table with his hand on my lower back. I like this regular, human side of Silas. It's a side that's not always jockeying to have the upper hand. This side is normal and polite, even witty. However casual his touch is meant, it still lights my nerve endings like a Christmas tree.

As we slide onto our stools, I ask, "Were you guys talking about a club event this weekend?" I try to sound only mildly interested, but Silas sees through me like a pane of glass.

"Yes, it's a little bit like a grand opening but without the banners and balloons," he grins.

I hold the drink skewer of olives, leisurely stirring my martini before I meet his eyes then pull an olive off with my teeth, salty as the Pacific. Chewing the olive, I say, "Tell me more about this club event."

"I plan to," he says, then takes a shallow sip of his drink. He is looking at me with a devious, sly smile. "But first, have you found 1462 to your liking?"

I sense he is testing me, probing for my suitability at the club. "1462 is very much to my liking," I say formally. I feel the back of my head heat up just thinking about the lack of boundaries at the club, the naughtiness, the erotic tension.

To circumvent the blush running to my cheeks, I hide my face in my wide martini glass as I take a long swallow. The drink warms my throat and saturates my abdomen, permeating my brain through the walls of my stomach.

"Good, I was hoping you would say that," he gives me a heart melting, panty-dropping smile. "I was hoping you would model for the event."

"Model?" I say, having expected just about anything out of his mouth, except that. "Like, fetish wear?" I ask, as I picture myself in a strappy outfit, crisscrossing and framing my naked breasts and wonder if I would even have the nerve. I'm flattered but caught off guard, so I'm not sure what to say.

Silas saves me from the need to respond right away by asking, "Have you ever heard of Nyotaimori?"

"Pshh, of course I have," I say while playfully shaking my head no.

He laughs at my contradictory admission then says, "Its origins are from the Samurai period in Japan, in Geisha Houses women would have sushi served directly from their bodies."

"You want me to be one of the women serving sushi off our bodies?" I ask, incredulous. I would never dream of eating off of someone's body, hair, and dead skin cells--gross.

"No, I want you to be *the* woman, serving sushi off her body." As soon as Silas gets that out, before I can fully absorb what he has just said, I see Devin quickly approaching.

"There you are Jessie," and then with barely a pause, "I'm Devin, and you are?" he extends his hand in a very short and to the point, Devin kind of way. If someone didn't know better, it would come across as possessive or even jealous.

Silas, unruffled in a very alpha male kind of way, takes Devin's offered hand and says, "It's nice to meet you Devin, I'm Silas."

"Well Si-las, I was just coming to let Jessie know she is a terrible lure for my business needs if she refuses to stay the course." He says this with a mock harshness that makes Silas chuckle.

"I swear, he thinks he's my pimp," I say to Silas, not really needing to explain. I feel helium light and giggly and realize the two martinis have taken hold. A dopey smile on my face, I inform Devin, "Silas was just recruiting me to be a sushi model for an event at 1462."

Devin's mouth hangs open in surprise, "You mean *this* Jessie?"

Before Silas can answer, or Devin can out me as being too vanilla, I jump in. "Of course I said yes."

Silas looks into my eyes with a slow leer bubbling to the surface. "Fantastic."

What is this power he has over me? I find myself doing things I would never dream of just to prove to him that I can. I am long past seeing myself as prude or boring, so why am I going out of my way to prove this to him? He is sexy for sure, I'm buzzed for sure...but it's his witty sense of humor and his quiet confidence that makes me want to know him better.

There is a nagging sense of unease in my belly. Why was Devin so stunned when I told him? He looked as if he had been slapped with a cold, dead fish. What could be so bad about people eating sushi off of me?

CHAPTER NINE
Trapped

Standing here naked except for my plush cotton robe, I inwardly curse myself for the thousandth time. It took two quick martinis to agree to this but would take ten to calm my nerves.

My skin, still prickled and humming from my full body wax and raw from the exfoliation treatment, would take days to feel supple again, but I am as smooth as oiled glass.

Devin offered me a Valium when he broke the news to me that I would not be wearing a bikini. I declined, although I'm not sure why. Now, here I am, like a death-row inmate, ready to take that final walk.

A similarly clothed man approaches and says, "Hi sushi girl, I'm sushi boy. aka Thomas." He is tall and well built, has a square face, both supple and vibrant. His dark brown hair is buzzed on the sides and pulled back into a short ponytail. He reminds me of a guy I dated in college on a full ride scholarship for swimming--confident, able and proud.

"Hi Thomas, I'm Jessie. Have you ever done this before?" I'm so nervous I have to grind my teeth together to keep them from chattering. If I could come up with a feasible way to get out of this, I would shoot through the door with nothing behind me but a flutter of Thomas' robe. Not even a backward glance.

"Hell yeah, I would do it every night if I could." He's pumped, like an MMA fighter walking to the octagon. "Why so skittish? You beat everyone else who wanted to do it."

"What do you mean everyone else?"

Thomas laughs, "Tons of girls wanted to do this, so you must be something special." He winks and smiles broadly suggesting, he too is something special.

My heart swells, Silas chose me. *Tons of girls wanted to do this*, and he picked me. My bubble of pride pops as I realize all the extra pressure this information puts on me.

A sassy platinum blond woman in cut-offs and peep-toe heels sidles up to me. She is maybe 5'2, but I can tell she is a spitfire just by how she carries herself.

"I'm Tally, I'm gonna help get you all set." She clasps my hand twining our fingers together saying, "This way Doll."

She leads me into a grand banquet hall. People are bustling about setting up elaborate table settings and large centerpieces of orchids. She walks me to a long table covered in buttery smooth, creamy silk. "You will be head to head with Thomas; he's a favorite of the Dommes," she leans in lowering her voice, "They always instruct him to keep his enormous cock flaccid, and then delight in punishing him when he can't. It's huge, have you seen it?"

"Um, no," I whisper as Thomas approaches, all smiles.

"What's your record, Thomas? Four minutes?" Tally asks, taunting.

"I believe just a bit shy of that Miss."

"Well, we all know how you like the chastisement wrought by your failure," Tally says as she slides her hand between the flaps of his robe, reaching between his legs and pinching his scrotum right between his testicles.

He closes his eyes but otherwise stays perfectly still. She holds his robe open to me as if to say, *See what I mean, Huge!*

Thomas is a big guy, I believe Devin uses the term *tripod*, but what stuns me more is him being so blatantly objectified. No ramifications no permission, nothing. Just look and touch as you please.

Realizing I'm his counterpoint I start to feel lightheaded and trapped, with the walls closing in. A cold chill runs through me as I ask, "May I have a shot of whiskey?" I try to tamp down the panic, but it's pointless.

"No Doll, that would dull the experience." She sees the look on my face and adds, "Take some deep breaths; we will keep your robe on for now." She can't seem to register why I might be shy and nervous about the whole experience, she looks at me like a Husker fan whom you've just told you don't like football, it just doesn't compute for them.

As I gingerly sit on the edge of the platform, I look over and see Thomas, lying stark naked on the table--you would think he was at a spa, waiting for the massage therapist.

I'm pleasantly surprised the table is padded, but I'm still running through excuses in my head of how I can make this nightmare stop. Nudity doesn't usually bother me too much, but nudity in front of a crowd is bad... and nudity in front of an *interactive* crowd is really bad.

As I start to lie back, it occurs to me I should have asked more questions. I'm not even sure how many people would be here, and now, seeing the size of the room, I don't even want to ponder it. I'm getting deeper and deeper, with dwindling options for escape, my predicament is like quicksand, and it's swallowing me whole.

I had convinced myself that nothing would be worse than telling Silas I had changed my mind and watching his face turn smug, deciding I was an amateur after all. I couldn't turn back now, as bad as this was, I still wanted to show him I could do it. Damn him and the ridiculous hold he has on me and damn Devin for not shoving that Valium in my pocket.

Tally has me raise my head so she can separate my hair to either side as a very prim, older man walks up, sucking on his teeth. He brings Tally a cart full of makeup and curling irons of all sizes, as well as a massive tray of flowers.

"Gorgeous," he purrs as he runs his fingers through the left side of my hair. "Do you know how many women would kill or die for this color? It's rich and delicious and... natural?" he asks, as he takes hold of the bottom corner of my robe, parting it incrementally before Tally smacks his hand away.

"No peeking!" she asserts, as she winds my hair around a wide curling iron. "Actually, maybe just a small peek, if you go get me the lotus flowers from the fridge," she says through bubble gum colored lips.

By the time the man returns with the lotus flowers I am fully made up, my hair lying in loose waves, adorned with flowers.

My intense focus on the ceiling above me has drawn attention away from the fact that I will be naked to the world, it's as if denying the fact will make it go away. I find I am somewhat resigned to the idea now, I've decided to treat it like a trip to the gynecologist--quick and dirty, then done.

Tally holds up two stunning purple lotus flowers so vivid with color saturation, it looks like they should drip thick amaranthine syrup. Leaning over, she kisses me square on the mouth. "Goodnight sweet princess," she whispers in my ear as she places a lotus flower over each of my eyes.

They are startlingly cold on my thin eyelids. The flowers cool the jelly of my eyeballs and rapidly pull my attention away from my jittery heart, which is fluttering like a hummingbird's.

"Now I want you to take some deep breaths," Tally purrs in my ear as she loosens the tie on my robe. At this moment I can understand how a personality could split for someone suffering from severe abuse. The desire to will yourself away from a situation, to pretend with all your heart that it simply is not happening to you, to go so deep inside your mind that the circumstances default to someone else.

Of course, I understand perfectly well that I am not being abused, or rather that my 'abuse' is my own doing, but the desire to disconnect and go to a happy place is still incredibly pervasive.

As Tally draws my robe apart, I fight the urge to cover myself with my hands. The air against my skin is pronounced in an unsettling way. I hold my breath as she guides my arms out of the sleeves then directs me to raise my hips as she slides the plush terry cloth out from under me. My nipples tighten right away in acknowledgment of the exhibition.

Now that I'm naked and no longer fighting the anticipation, I feel marginally better. This is what I was afraid of, it's happened, now my parasympathetic nervous system can kick in with some soothing, stress relieving hormones...hopefully sooner than later.

"This is the most naked you will be, by the time everyone comes in you will be covered with fish and flowers." She cups my breasts and adds, "These will display nicely."

I lie there perfectly still, thanks to the paralyzing grip my self-consciousness holds me in. I'm grateful my eyes are closed and covered, that simple fact makes the whole thing easier.

Tally arranges my arms out to my sides, bending them slightly as if I were merely lying on some tropical beach.

"Jessie, I have a bolster for your knee, it would be tough to hold your pose without it after an hour or so," Tally explains while easing the round satin pillow under my knee. As she does this, she starts to spread my legs apart. "Relax, I'm going to spread them a bit more but don't worry, you will have flowers covering your pussy."

I'm grateful for her explanation. If not to ease my discomfort, at least for her soothing voice, though her use of that word is jarring to my ears.

"This will be cold, it's a banana leaf," Tally says as she places the chilled leaf down my sternum from collar bone to belly button. It is firm like cold plastic but adheres to my skin as my body warms it, my nipples growing hard as acorns. She places another clammy leaf down the thigh of my straight leg, leaving goose bumps rioting against the chill.

Next, she places a star-burst pattern of leaves that encircle my belly button and run hip to hip. "Are you allergic to latex?" Tally asks, more as an afterthought.

"No," I say, and it's almost a chant I'm working so hard to relax.

"Good, this is liquid latex; I will use it to adhere the flowers to your legs, so they don't tumble off."

"K," I whisper. The sensory stimulus of not being able to see, added to the freezing cold leaves, on top of an intense fight or flight response, has worked as a trifecta relaxation technique. It reminds me of a Russian Banya treatment I had last year--the hot and cold, melting honey, and beating with leaves--same idea, same mental zone.

Tally says in a monotone voice, almost hypnotic, "I want you to be able to picture what you look like, so listen very carefully to my voice."

"Ok," again, my voice is a whisper.

"These are fuchsia pink Peonies; they will start at the top of your left thigh." As she explains, she dabs the pungent smelling latex against my skin and presses a chilled flower into it. The methodic outlay of flowers effectively snuffs out the sharp, tangy smell of the latex. The latex smells like a hamster cage with the sweet, ethereal scent of the flowers sprinkled over it. "A whole row of them will follow the rise of your leg to the summit of your knee," she speaks as she dabs and flowers three more spots along my thigh. "They will flow down your shin, across the top of your foot in descending size. It's really beautiful; I wish you could see it."

With the wispy assortment of sweet smelling flowers hanging in the air, Tally prattles on, "Magnolias in your dark red hair make the perfect contrast...Oh, I nearly forgot!" she says with mild alarm, "The rules, there are not many, but they are absolute and completely rigid. Also, you need to keep in mind that there are those here who would love to see you punished for breaking them," her tone is serious now, she almost sounds like another person.

"You may not talk, and you may not move. Do you understand?" Before I can respond, she continues. "Now, bearing these rules in mind, you need to remember the ones that will try desperately to make you move or talk. You mustn't break."

"What types of things?" I ask, listening carefully.

"Nothing malicious--"

"What do you mean malicious?" I interrupt.

"Well, like figging. That's never been allowed."

"What is figging?"

"It's when a freshly peeled ginger root is inserted into your pussy. I've heard it burns like hell. It was used as a form of torture at some point."

"OhmyGod!" I gasp, horrified.

"I told you, nothing malicious. Just some light hearted attempts to tickle or perhaps...surprise you," she says and then continues, "Here, I have something to help remind you to stay perfectly still."

I feel her slide a headband through my hair onto my head. After fiddling around a bit, she bends some sort of headband *prongs* into my ears. A shudder trickles through me as the little prongs tease both ear canals. The sensation is indescribable, both a tickle and a torment but a threatening reminder just the same.

Once my body is completely adorned with leaves and flowers, Tally places some type of botanical between my legs, finally obscuring my vagina. It's too firm to be a flower, and it has pointy tips like an artichoke. I assume it must be some sort of succulent but the nature of the plant means very little to me at this point.

The plant has the same effect as the ear prongs, absolute stillness, because the slightest movement causes a sharp poke to my inner thighs--my upper, inner thighs. Its dangerous proximity to my very bare, very waxed and unprotected flesh makes me hold my breath. I wiggle my cold eyeballs around under the thin lids in an attempt to redirect my focus.

"Just take slow breaths, ease into it," Tally instructs.

"She looks beautiful Tally." It's a voice I recognize immediately as Silas'. Although I am mostly covered in leaves and flowers, I have not forgotten that my breasts remain exposed and now here is Silas standing over me.

I feel like my nipples are blowing fog horns, or flashing neon lights the way I can feel his stare.

"Tally, go tell Akio she is ready for him," he instructs. Then to me, he says, "Jessie, you look amazing."

I pause, then ask, "May I talk?"

"Of course, how do you feel?" he asks, taking my hand in his firm grip but not raising it from the table.

"Honestly? I feel a bit like I'm laid out for the medical examiner."

Silas snorts, "I'm going to try to forget you said that while I'm eating Ahi off your tits." I groan inwardly and clench my kegel muscles. There is a long pause before he continues, "See if you can tell when it's me who's touching you," he murmurs in my ear, making the prongs sing. Then, with a little squeeze of my hand, he walks away, dress shoes tapping his swagger on the freshly polished floor.

The memory of his voice in my ear makes the cilia dance and the prongs threaten a sharp jab.

The next footsteps I hear are quick and muffled, like slippers slapping against the floor. A hurried voice says, "Konbanwa--Good Evening." Right away he begins to lay sushi on the leaf between my breasts. He continues to jabber on the whole time he decorates my body with sushi, but all I can think about is Silas; his ticklish whisper in my ear and his challenge. *See if you can tell when it's me who's touching you.*

The strips of raw fish are ice cold and still partially frozen as Akio places them lightly on my breasts. The placement is in a sunflower pattern, with something firm in the middle, covering my nipples--shrimp maybe? He repeats a similar pattern around my belly button then fills the center with what he says are smelt eggs. The slippery coldness inside my belly button feels like a cold rod straight through my body.

When he is finished, he gives a quick, "Oyasumi Nasai--Good Night." And then he is gone, with a flurry of his slippers across the floor.

The room has grown very still and quiet, even the clamor of ice in glasses can no longer be heard, it's as if the bartenders have also vanished.

I already feel a sick compulsion to move, but I'm afraid to, so the torment rolls through me like an earthquake on a seismograph. I hope the straight jacket effect of the sushi and rigid rules will let up some. There is something about being told to remain still that makes me feel like a bag full of slippery eels, it's like I have restless leg syndrome or something.

"Thomas?" I loud whisper, making me sound like an elderly woman speaking to her friend during a funeral. I know he is there but can feel only the faintest essence of him.

"Shhhhhh," is all I hear in reply.

The sushi is beginning to feel heavy, making me feel like a trapped animal. I clear my throat and wait.

There is muffled cheering and applause from another room and then without further fanfare, the doors to the banquet hall swing open. The room is suddenly alive with a matrix of conversations. I can't see their faces, but with my hearing sharp as an owl's, I can hear the electricity in the air.

Inwardly, I feel like all my nerve synapses misfire all at once. I wish I could sink into the table, just have it swallow me whole, like that device that lowers caskets into the ground.

I'm trying to focus on the easy banter by the bar as ice clinks into glasses, alcohol splashing behind. The problem with this diversion technique is that I am also picturing the bartenders as Chippendale's dancers. The dancers I am picturing are wearing tight, lustrous tear-away pants, with their bare chests and tight bow ties. The problem is, the dancers in my head are not *sexy* bartenders, they are the cheesy, hip gyrating and overdone thrusting kind of dancers. So when I feel the giggle roll up my spine, I recognize it right away for what it is--the inappropriate laugh. The one that happens when you see someone very unpoetically slip on the ice, or when you see a runway model teeter on her high heels and fall down--it's the highly inappropriate... church laugh.

When the smile curls my lips I try to swallow it, pinch it together, ignore it--all in vain, because the harder I try to stifle it, the more demanding it becomes, like a door to door solicitor.

The giggle is barely contained, and my smile is maniacal, reminding me of the time when I was a kid in Catholic Mass. Back then, the priest had begun singing a chant he was especially bad at. Of course, my brother and sister heard it too and were similarly plagued with the giggles. I had tried biting the inside of my cheek, tried holding my breath, nothing could stop me, even the ferocious glare and the silent threat from my dad couldn't stop my stifled snickering. The three of us would finally control ourselves, but inevitably, someone would think of the dying animal sound the priest had made. One of our choking giggles would fuel the others, causing the whole dam to burst again.

The same cycle is plaguing me now, it seems the more inappropriate it is to laugh, the more I feel like I have to. I'm squeezing my lips together in a tart, sour pout trying to keep it at bay but the thought of gyrating hips while shaking martinis is pushing me ever closer to the edge.

I feel a warm hand on my bicep give a gentle squeeze as a familiar voice hovers just above me, "Jessie, you have to stop," he whispers just above my face, his breath an imperceptible tickle on my skin. Silas presses a kiss to my pinched lips.

"Sssssstttoooopppp," he murmurs, this time holding his lips against mine longer, to allow me time to relax my face. Another gentle squeeze then his touch vaporizes into the ether, the slow burn of his lips left to tingle on my mouth.

"Ah, Bishop, one of your pets?" A male voice questions and it sounds like he has rocks in his mouth.

"She's not mine. She's too undisciplined," Silas responds with a total lack of sentiment.

"Undisciplined? Well, we will have to teach her a lesson," the man garbles out. I can visualize the frat boy nudge he undoubtedly gives Silas.

"Gorgeous, silky skin," says a female voice, it's filled with liquid satin. "I believe I shall start right here." I feel her hand drag up the inside of my right leg, ankle to thigh. Her hair tickles my skin as she closes her mouth on a piece of fish, grazing my flesh lightly with her lips. "Mmmmmmmmmm," she moans.

"Not me," comes a slow growl in my ear, "I'm going to skip the sushi and eat your snatch you haughty little wren."

I hold my breath a few extra beats, no longer feeling like laughing. Is that a threat he would see to fruition?

I feel the glide of chopsticks as a piece of fish is peeled from my breast. Light and easy conversations are happening all around me, mostly boring, mundane chatter. One such group discusses stocks and futures, another group, bone fishing in Mexico. Surprisingly, more than one conversation is about kids, soccer games, piano lessons, tutors, teacher conferences...not quite what I expected to hear.

As the night wears on, I realize, with the exception of a few hardcore players, the room is filled with regular, everyday ordinary people. No one seems hell bent on making me move or talk, so I kind of ease into my role. I remind myself that I look good naked, and the sooner they all eat the sushi, the sooner I can move.

Basically, I have a skirt of leaves, flowers, and fish with the poky succulent between my legs, so I feel somewhat covered there, more at ease now.

Due to my insipid preoccupation with the need to shift my weight, I find myself eager for the sushi to disappear, even with each bite increasingly exposing more of me.

Some time later, it is with confounding relief that the last bit of sushi is peeled from my breast, leaving a dampness behind to chill in the air. My skin is clammy and chilled, nipples hard and at full salute, as I feel the smooth edge of chopsticks grab, then tug my left nipple.

It doesn't hurt exactly, but the tug is relentless. Each time my nipple springs free, the chopsticks snap together, and the wood scrapes against itself. The sound of the grating wood makes the hair on the back of my neck prickle to life. It gives me the gnawing shivers like when you would bite a wooden Popsicle stick as a kid.

My body stiffens while the prongs in my ears remind me to keep still. There is a simmering ache growing between my legs as the attention on my nipple increases. *Is it Silas?*

The laughter and general joviality in the room heightens as the drinks flow freely, making the crowd less polite and more insistent.

I feel the long banana leaf that runs down my torso begin to slowly peel back revealing a layer of sweat beneath it. As my skin grows cold, I feel a warm, wet tongue trail up the path vacated by the banana leaf.

My teeth clench, the ear prongs hum their presence against my cilia and the plant between my legs pokes infinitesimally at my intimate parts.

A deep voice boasts, "Watch, I'll get a moan from her at the very least," as I feel his mouth close around my right nipple and suck. Simultaneously, I feel fingers tapping on my left nipple. At the same time, fingers tickle up the inside of my arm.

Ironically, the entire night while countless people ate sushi off my naked body, I had felt like less of a buffet than I do now. The man mercilessly sucking my nipple releases it then flicks it harshly with his finger. I suck in my breath as the pleasurable pain shoots to my core. The breath, a tiny motion but enough to make the ear prongs poke the inside of my ears, freezes me mid-breath.

Warm liquid pours into my navel then is licked and sucked out. Through all this, I remain absolutely motionless, not because I've invoked some strict new standard of discipline, but because I am terrified of the ear prongs, they feel dark and menacing as they tickle and threaten.

At any given time hands, tongues and mouths are on me. I am completely preoccupied trying to decipher Silas' touch. It excites me to think he may be touching me now, rolling my nipple around between his fingers, licking Saki off my body, hands roaming lower and lower.

The fevered rush all around seems to be closing in on me, a pack of wolves descending on its prey as a gruff voice announces, "I'd like to see your pretty mouth around my swollen cock."

At the same time, I feel a hand wrap around the ankle of my outstretched leg and pull it to the side. The movement causes the plant to bump and poke me in twenty tender places at once, as if on accident before it is taken away, exposing me to the world.

My heart is churning, I feel like I've just gone over Niagara Falls in a barrel. On one hand, I am mortified and filled with embarrassment--on the other hand, my body is reacting and loving the attention. I'm turned on from every direction, but my inner sanctum is at war. I don't even know these people, and here I am acting like their little toy.

More and more I am deciding to let go, to give in to the eroticism. I need to allow myself the sexual torment, give myself up to the experience.

I feel a stern slap to my breast, and before the quaking of my flesh stills, another as the soothing voice of a woman penetrates the air, "Here, let me try." There is a slow drag of soft leather from my neck, between my breasts, across my belly and finally lightly grazing my sex. I'm guessing she's using a riding crop because it feels like soft leather. Then, just as I'm relishing the sweeping caresses, I feel a sharp, straight on slap to my nipple. The crop then makes circular, ticklish rounds around the hard peak, then crashes down again.

The stirring in my core is immediate, I have given myself over to these people, but my body is not used to such willful ministrations, such sexual skill. I don't trust myself as my body dissolves deeper and deeper into the harsh pleasure.

Once the crop stops its' erotic torment, I feel soft hands caressing both breasts, palms cupping them, rubbing and pressing them.

I have learned that gentle touches give way to pinching and twisting, so my whole body hovers on the knife's edge of anticipation and dread. I ache with an unfamiliar need I never would have expected when I agreed to this. I feel strong waves of both mortification and thrilling exhibitionism, but desire…I never would have thought it possible.

As my nipples are tweaked and fondled, someone's wandering fingers prod lower down my body. After finding my clit, they exert a consistent, mild pressure. I feel the touch of chopsticks at my exposed vagina as the tips tenderly spread my lips. "Ah, wet as a juicy pear," says an eager male voice. Before my shock registers, the finger on my clit begins to rub slow circles, and I forget about the chopsticks.

More warm liquid is poured into my navel and dribbled across my breasts to be licked by solicitous tongues. I no longer care about my predicament, no longer feel ashamed. My body is singing and has never felt so alive.

I'm beginning to realize for the first time, that they won't stop--not until I move, or cry out, or...release.

Tally had warned me about moving or making a sound, she emphasized how they would delight in punishing me if I broke. Having seen their methods of punishment first hand in Declan's dungeon, I am diametrically opposed to letting it happen, but how do you stop a runaway train? There is absolutely no ignoring the building pressure in my core, it is relentless and getting stronger.

As tongues lap and flick at my nipples, the fingers continue their methodical circles around and around my clit. My orgasm is building tumultuously--higher, higher.

Suddenly I feel a thick finger slide deeply into me followed by a ferocious voice, "Marcus!" the angry voice barks, "Out! Your membership has been revoked!" It's Silas, and he can barely contain the viciousness tingeing his voice.

"But..." is all Marcus can stammer before a swift bustling in the crowd removes him quickly and succinctly from the room.

I am thankful for the commotion because blessedly, no one had noticed my body jerk away from the rogue fingers' intrusion. Strangely, after several moments I can still feel the plunge of the finger, like a phantom limb though the offender had been removed.

Hands and mouths hardly skip a beat, warm Saki is being poured all over my body. It tickles my neck as it curves around the arc of my throat, dripping off the back of my neck into the silken sheet. Someone is sucking at my throat, stopping only to mutter, "You are going to cum very soon." Following the taunting, heated Saki is poured between my legs.

The rubbing fingers are replaced with a firm, probing tongue. *Oh, God! Is it Silas?* I clench my body, fighting against even the thought of having an orgasm. The tongue is masterful and requires very little time to bring me to the edge of the abyss considering how intensely stimulated I already am.

I'm at the threshold of my release. There is no use trying to stop it, I just need to concentrate on keeping still and quiet. So I squeeze my eyes shut beneath the Lotus flowers just as the spasms begin. They start just below the surface, a quiet rumbling before my body fully gives in. The orgasm is unstoppable, but is somehow restrained through my pure strength of will.

The prongs itch in my ears as my body goes liquid-- though I remain stiff as an iron maiden. The orgasm rolls off me in dizzying torrents, my skin is electrified, sparking in short rhythmic pulses.

Once my body fully quiets, I begin to shiver against the cold dampness left by Saki, long since licked off. My teeth are chattering, and my lips are trembling. I'm completely wrung out by the need to keep still, so I find I no longer fear the repercussions of my movement.

Tears I hadn't noticed trailing down my temples begin to pool in my ears. I'm trembling all over as voices wander off, the crowd finished with me, on to the next chapter.

Someone drapes a plush, velvet blanket over me, a warm cocoon for my quaking, shivering naked body. The ear prongs are slowly bent back from my ears, and the headband is pulled free of my hair, with only a few strands resisting its desertion.

I feel the flowers plucked from my eyes, still laden with false eyelashes. Keeping my lids shut, I feel a feather light kiss, on first one eyelid then the other. Slowly opening my eyes, I have to squint against the sudden light flooding through my lids.

Silas is next to me, his warm smile and bright eyes look comforting and tender, almost protective.

"Tally is going to take you to the bathhouse for your aftercare. I will check on you later, Ok?" His soft nurturing tone is enough to slow my trembling.

Somewhere in my muddy brain, at that exact moment, I realize Devin was right about what I needed.

CHAPTER TEN
Bathhouse

When Silas said *Bathhouse*, he wasn't kidding. The massive room looks just like an ancient Roman bathhouse. A steaming bath the size of a swimming pool monopolizes the stone walls and floors. There are eight or so huge marble pillars, reaching to the dome-shaped, two-story ceiling.

The rounded ceiling is painted with an elaborate fresco painting depicting ancient Roman gladiators, chariots and the Colosseum. It looks hundreds of years old, with chipping paint and disintegrating sections.

Four cherubic statues are lining the far end of the bath in various angelic poses and spouting water from their mouths or tiny penises.

The air is thick with humidity, soggy to breathe and sticky on my skin. There is a mist that obscures the room, making it feel otherworldly and dizzyingly ethereal.

Tally once again helps me out of my robe and guides me to step into the steaming water. Sinking down to my chin, I sit on a pebbled rock ledge that must ring the inside of the stone bath.

The hot water loosens my tight joints, having stiffened like rusty hinges after my forced stillness.

"I'll let you soak for a bit," Tally says, as she disappears into the steam like an apparition.

The steam rises from the surface of the water enveloping me in an earthy smell like sage; it's soothing and blissfully warm. As I'm leaning my head back and closing my eyes, I notice a figure slowly sloshing towards me. Emerging from the plume of mist I see the male sushi model, Thomas.

"How did it go?" he asks.

"Well, it was a lot more than I expected, that's for sure."

"So what was all the ruckus?"

"The ruckus?" I lean my head up from the stones to see him better. I am confused because it was all ruckus to me.

"Someone had their membership revoked?" he prompts.

"Oh, yeah...someone fingered me," I say, too depleted to be elusive.

"And?" he asks while twitching his head to the side genuinely puzzled.

"And what? I guess no one was allowed to actually penetrate me." I loll my head back again, finished with the conversation and close my eyes.

"That would be a first," he scoffs.

Suddenly interested, I sit up and face him. "What do you mean?" I ask pointedly.

"Just that I was penetrated upside down and sideways. That's just never been a rule before. I mean every orifice of mine was entered...fingers, tongues, anal beads, dildos, you name it," he says this conversationally though his smile is one of pride, not mere acceptance of being so thoroughly violated.

Even after my shocking experience of very public sexuality I somehow feel like it pales in comparison.

"Did you cum?" he asks boldly.

"Yes, but I stayed mostly still, and I kept quiet like Tally said. Did you?"

"Oh Yeah. It's not so easy for men to hide their orgasms," he says with mock smugness. "Anyway, I like to be punished," he winks, and then sits right down next to me--close, almost touching though there is room for twenty. Devin would say he was in my hula hoop.

Thomas is very good looking, with his short ponytail now taken down; his hair is rangy and turbulent. He's hung like a horse and likes being punished, to think if I met him on the street, I would only know he was hot.

"Thomaaaas," sings a honeyed woman's voice. We both look up to see a leggy blonde with huge perky breasts drop her robe and slink into the water on the other side of the bath. She swims the length of the pool underwater, surfacing right in front of Thomas, her breasts bobbing just above the water.

"Let me take care of you and your huge cock," she purrs with a Russian accent. She leans in, skimming her nipple across his chin before he takes it into his mouth.

I can feel his thigh pressed against my leg, and I'm suddenly uncomfortable to be so close. As I start to scoot away, Thomas slides his arm behind me and places his hand on my waist, keeping me close.

The Russian woman stands, waist deep in the water and waves her breasts at me while she slowly pivots at the waist, back and forth, like a lighthouse beacon. "Do you like my beautiful big titties?" she asks through pouting lips as Thomas loosens his grip to caress my side, hip to armpit and then back down.

"Ah, I'm really more of an ass girl," I respond, profoundly discomforted by her question. Thomas throws his head back and laughs heartily at my response.

A bark of laughter, followed by a slow clap alerts me to the newcomer in the room. It's Silas, and he is also humored by my reply.

The Russian, undaunted croons, "Ooooooo but my big, huge tits are aching to be touched by a beautiful woman." She backs up while Thomas pulls me swiftly, almost weightless in the water, onto his lap. His stiffening dick is now pinned between us, and his hands are stroking my inner thighs, savoring the smooth skin.

Silas unbuttons a couple top buttons on his dress shirt then pulls it over his head then drops it to the stone floor. Next, he unbuckles his belt, quickly followed by his slacks. All while staring at me with a flirty smile, his pants dropping into a heap around his bare feet. His boxer briefs are hardly able to contain his stiffening cock.

Sitting on Thomas, my own breasts hover above the surface of the water, in full view of Silas. I return his provocative smile and watch with reverence as he drops his underwear.

He walks to an alcove in the stone wall, while displaying his perfect ass then returns with a couple of bottles. Slipping neatly into the pool next to me, he hands me a bottle of water.

Breathless at his nakedness and grateful for the drink, I sip it then set the bottle on the edge of the stone bath. At the same time, I try to shift myself off Thomas' lap.

Instead of allowing me to move off of him, Thomas holds my thighs, coaxing them apart so the Russian can move forward.

I hear Silas chuckle, and I realize, he too is curious how this whole scene will play out. I have to remind myself, with a careening wave of disappointment, that Silas is not a regular guy. He probably has no qualms about sharing women and most likely has no strong feelings toward me beyond what's right in front of him. He is a man who owns an S&M club, so all normal rules of engagement do not apply. I will definitely need to modify my playbook if I'm going to dabble in his league.

I have never so much as brushed past a woman in a sexual way, so I am going to have to muster the strength of will to do so now. Having made my decision, I playfully wink at Silas and rest my head back on Thomas' shoulder, forcing my breasts up and forward.

Thomas groans and reaches up to cup them, swiping his fingers across my pert nipples. He bumps them with each finger then claims them with greedy palms. "Aahhh," he groans in my ear, "Your tits were made to be played with." He thumbs them rigidly then tugs them.

I reach to my side finding Silas, barely two feet away. Touching the silken skin of his forearm, I let my fingers trail down, feeling his ropey veins as my touch trickles down to his hand. He slips his fingers between mine and gives a gentle squeeze.

Thomas lifts my breasts as if in offering to the buxom Russian. She moves in, placing her hands on my thighs and leaning down to brush her nipples across mine. She rocks her right shoulder forward then back as her left shoulder comes forward, causing her nipples to trail slowly side to side, bumping and dragging against mine.

I'm immediately conflicted, my mind at war with my sexuality. Devin once said if he had to be with a woman sexually, he would throw up in his mouth. I don't feel quite as strongly, I'm more indifferent. I'm not turned on by her, but what does get me going is seeing the guy's response.

It's noticeablyly turning them on. Like moths to a flame they sit riveted to the dueling of our breasts, mesmerized, almost drooling like dogs.

I quickly realize the tremendous power this affords me, as well as recognizing that the interplay is not between the Russian and me but very much between Silas and me.

It's clear to me; now more than ever, that sexual power over another doesn't have to involve whips and chains, and you certainly don't need to be a Dom to have that power.

I would describe myself so far as a begrudging submissive, but I'm starting to see I still have power to wield. This sudden epiphany helps me to see myself, not as a pawn on someone else's chess board but in a leading role--with Thomas and the woman as my props.

Satisfied with my discovery, I play into the woman, letting out a soft moan that reverberates off the damp stone walls and ratchets up the simmering sexual tension. I arch my back further and reach up with my free hand to grab Thomas by the hair. His face is sunk into the crook of my neck, kissing and nipping my flushed skin from behind.

The woman leans in and sucks my nipple into her mouth. Silas gives my hand a squeeze, as he involuntarily winds up like a Jack-in-the-box ready to spring. She slurps and flicks at my nipple, moaning her delight as I writhe against Thomas and his hardness.

The stone room has an echoing stillness to it, punctuated by rhythmic drips falling from overhead and the peaceful sound of sloshing water.

The echo from my next contented moan brings Silas from his noiseless amnesty.

He sits forward clearing his throat and announces, "Well now, it seems as though it's time to finally see to your aftercare." He has a flustered look on his face. His light brown hair is wet and perfectly disheveled, so it partially obscures his simmering eyes.

Silas reaches over and with an easy tug; I slide from between Thomas and the woman, their bodies closing together against my vacated space like a bear trap, eager and hungry for each other. Her mouth closes on his in frenzied abandon.

Silas pulls me sideways onto his lap, my shoulder against his bare chest before I move my arm to drape it over his shoulders, and lean into his muscled chest. He says into my neck, "Tally had to get home to her kids, so I will take care of your aftercare."

Something about the way he says this makes me smile a sly, knowing smile. His tone is soft and the way his arms circle my waist and cross loosely at my hip, speaks to a softer side of Silas.

Well, not really soft, but not the bossy, demanding Dom of his alter ego. Caught in his tranquil, enchanting spell of kindness, I feel completely drawn to him. I like his powerful, commanding side, but more and more I'm getting glimpses of his benevolent, regular guy side. I'm being sucked into the Yin and Yang of him.

"What do you mean my aftercare?" I ask through glazed eyes and a growing lightheadedness from too much time in the hot water.

He laughs freely, really more of a rumble in his chest. "Jessie, aftercare is an important part of coming out of subspace," he explains while raking his fingers through his wet hair. The movement of his arm jostles me just enough to remind me I'm sitting naked on his lap as his thigh moves incrementally against my bare sex.

"You have to be able to let yourself go and trust that you will be taken care of, not only during play but after too. We can't exactly just high five you and send you on your way. That would break the trust and ruin your experience…and mine." He waggles his eyebrows, lifting me and carrying me like a newlywed to the other side of the massive bath.

I'm supremely grateful for the chilled air against my steaming skin. I'm also relieved by the distance from the other couple. He sets me down on my feet, turning me to face him with only our lower bodies submerged.

"Plus, you have Wasabi in your hair," he says with a smile. "I left the shampoo and body-wash over there," he indicates towards Thomas, with the Russian bobbing up and down on his lap. "But I'm not going back over," he says, as if suddenly shy of their sexual activity.

He moves to the edge, steps on the rocky seat running the perimeter of the bath and strides out toward another stone alcove. He reaches for a couple of plastic bottles as I watch the water bead up and trickle down his taut, muscular back. Mesmerized by his muscle tone and the smooth way he moves, I find myself gaping at him open mouthed.

I slam my mouth shut, replacing my awe with a guise of indifference as he turns around, grinning at me as if he knows I was staring at him. The sight of him naked from the front is equally impressive, but the sheer cockiness that reads on his face forces me to remain undaunted.

His penis isn't hard, but it's not soft either. I can't be sure if he is at war with himself to keep from becoming hard, thereby showing his hand, so to speak. Or if he's struggling to get hard with a lack of desire. Either way, his body is impressive, and he knows it.

Stepping back into the water, he twists the top off of a large Aquafina bottle and hands it to me. I swallow a long gulp and then hand it back for him to drink.

"Thank you," I say, wiping the back of my hand across my forehead and mopping off the beads of sweat. Even with the upper half of my body out of the hot water, I can still feel sweat trickling down my temples.

Silas notices, he has his chin tipped down but looks at me through the tops of his eyes; through thick, dark lashes. His wet hair is also clinging to his forehead.

His look is thoughtful, as though he is measuring something in his head, but also intense, like he wants to eat me alive. He is holding the water bottle in one hand, and the body wash in the other before he sets the body wash down between us, to float like a bobbing life raft.

He carefully brushes my long hair back, over my shoulders, then begins to gather up the damp waves with his free hand, lifting them off my back while simultaneously pulling me closer to him.

With hair no longer obscuring my breasts, save for a few rogue strands, and a disarming twinkle in his eyes, Silas reaches forward with the water bottle and trickles cold water down the back of my neck. It trails down like icy fingers of glacier water, cutting through the engulfing heat like a machete. I gasp and stand up straighter, slapped out of the looming heat stroke in a flash.

His wry smile broadens as he sprinkles more cold water across my shoulders. The water dances down my back and trickles through the valley between my breasts. He playfully takes a sip then pours the rest directly onto my breasts. This calculated act, causes another jolt from the intensity of the cold water on my flushed skin and causes my nipples to draw even tighter.

I step closer to him wanting him to touch me. He lets go of the gathered hair, letting it fall down my back. This time, instead of feeling hot and sticky, it feels fresh and tickles my back.

He squeezes some body wash into his hands, lathers them together then reaches out a hand to cup my face and stroke my ear with his thumb. "Wasabi," he says, by way of explanation.

"Oh," I say, and my eyes drift closed.

He gently washes my hair, massaging my scalp like a pro, then fills the empty water bottle by submerging it under the water. Then he rinses the suds out while tenderly tipping my chin up, to let the soapy water cascade down my back. Once my hair is thoroughly rinsed, he soaps up his hands again, then begins to wash my body. He is prudent at first, making sure my arms and back are free of Saki and soy sauce but his hands linger over my slippery breasts.

When his roving hands move to clean my submerged legs, he is less thorough, until he reaches my upper thighs. Here he teases me by lightly grazing his fingers through my folds. His eyes are taunting, as I melt into him, hardly able to stand up.

After a while, it becomes apparent that bathing me is his only intention, so I ask softly, "Why did you revoke that membership?"

"It's too hot in here, let's get out," he says, taking my hand and turning to walk over to the side, effectively dismissing my question.

Dripping, he leads me to a stone niche. There are thick, white terry cloth robes hanging from what look like rusty railroad spikes, driven into the slab of rock.

He helps me into my robe, carefully tugging my hair free and letting it fall down my back in ropey waves. He dries his face on his robe before sliding his arms in and loosely tying the sash.

I am so tired and wrung out from the heat; I don't have the energy to press him about the withdrawn membership, but just when I'm certain he isn't going to answer my question, he clears his throat. "Jessie, I own this club, and I demand absolute obedience from the members. Not just from the subs, but from everyone. I expect my rules to be followed." He says this while sliding his hands up and down my arms in a somewhat awkward attempt to dry me off.

I can tell he is still feeling surly about having been disobeyed.

"Thomas said penetration is part of it. That it's expected," I say, raising my eyes to his intent blue gaze. "Why am I different?"

"You just are Jessie. Now let's go before we pass out in the grotto and knock ourselves out with the fall," he says while backing up, a glaring attempt to elude my question.

"Silas?" I ask, and then lose my nerve, leaving his name hanging in the air like an old forgotten wind chime.

Disarmed, he looks at me, "Do you like Thai food?" he asks in a rush, as he tugs on the hip pockets of my robe drawing me closer to him.

1462 South Broadway

CHAPTER ELEVEN
Date

"I can't believe Dom boy is taking you out on a date," Devin says, shaking his head in disbelief. "Will he be dragging you around on a leash? Flogging you for forgetting to call him Sir?" he asks, completely unable to keep a straight face. Then he doubles over laughing as the visual in his mind solidifies. "This guy has no idea what he's in for," he says, eyes brimming with gleeful tears as he really lets go.

"You are making me nervous you little toad," I say through clenched teeth while glaring at him.

"Wait, Jessie, wait," he pinches out between fits of laughter. "Don't go! I am visualizing you with a bit in your mouth and a horse tail, anal plug in your ass." He howls with laughter then dramatically falls into a heap on the couch.

"You are a horrible, horrible man," I counter, but it breaks off with my own giggle. I throw a shoe I'm holding at him, then the other. He catches the first and bats the other one away.

"Which one?" I ask, referring to the thrown shoes.

"The taupe, strappy ones," he says without hesitating, then settles himself into an overly casual slouch, with his fingers laced behind his head.

"Devin, can you be serious for five minutes?" I ask, walking to my room to retrieve a newly purchased item.

"Of course Shortcake. I think I have it all out of my system," he says, still too playfully to sound completely ready to be serious.

I remove a small black box from the bag as I walk toward Devin. Opening the box, I pull out some lace and toss it at him.

Devin holds up the panties saying, "Sweetie, these will never fit me."

"Devin," I say with mock seriousness, as I place a hand on his leg, "I know, I just wish you would stop trying."

He starts to say something tart but then looks at me genuinely puzzled. "What's this hard thing?" he asks while pinching the crotch of the panties.

"They are remote-controlled, vibrating underwear, that's the bullet that vibrates," I explain, then wait for the meaning to dawn on him.

Opening his eyes wide with a congratulatory look he says, "It appears I have underestimated you."

"Do you think it's too much?" I ask, suddenly unsure of myself. It certainly would be a bold first date move, but I can't stand Silas thinking I'm too soft for 1462. That I want or need special rules that only pertain to me.

I have to keep reminding myself this is not a normal guy, kink is second nature to him. Something seemingly bold to me may be terribly passé to him.

Devin breaks into my thoughts, "No, It's definitely not too much. Just don't ask me to install a stripper pole or a sex swing in your room, because I like you the way you are. Don't

108

turn into someone you're not just to please a man. I would hate for the real Jessie to get lost," he says with real emotion.

"So…they are too much?" I ask, touched by his words but not wanting it to show.

He sighs and starts again, "No, they are perfect, it will surprise the hell out of him. It's sexy and playful--and any red blooded male would love it. Even me," he winks, and then shifts back to serious.

He sits forward and takes my hand. "However, if you really are going to get into a relationship with him, I don't want you to become something you're not. I pretended to be something I wasn't for a long time, and it ate away part of my soul." His hazel eyes are beseeching and look mossy green, just like his ratty t-shirt.

"Jessie, men love you in case you haven't noticed. There are a million of them out there that would treat you right."

I lean forward and kiss him square on the mouth. "I don't need other men when I have you." Then, breaking the sentimentality, I blow some wisps of hair out of my eyes.

"You will always have me, but I'm crazy about your fierce spirit and I don't want you to lose it, so he can debase and devalue you for his own pleasure that's all," he says, raising his hands in surrender.

"I know but it's not like that, I'm telling you he is different. I really do feel powerful when I'm with him…well, except the first time, that was a dirty power trip."

"Exactly. I know you. You will let him boss you around for about five minutes. Then you will try to top. He won't like that. The relationship will implode. And boom, I have a crying Jessie in my lap. There you go. That's the Reader's Digest version. You're welcome." He gives me a tight smile daring me to challenge him.

"I told you, it's not like that," I drag my fingers through my hair in frustration, knowing I will never be able to make him understand. "I like a powerful man, a man that oozes confidence and knows what he wants. Even when I have been bound or forced into a sub role, I still felt powerful and cared for. Almost like the experience was *given* to me."

"So, let me get this straight," Devin says with a wisp of a smile. "You felt powerful, totally naked with strangers eating sushi off you?"

I sigh before responding, "No, I felt vulnerable and exposed, and that heightened the experience to a level I can't even explain because it was so intense."

"And that felt powerful?" he questions with raised eyebrows.

"Yes. And by the way, who are you? I have heard about so many of your sexual exploits, my ears are still hemorrhaging, so don't go and get all high and mighty on me," I grind out. I am over his condescending tone, not to mention his hypocrisy.

"It's just a fucking date!" I toss over my shoulder as I storm out of the room.

Forty-five minutes and three dress changes later, I'm standing in front of the full-length mirror, mostly satisfied with my reflection.

A quiet knock precedes Devin through my door. He sharply sucks in his breath, "Wow, I came in to apologize but can't remember why now." He takes in my backless, plum colored dress with a gaping mouth.

"Oh stop it. You are going to get a boner, and I don't want to have to explain that to Corey," I tease, happy to have his support finally, begrudgingly or not.

My hair is in a messy bun with one long braid wound through it. Admittedly, it took far too long to achieve the look of effortless chic. The 'effortlessness' of my hair is laughable because it took thirty minutes and no less than seven tries to get it just right, but the result is really beautiful.

Having last seen Silas in a steamy Roman bath, with all my makeup dissolved off my face, I'm not taking any chances. Tonight my makeup is perfect. I used deep plum and shimmery gold tones on my eyelids, which has a dazzling effect on my green eyes.

"What jewelry are you wearing? You need something on your neck...so he isn't tempted to slap a collar on you," he says in hopes of breaking through my nervous tension.

"I'm not really wearing any, just that jeweled, leather cuff on my wrist...I don't want to overdo it, short, backless dress, high heels--that's plenty," I say with certainty while tugging the dress down my thighs in nervous anticipation.

"Well, either way, your Chariot awaits."

As I walk into the living room, heels tapping my entrance on the wood floor, Silas rises from his spot on the couch. I'm grateful when I see that Devin had been gracious enough to at least get him a beer.

When Silas sees me, he almost looks shy, but his bashful look quickly turns devilish as he walks toward me. Leaning in to drop a kiss on my cheek, he says sweetly, "You look beautiful."

He is wearing dark slacks and a blue dress shirt that draws crazy attention to his eyes. His tawny brown hair is perfectly mussed and it makes me secretly wonder how long he worked to achieve his own look of effortless perfection.

"And you...you look dangerous," I say through a smile, feeling a little shy myself.

"Devin, it was good to see you again buddy, thanks for the beer," Silas says, as Devin glowers through a smile.

Silas takes my hand, threading his fingers through mine like it was the most natural thing in the world.

"You too Silas. Where are you two headed tonight anyway?" Devin asks, way too casually. I have to suppress a groan.

"There is a great martini bar right down the street--I know how Jessie likes her dirty martinis, I thought we would start there. Have you been?" Silas is breezy, Devin is coiled like a snake ready to strike. I'm sure he thinks Silas' plan is to get me drunk and then take me to the club.

"Um hmm," Devin grinds out, between pinched lips.

I abruptly jump in, "Ok, well then. See you later." Then I hurry toward the door, nearly dragging Silas behind me.

As he closes the door behind us, he asks, "Are you sure he's gay? He almost seemed jealous." Luckily, Silas is at least half joking, based on his huge smile.

"Yep. As the day is long," I quip then continue, "He is not jealous, just...um, protective," I say, trying to explain Devin's parental demeanor.

"Well, he should be. I mean you, in that dress," he says through a dazzling smile.

As we settle in at a cocktail table in the martini bar, I take in the comfortable, loungy feel of the place. "Did you know this

112

used to be a Speakeasy back in the prohibition days?" I ask, while secretly wishing I could take down my hair to cover my exposed back.

"I had heard that," he answers, "I kind of like the rebellious, supper club feel it still has." He looks comfortable and totally at ease, unlike myself--I feel like I'm on a date with a superhero, not a regular man.

As if to imprint the Speakeasy feel even deeper into our consciousness a quiet, bluesy music plays in the background amidst all the chatter and clinking forks against plates.

Our waiter approaches with a slight hesitation as he looks me up and down, finally welcoming us and asking what we would like.

Silas orders me an extra dirty martini and a single malt scotch for himself, then slowly chuckles as the waiter walks away.

"It's too much, isn't it? The dress, I mean," I say as more of a statement than a question.

His eyes alight, he says, "I'm starting to worry that it may not be enough."

"I knew I should have stuck with yoga pants. They felt sooo right," I say while rolling my eyes and trying to tug my hemline down a bit.

"Jessie, it's perfect," he says, laying a hand on top of mine and leaving it there. "You shouldn't be surprised when people notice you, especially men."

"I only wanted you to notice," I say, looking him straight in the eyes.

"Oh, trust me, I've noticed," he says, scooting his stool closer to mine. "Long before that dress, I noticed."

Our waiter arrives with our drinks, and I take a long swallow before he even walks away. I can finally relax a bit as the warmth of the liquor seeps through my body.

"How was your week?" he asks conversationally before taking a tentative sip of his scotch. "What is it that you do for work?"

After another fairly aggressive sip, I clear my throat and answer. "I'm a Landman for an oil and gas company, so I negotiate for the acquisition or divestiture of mineral rights. It's terribly boring I'm afraid."

He sets his glass down saying, "It doesn't sound boring, in fact, it sounds quite a bit like what I do in commercial real estate. Contract negotiations, managing rights and obligations, tedious stuff like that right?"

"It is similar. Although, I have to say I'm glad you led with your real estate career and not the other," I say while widening my eyes on *other*.

"Oh, that reminds me," I say, feeling my body loosen up, thanks to the rapid consumption of vodka and olive juice. "I have something for you." I reach into my purse and pull out the small remote control for my panties.

He takes it, turning it over in his hand as realization dawns on him. He slowly looks up with a wolfish grin. Then promptly presses the button. Right away I feel a persistent hum between my legs.

My eyelids drift closed, then slowly open with my own sly smile.

The vibrating stops, then he drops the remote into his pocket. "I'm going to have some fun with this," he promises just as our waiter brings another round of drinks.

My eyes widen, I'm already feeling the effects of the first martini. After a small sip of the new drink, I say, "Wait, that doesn't taste like green curry."

Silas chokes on his sip of scotch, laughing. "That's funny, you're right, this doesn't taste like Pad Thai either." His eyes are shimmering with mirth.

"You should know, I'm a sloppy drunk," I say while chewing on an olive.

He gently squeezes my hand, "Trust me, if I was going to take advantage of you, I already would have," he says in a very low voice.

My heart stops beating for a minute, then starts again with a whoosh of pounding, pumping blood.

"You're right. You've had several opportunities. Declan too. Do you know what he did to me?" I ask.

Silas looks me dead in the eyes, leans in and answers, "Aye Lass, I doo."

I drop the olive skewer back into my drink, gaping open-mouthed at him as the last cog falls into place in my mind. "The cowled stranger, it was you," I say, almost inaudibly.

"Thas a bra lassie," he whispers, as he leans into my ear. A wave of searing heat crashes through me as his breath warms and tickles my ear.

"And the pearls?" I ask.

"No, no, the pearls were not me. But I enjoyed watching very much." He laughs at the abashed look on my face.

"Is it super hot in here?" I ask fanning myself with the happy hour menu and shifting on my stool.

"Yes, suddenly it's very, very hot. Let's go get some dinner," he says, polishing off his drink then pulling a few twenties from his wallet and dropping them on the table.

I slide off the stool, tugging at my hemline as Silas places a hand on my low back, leading me outside.

His palm is against my bare skin before he becomes uncomfortable with the presumption then lowers it to the draping fabric at the top of my ass. Once realizing his hand is, in fact on my ass, he drops it all together, taking my hand instead. It's cute; he's being such a gentleman.

"How long have you known Devin?" Silas asks as we meander down the lively city sidewalk in the direction of the Thai restaurant.

"My whole life, we were neighbors growing up. I used to get in fights defending him," I say with a nostalgic smile. "Kids were horrible to him, to me too, with my red hair. So we were good together, two social outcasts."

"Now I can see why he is so protective of you. Was he picked on for being gay?" he asks.

I scratch my shoulder where a wisp of hair is tickling me and say, "Kids can be such assholes, you know? They will find anything to pick on you about. Devin was different, but nobody really understood what gay was when we were kids. They just knew something was...off. As we got older, the teasing got worse, and he spent most of his teenage years getting beat up."

"It's such a shame no one bothers to teach kids compassion and acceptance. Yet, they teach cup stacking in schools, because we all know how valuable that skill is." He shakes his head and slows our pace, "Tell me more."

"His parents knew he was gay, but they figured he had the grim misfortune of choosing to be that way. So they mind-fucked him through most of his formative years, it was awful to watch him go through so much. One time, his parents told him he couldn't go to church with them anymore and that God was disappointed in him."

"That's messed up," Silas says with real emotion. Our palms still clasped together as he swipes his thumb gently up and down mine.

"I told him he was going to go to church with me from then on because my God loved him and created him exactly, perfectly the way he was. I was 13 at the time but had more of a grasp on humanity than a lot of adults."

Silas clicks his tongue and lets go of my hand so he can wrap his arm around my shoulder and tuck me into him.

"He was seventeen when he tried to kill himself," I say through the lump in my throat. The statement hangs in the air like a lead balloon before I continue. "When I went to see him in the hospital, his wrists were wrapped where he had cut them. He was sleeping, so I crawled up next to him in his tiny hospital bed, wrapped my arms around him and held him like a child. I had tears streaming down my face, I was begging him not to leave me, and I told him I would die without him. I begged and pleaded with him for what felt like hours. I knew the cuts on his wrist wouldn't kill him this time, but I also knew that next time he would be that much more certain to finish the job. So I begged him for his life and for mine too. It was late into the night when I felt him shaking against me, sobbing. Then I knew he was conscious and could hear me pleading with him."

"Jessie," Silas stops walking and turns me to face him. He notices I have tears in my eyes, so he pulls me in to engulf me in his arms. I can smell his sporty deodorant and his warm skin, and it soothes me while I blink away my tears.

"The thing is, Devin is the most amazing person I know, it's just such a shame so many people had to miss out on him for so long."

"What happened after the hospital?" he asks with genuine curiosity, as we start walking again, in no hurry to reach our destination.

"We moved. I told him his way wasn't working so we were going to try my way. Then we moved to a new city and got an apartment together. I thought my parents would have simultaneous strokes when I left high school in my junior year. To their credit, they understood my circumstances better than I knew. Anyway, I finished high school online while working at a dingy biker bar."

"Your parents sound pretty great. They obviously love Devin to sacrifice so much, you know, to let you go," he says.

"Well, they still had their hands in my pot, you know. Without being too pushy, they let me know college was still expected of me. They sent college applications and financial aid packets along with cookies or brownies," I laugh just thinking of it. "But Devin thrived outside of the poisonous environment, and as he started to embrace who he was, the oppressive shell broke away," I finish.

"You saved his life, Jessie, he is lucky to have you." He holds me close against his side. "I have an amazing new appreciation for you...well, actually I think I just admire the hell out of you altogether."

Silas pulls the door to the Thai restaurant open for me, and we enter into a much more animated crowd than at the martini bar. People are clustered around small bar tops, spilling the end of work week joviality out in thrumming stories, boisterous laughter and hearty thumps on the back.

Sinking into a plush booth beneath a spray of bamboo stalks, I say, "Sorry for the heavy topic, I just wanted you to understand my relationship with Devin and how important he is to me."

"That I do. It's obvious how much you care for each other. He kind of falls somewhere between a protective brother and a jealous girlfriend," he laughs, but he's not too far off the mark.

I don't want Silas to know how much Devin distrusts him, how leery he is of him, so I smile and prattle on. "As long as you are not homophobic, we should get along nicely," I say with a broad smile and reach for the menu.

"Are you kidding? I'm not prejudiced against anyone. In fact, I don't judge anyone for anything. Just look what I'm into--" He leans in animatedly. "People judge me based on that all the time," he says and raises his eyebrows accusingly.

"You mean you really are just a normal guy under all that depravity?" I ask with mock pretentiousness. I'm feeling relaxed and languid from the drinks but also from the surprisingly easy company.

"Well, I tend to cast a pretty wide net around what's considered normal. But yes, I am just a regular guy." He allows a lascivious grin while his dark blue eyes swallow me whole. "In fact, Jessie Hayes, *you* judged *me*. You called me old-timey and said I was a juicer."

My smile broadens; I had wanted to put him down--to knock him off his high horse then, back when I thought he was a narcissistic prick... "That wasn't all because you're totally controlling and super disciplined...it was a little because of your hot bod. It just doesn't seem like you have a lot of carb load days, that's all."

He laughs at my attempt to recover but adds, "You still judged me."

I pause, smiling playfully, lean in and say in a lowered voice, "Don't kid yourself, I'm still judging you."

He laughs before saying, "I'm starting to think we get our own drinks here." He glances around for a server, but finds none amongst the throngs of well-dressed people.

"Easy tiger, I'll go to the bar," I say as I snag my purse. I shimmy sideways on the seat while my thighs stick to and then shuck the leather of the booth. Finally freeing myself, I stand and straighten my dress.

"I don't want you to have to do that…but I want to watch you go," he says, settling back and casually propping his elbow on the back of the booth.

I make my way through the crowd like the cleaving hull of a ship, parting the masses with murmured apologies and polite interjections. The crowd at the bar is mosh-pit deep, and the bartenders are hustling around with an almost choreographed ease amongst each other. Bar-backs are dumping ice from huge drums and bringing out clean glasses by the crate full.

I skillfully make my way to the bar where an oaf of a man sits with his meaty hand around a chilled pint glass. Molted skin around his watery eyes speaks to his repudiated intolerance of the sun. He is obviously wealthy, with diamond cuff links, fat rings on most of his fingers and a choking amount of cologne. Perhaps these displays are his siren's call to anyone of trophy wife material, or possibly just a simple gold digger in the vicinity.

He eyes my cleavage then speaks through his trout lips, "Allow me, Sweetheart. What are you drinking?" As he speaks, he snaps his fingers in the face of a clean cut bartender, all while keeping his eyes fixed on my chest.

The bartender rolls his eyes, apparently accustomed to this man's behavior, but still not happy about it. I look at him apologetically as he notices me for the first time.

"What can I get you?" he asks with a friendly smile.

I order our drinks while turning my back to the fog of cologne. The bartender is quick with the drinks and generous with his pour. He sets the cocktails in front of me while smiling gallantly. "These are on Felix," he says with a curt nod to the brute next to me, and a wink.

Making my way back to the table, I'm stopped by a tall man with brown hair combed neatly back and wearing a very expensive suit. "Where are you going in such a hurry?" he asks.

"To my table," I respond lightly with a friendly smile.

"I was hoping I would get a better look at that dress, and now here you are," he says with his own friendly smile.

"Yep, here I am. But look quick because I'm--" Suddenly there it is, the vibrating bullet in my panties. I suck in my breath at the insistence of it, spilling a few drops of my drink.

I look down, smiling at Silas' ironic audacity then shake my head slowly back and forth. Silas is having fun with this. That wicked, wicked man.

"Um, so...yea. Uh, what were you saying?" I stammer, struggling with the sheer force of the bullet directly against my clit.

"I just didn't want you to rush by before I could introduce myself. I'm Alexander," he says as he drags a hand lightly up my bare arm.

"Nice to meet you uh, um...Alexander," I strive to meet his eyes but only succeed for a fraction of a second.

"And you?" he asks.

"Me what? Oh," I tilt my head back with equal parts of frustration and stimulation. Alexander evidently fears I will topple over, because he gently takes hold of both my arms saying, "Easy Babe, do you need help getting home?" He says this in a gentlemanly manner, not a skeevy, date rape kind of way; which I'm grateful for.

"N-No, I'm, no..oh God no. I'm fine. Thank you, really...I'm fine," I respond, completely aware of how breathy I sound. Alexander looks puzzled, but he doesn't want to seem too pushy, so he nods and drops his hands.

Blessedly, the bullet stops vibrating. I round on my heel and march toward Silas. I immediately see his laughing face and his hands raised in surrender. He looks like a kid who just put a Whoopee cushion on the teacher's chair. My stern face is met with more giggles as I slide back into the booth.

"That was a dirty trick," I say in a hushed voice.

Still chuckling, he opens his menu then says, "Thank you for fighting through the fray to get our drinks." He takes a sip and asks surprised, "Is this Lagavulin? This is expensive stuff."

"Yeah? I wouldn't know," I say as I peruse the curries on the menu.

"Someone bought you these?" he asks, now his curiosity is piqued.

"Not on purpose," I say, almost under my breath.

"Ok, I was just wondering if I needed to go all alpha male and kick someone's ass," he says, his crooked smile evidence that he is only kidding.

I hardly touch my drink while we wait for our food to arrive; our conversation is so natural and fluid.

"Tell me about your family," I prompt.

"I have an older brother who is a stock broker at a big firm in New York. We have a super strong bond, but I don't see him much. As kids, I was the typical bratty little brother. I always wanted to do whatever he was doing, and he never wanted his twerp little brother hanging around."

"Aawwwww, that's typical."

"He used to roll me up in a blanket like a burrito, lean me against a wall inside our bedroom closet and close the door. He would tell me that when I freed myself; I could play with him and his friends." He smiles brightly, his eyes alight. "As I got faster and faster at getting out, he would do more and more to stop me. He would add belts and scarfs and tie me tightly."

"So that's where it comes from!" I tease.

"I doubt that. One day he wrapped me in a thick carpet, you know, like a big area rug and secured it with bungee cords then shimmied me to the back of the closet. Well, in the beginning when he would roll me up, I would push my arms out from my sides and widen my legs to create extra room inside my little burrito, so getting out was easy. Sometimes I even waited in the closet after I had freed myself so he would think he did a great job." He laughs at the memory, while a slow rumble quakes his shoulders.

The waitress approaches and sets our food down in front of us. After some quick words of appreciation, she is swallowed back into the crowd.

"So, the game changer this time was the rug, it wasn't pliable, and I hadn't managed to create much extra space. So this time, I completely exhausted myself trying to get free, struggling and fighting in vain. I had sweat dripping in my eyes, I was calling out to my mom to rescue me, but she couldn't hear. I started to really panic and got frantic with my struggles. Jessie, this rug was like a straitjacket, and inside the closet, the air was so hot and stifling, it was like a crypt."

"How did you get out?" I ask, completely engrossed in his story.

"I either fell asleep or passed out and pitched forward, crashing through the closet doors. I knocked them both off the tracks." Silas is so animated in his telling of the story; I completely lose interest in my food. "So, of course, my mom heard the commotion of the closet doors crashing to the floor, so she burst in screaming, 'God damn it boys, what are you up to now!?' and Jessie, if you knew my mom, I swear you would be able to hear her right now. She said those words more than anything else while we were growing up. Oh, how we tormented that poor, sweet woman."

"What happened after she found you?" I ask as he sucks in his breath.

"Holy shit this is hot, *Thai spicy* really brings spicy to the next level," he says while wiping his mouth with his napkin. I slide my ice water over to him, as he has already drained his then urge him to go on with his story.

"She blistered Sam's ass, she was so angry." He sucks in some air seemingly to quench the fire in his mouth then goes in for another torturous bite.

"How old were you guys?" I ask before taking a bite of chicken, dripping with green curry.

"Like eight and twelve, but we were ornery kids our whole childhood. I told you we tormented our mom. Once Sam and his little cronies put me in a truck tire and rolled me down our huge sledding hill, I still remember barfing carrot and raisin salad. That's when we coined the term 'Un-swallowing' to use in place of puking. Oh, sorry," he gestures to my food as if talk of puke crosses the line.

"Oh my goodness, you were such a little brother!" I say laughing at the tire story.

"I know, but I was trouble on my own too, I used to flush cherry bombs down the toilets at school, or put a brick in a brown paper bag and leave it on the street so people would drive over it thinking it was just a paper bag and jack up their alignment." His amusement is infectious, and we both laugh at his antics.

"Oh, your poor mother, two trouble maker boys. What about your dad?" I inquire, wondering if the boys got their sense of mischief from him.

"He was always at work. He would come home smoking his pipe, eat dinner and watch 60 Minutes on TV. As far as he knew, we were angels."

"You should do something really nice for your mom on Mother's Day," I say, not at all joking.

"I should. I'd need a gift that really delivers the message 'Thanks for not putting me in foster care,'" he says, and I laugh. It makes me choke on a sip of martini, but I love his witty comeback.

"It sounds like you had a healthy, happy childhood. Some would believe kinky Dom's were all abused or somehow messed up in childhood, but you don't seem, you know, messed up," I finish lamely.

"Jessie, there are some seriously fucked up people involved in BDSM, but that can literally be said for every segment of society. Priests, Boy Scout leaders, teachers, doctors, therapists--literally every segment of society has its bad eggs. For the most part, people in the scene are regular, high functioning, reputable people."

"What about me?" I ask.

"I'm not sure. I haven't quite figured you out yet," he says while sliding his empty plate to the edge of the table.

"You don't think I'm ready for 1462?" I challenge.

"I think you are ready for *parts* of 1462," he says delicately, then adds, "Tell me the craziest thing you have ever done sexually." He leans in toward me, eyes locked on mine.

"Let's see... I bent over naked in front of a stranger so he could tie me up with my panties and then twist nipple rings on my girls," I say with a quick nod to my breasts.

"I mean before the club, and I don't mean the strangest place you have ever had sex, it doesn't even have to be about sex. Just tell me something sexual you have done that would surprise me," he says, sitting back with a satisfied look.

"Um, well, ok. I was on vacation in Maui with my girlfriend Heather, who lives in Chicago now. We were lying by the pool having some Mai Tai's when Heather pointed out some window washers a few floors above our room. She told me if I could stop them at our floor and keep them there for ten solid minutes; she would pay for our rental car."

"I'm listening," he says, still sitting back with a devious grin parting his lips.

"I sat there for a minute thinking, because ten minutes is a long time, but they were moving pretty quickly, so I had to make a decision fast. I grabbed my cocktail and our room card and said, 'see you in fifteen' and went up to our room." I pause for effect.

Silas says, "Now you really have my attention." He nods for me to go on.

"So I got to the room, and they were still a few floors up, so I just paced around nervously, because seriously, ten minutes is a long time."

The waitress gathers up our empty plates and Silas orders two orders of mango sticky rice and two Thai coffees. Then he drums his fingers on the table, impatient for me to continue.

"When I finally heard the pulley system lowering down, I was waiting for them. The balcony was around the corner off the main room, but the bedroom had huge windows, those were the ones they were cleaning. Anyway, I heard them outside the window and pulled the curtains back, like I had no idea they were there, just going about my business in high heels and a string bikini," I giggle at the memory.

"When they saw me, I smiled and waved. Now, I'm sure they were instructed not to interact with any hotel guests while cleaning the windows, but when they didn't wave back it gave me a great excuse, so I stuck out my bottom lip and pouted. I turned my back coyly to them and pulled my hair forward over my right shoulder so they could see me toy with my bikini tie. I slowly pulled the bow down my back, but before I undid it all the way, I playfully glanced over my shoulder at the two guys. One had put his sunglasses on top of his head, and the other was squeegeeing the dry window, both totally watching me."

"Of course they were. They would rather have been fired than miss the show," Silas puts in.

"I finished untying the knot between my shoulder blades but the ties around my neck were still fastened, so my bikini top hung down still partially covering my breasts. I walked to the nightstand which is where I had strategically put the ice bucket."

Silas groans and shuts his eyes for a long moment.

"Then I just tipped my head back, dragging some ice all over my neck and belly. By this time they had both leaned in closer, and their breath was fogging two crescents on the glass. Anyway, my breasts were still mostly covered, but my nipples were super hard from the ice and the water droplets that had trickled down my skin. Then I shimmied my hips a bit so the bikini top would shift just enough for my nipples to poke out from behind the fabric triangles."

Silas sighs, "Go on," he prompts, his eyes darkening.

"The window washers were not going anywhere, but it had only been a few minutes, so I teased them some more then slowly untied the neck straps. The top dropped to the floor, and I grazed over my tits a few times with my hands, taunting the guys."

I lean in and lower my voice. "I started pinching and tugging at my nipples, slowly rolling them between my fingers and thumbs. After a few minutes of that, I let my hand slide down my stomach into my bikini bottom. I looked right at the guys, licked my lips and chewed on the bottom one in my best porn star rendition. Then I hooked both thumbs into the ties at my hips, danced and twisted around a bit to tease the guys but also to burn more time. Finally, I bent over in front of them, sliding my bikini bottom all the way down my straight legs. I turned and sat on the bed with my feet still on the floor but my legs spread wide, open to their hungry stares."

I lower my voice even more so Silas really has to strain to hear me. "Then I began to circle my clit with a finger, round and round, careful not to obscure their view. For good theatrics, I brought my finger to my mouth and licked and sucked it."

Leaning in further, drawing Silas in closer as well, I continue. "I spread open my legs so far I thought my hips would pop out of joint. All the while circling and stroking my clit and pinching and twisting my nipple with my other hand. My orgasm had been building just from the exhibitionism, let alone my fingers, but I wasn't sure if ten minutes had elapsed yet, so I slowed down and writhed, arching my back and moaning, increasing the speed of my circles until I came for them. I was pulsing and crying out while the orgasm clenched and sparked my body," I finish.

"What did they do?" Silas asks.

"They just stood there watching, like two slack-jawed chumps."

"It's because they had both just popped off in their shorts and were not sure what to do next," Silas says as he sits back heavily in the booth.

"When I came back down to the pool, everyone started cheering and clapping. Heather yelled out, 'eighteen minutes!' People were whistling and congratulating me, sending over drinks."

"What did you do once you found out the whole pool knew what was going on? Were you embarrassed?"

"Not at all, I did a deep curtsy, waved and blew kisses of course," I say, smiling at the scandalous memory.

I eye him for a minute before he says, "I have a massive hard on right now."

"Yes, but are you surprised?" I ask.

"Huh?" he says and looks genuinely stumped.

"You asked me to tell you a sexual story about myself that would surprise you. So you could decide if I'm right for the club," I add helpfully, cocking my head in a questioning taunt.

"Just so I'm clear, you want a full-fledged BDSM experience at the club? No holds barred?" he asks, as he shifts in his seat.

"Yes," I say, "With you," I add almost shyly. "We can do a formal contract and everything."

He is so handsome the way he looks at me, I feel like my heart will break if he says no. My eyes have been opened. Despite the discomfort I felt at 1462, the experiences have always been intensely gratifying.

I am also falling fast for this man; there is no denying that fact. I am ready for the sexual wonderland 1462 lays before me, and I want to embrace my new found eroticism and learn the intricacies with Silas.

"Ok Jessie," he says, not taking his eyes off mine while the waitress sets down our mango sticky rice, Thai coffees and the leather booklet with our bill.

Silas thanks her without looking away from me. Heat is creeping up my neck and cheeks, but before Silas notices, his brow furrows. He reaches into his pocket and produces his phone.

"Hi Analise, is everything Ok?" he says hastily. "Of course. (pause) No. Absolutely (pause) I'll be right there!" He hangs up, looking stricken.

"Jessie, I'm so sorry, I have to go." He speaks absentmindedly while pulling his wallet out with one hand and hurriedly texting with the other. "I'll have an Uber out front in a minute to take you home." He flags down the waitress then hardly glances at the bill before stuffing the money in and handing her back the leather booklet.

"Is everything Ok?" I ask, slightly affronted.

"I think so, but I have to go right now, I'm so sorry." He jumps up and practically tugs me from the booth as he grabs my hand and propels me through the restaurant and out the front door.

He packs me expeditiously into the black Chevy Tahoe Uber and says hastily, "I'll be in touch." Then he closes the door, immediately turning his back to me and melting into the crowd.

The tornado that was the brash ending of our date spins my head and has me wondering, *what the hell just happened? And who the fuck is Analise?*

CHAPTER TWELVE
Steampunk

"What is Steampunk, anyway?" I ask Devin and Corey while staring at the formal 1462 Fetish Ball invitation. It was hand delivered with a box I have yet to open. The invitation itself looks very old and delicate; it's as frail as old tissue paper and even looks burned in sections. There is also an irregularity to the yellowing paper that looks like someone spilled their tea on it. The faded background has a sophisticated system of gears that lends a Victorian Age feel to the delicate paper. It reads:

Mr. Silas Maxwell Bishop Requests

The Honor of Your Presence

At 1462 for the Annual

Victorian Fetish, Steampunk Ball

June 10, 8 pm

"Are you kidding me? You have never heard of Steampunk?" Corey intones while rubbing his newly shorn buzz cut with one hand. It's a confused gesture that tells me he is disappointed in me.

"Corey, let's not forget our young Jessie is an innocent. She is unschooled in the art of fetish balls," Devin says while settling himself next to Corey on the couch.

"I'm not *that* innocent, I know what a fetish ball is. I just don't know how to dress Steampunk. Something tells me traditional fetish wear is not what they are looking for. Was there even latex in the Victorian era?" I ask only half joking, making my way to the kitchen for a bottle of water. When I return, Devin and Corey are looking at me conspiratorially.

"What?" I ask, with an inflection sounding harsher than I mean it to sound.

"Do you trust us?" Corey asks.

"I think so, but I'm not going to commit to anything until I hear what you two are cooking up. You look like two foxes in a hen house."

They look at each other then sit forward stoically in an unintentionally synchronized move that reminds me how in tune they are with one another.

"Let us help you," Devin says, hair flopping in his eyes unnoticed.

"Yes, you need us. The ball is only five days away," Corey says. "We can do this for you, we know our fetish balls." His warm brown eyes are petitioning me.

"Don't you see this is your big night? This is Silas' invitation to play with you!" Devin explains, like I'm a child.

"I'm not even sure I want to go. He hasn't so much as called since running out on me," I say, the hurt in my voice betraying my studied indifference. I snap the twisting lid off my water then realize I no longer even want it. I prod the guys, "Tell me more about fetish balls. Are they giant orgies?"

They look at each other, then both burst out laughing, dramatically falling into each other.

"No, absolutely not. Not in the open anyway, there are playrooms for that. In fact penetration of any kind is not allowed in the open areas," Corey explains.

"Nudity is not even allowed if alcohol is served and I'm talking ass cracks and areolas," Devin pipes in.

"There are usually bands or DJ's, and fetish wear fashion shows or drag shows. Jessie, It's just a very uninhibited costume party, and people get VERY into it," Corey explains.

"This will be perfect for you because the costume element will help you get into character. With this being your first real scene with Silas, it might be easier if you are *Steampunk Girl* rather than *Plain old Jessie*." Devin winks to soften his words, but I know he is right.

Ever since our ill-fated date when Silas had agreed to a scene with me right before running out, I had wondered how we would transition into it. I feel incredibly awkward just thinking about it because he had seemed so *normal*.

"We will handle your outfit. Now as for you, you need to open that box." Devin gestures with his head toward the box that accompanied the invitation.

"Oh, I nearly forgot," I say, as I retrieve the little box from the slim marble entry table in our pseudo-foyer. The box is the size of my palm, thin and made out of sheet metal. It has burn marks and sloppy welding bubbling through the edges. On top is a rusty gear box, which Devin admires unabashedly.

"It's beautiful," he says, immediately intrigued with the industrial look of it. "I like the look of the rusty gears for the Dawson's loft project," he muses while taking mental notes.

"I get it that Steampunk is mechanical and industrial, but you two have to make sure I look good…and sexy, or I'm not going. The last thing I want to look like is the Bionic Woman at a Steampunk party," I say sternly. They both smile at me wickedly, so I repeat even louder, "Or I'm not going!"

I slowly open the box, not sure what to expect. You would think a severed finger the way I cautiously tip back the top causing old stiff hinges to come to life. As the box creaks open, the gears start to turn. An ominous shudder runs through me as I realize I have literally as well as metaphorically just opened Pandora's Box.

Inside the box, there's an old, historic key and a membership card with a magnetic strip across the back.

CHAPTER THIRTEEN
Fetish

I decide to leave work early on the 10th. The anticipation alone is destroying my ability to concentrate, it's almost too much to handle. The contracts are blurring before my eyes as I read and re-read the addendums. I'm completely unable to make sense out of them.

Taking my fiduciary responsibilities very seriously, I conveniently decide that it would do my clients a massive disservice if I continued to sit at this desk, fumbling through the day. So, with nary a look back I leave my office.

I have a downtrodden look across my face though inside I am skipping past the other offices. I do, as an afterthought, poke my head into Salinger's office. It's only fair to let him know I'm leaving. As my land technician, he and I maintain a very symbiotic relationship together, he needs me, and I need him.

"Hey there, I'm going to bust out of here and take some department time...you ok with that?" I ask as a courtesy, not for permission because technically he works for me.

"Whatever you say, boss, I figure I'll just stay here and work on my carpal tunnel syndrome. It's coming along nicely with all these figures you sent me," Salinger says with a broad grin. His perfectly combed hair is flawless, never a strand out of place.

He recently went through a messy divorce after his wife cheated on him, but he never seems rattled, ever. He spent some time in the Middle East as a Marine, so I figure his perspective on life is weighted against war and carnage. I guess after that, nothing is all that bad, even a cheating whore wife.

"Ok then, carry on," I say, smiling because I just told him to carry on getting carpal tunnel. The fact is, he's a good-looking, funny guy. He makes work enjoyable, and with the exception of actual work, we are hardly ever serious. He's amazing; his wife was crazy to screw that up. I always had thought of her as a snobby, Stepford wife; add cheater to that and you have the image about right. He was way too good for her.

It's just past 11:00 when I step into my apartment, nine hours to go. I'm feeling conflicted about the evening because it's shrouded by the party. Was this Silas' way of not really giving me a full experience? The fact that he has been MIA since our date leaves a sour taste in my mouth.

The date seemed perfect, serious at times, playful at others. His BDSM side was still an enigma, but the encounters with him at 1462 were hot. I want the experience with him at the club, but I'm certainly not sure of my need for BDSM as a lifestyle.

I am still in the curious stage, but in the interest of full disclosure, I'm feeling more and more like it is Silas I want, not necessarily the kinkster scene. I have no doubt they are not mutually exclusive to him, and to have one, I need to embrace the other.

"Jessie, you're home," Devin says, as he rounds the corner, startling my daydream into an evaporative mist.

"Shit! Damn Devin, you scared me!" I say with my heart in my throat. "I thought you would be at work."

"I'm an independent business owner, I work when I want to. Come check these out," he says, as he grabs my hand and drags me excitedly to his room.

He turns around, hastily pulling on some ridiculous goggles then turns back toward me. "What do you think? I'm obsessed with these." He's as giddy as a kid on Christmas morning.

"Devin…they're ugly, and I'm not wearing goggles on my face," I say with disgust. They are coke bottle thick, round goggles made of bronze, flanked by a broad leather base, covered in cogs and rivets and made of copper. The round lenses are blue…deep, intense, undeniably blue. The leather base hugs his forehead like a snorkel mask and rims his eyes, both occluding the light and holding them at an obnoxious distance off his face.

"What?" he howls, "These are post-apocalyptic, crazy Victorian scientist goggles, and yes, you are wearing them. Just not on your face," he smiles, holding up a finger for me to wait. He hurries to his closet and pulls out an old, brown leather, undersized top hat.

The hat has the same bronze and copper rivets as the goggles, but the decorative set of cogs on the side are shiny brass and brushed nickel. There's a plume of brown and white speckled pheasant feathers flaring out from the mechanical cogs. In design and style, it has Devin's name all over it. Chic meets industrial, as he is constantly explaining to clients at his endless dog and pony shows, it's the hallmark of his design aesthetic.

137

He slips the goggles over the top of the hat, careful not to disturb his cog and feather creation and situates them at the base of the hat. Now they rest post-apocalyptically on the brim. He raises his head haughtily, settling the hat slightly askew on his head. Sucking in his cheeks, he asks through pinched lips, "Isn't it fabulous?"

After seeing it together I have to agree, it is pretty fabulous. My excitement for the evening catapults to the next level, never mind the knocking of my knees. "Show me more," I say, flopping down on his bed.

"I can't, not without Corey here. Besides, the building anticipation is delicious, no?" he says, as he crawls up next to me. He settles in lazily, with his fingers laced behind his head and one knee bent, protruding up like a shark fin.

I roll to face him, but I'm unable to make eye contact. He's bare chested with gray sweatpants tugged up to just below his knees. "Devin," I whisper, "Am I doing the right thing?"

He exhales heavily while pondering what to say. "It's hard to say Hon, he would be really great if you could disregard his penchant for domination," he smiles weakly as I finally look into his hazel eyes.

"I can't forget that, it's a part of him, and I think I like it, I'm just not sure if I love it, or like it all the time," I say.

"Don't get too carried away, he may not *need* it. I mean, I like CBT but even my cock and balls can only take so much. Maybe you should just look at it as spice, you know? Something you can use but don't have to," he offers helpfully.

"That's a terrible analogy, he owns a BDSM club...I think it's more than spice to him," I say, feeling a little defeated.

"Well, keep in mind he is a man underneath all his labels and titles, and he is human under that, so don't let one thing about him conceal everything else," he says, as he rolls over to face me.

"Like you?" I whisper.

"Yes, I am many things, but only one of those things is a fag," he whispers back, draping his forearm across my hip. "Try this. Try his particular *spice,* if you don't like it, or he is disrespectful, then you come home and drink copious amounts of wine with Corey and me." Then he quickly adds, "Or, I could make a bumper sticker that says, 'I Love Wanking.'" His eyes light up at the thought.

"What does that even mean?" I ask, not sure I really want to know.

"Most clubs have rules against wankiness, it's the weirdo in the corner masturbating to someone else's scene. You know…the *creepy* voyeur," he explains with the same patience he uses with me when describing all types of sexual conduct. He is the big brother, but instead of teaching me how to punch without breaking my thumb, or changing a tire, he teaches me about rimming and wankiness.

"Let's go grab lunch, then we can swing by my buddy David's salon so he can do your hair. Corey wants to do your makeup, but I'm afraid the two of us would massacre your hair." He says this as he pulls me into a sitting position.

"It's like you are getting me ready for prom," I say as I allow him to tug me to my feet.

"Yes, and this year's theme is *Bondage Under the Stars.*" He grabs a navy T-shirt from his immaculately organized closet then pulls it over his head, ruffling his already disheveled hair. He is somehow always able to look deliberately handsome without even trying. He looks rugged, like he lives on a ranch and throws hay bales all day.

"What about *Moonlight Submission?*" I throw out, as I head toward the door.

He smiles and widens his eyes, "*Enchantment on a Berkley Horse*...I like that one."

CHAPTER FOURTEEN
Corset

I am skeptical of the corset Corey and Devin have chosen. It looks like a child's size for sure, as well as a torturous device to preventing breathing entirely. It makes me regret wolfing down a crab cake sandwich at lunch, dripping in Siracha mayo, with a plate of fries as big as my face.

To be totally honest, the outfit the guys put together and laid out on my bed is beautiful. I needn't have worried about it not being sexy because I would have been sent home from anything but a BDSM club. The vision I feared was more of a 'Mad Max Beyond the Thunderdome' look, with big pointy shoulder pads and platform Moon boots, but the guys had assured me I wouldn't be disappointed.

As I stand here in my bathrobe, I can't help but get excited, a flutter blooming in my stomach. After my day with Devin, I am feeling confident about my evening with Silas. Devin had a calming effect on me while convincing me that Silas couldn't really have blown me off after our date, seeing as I was personally invited to the fetish ball and "lest we forget" the membership card I had been granted.

So I decided Silas was in fact interested in me. I also stopped all the teenage girl, back and forth rumblings going on in my brain. Effectively shifting gears, I put my mind to blowing Silas'.

The outfit, no question, will do the trick. The boots are black Victorian looking, mid-shin height with eyelets and laces all the way up. There is a thick buckled strap across the arch of the boot, giving it the look of having spats and another two around the top that will hug my calves.

The thigh high stockings have wide alternating vertical stripes of black and taupe and thick lace spouting from the tops, hiding the small clasps for the garter.

Next is the skirt, it's a flouncy, heavily ruffled, cream colored high-low skirt and by "high-low" I mean extremely high in the front and extremely low in the back. In fact, I suspect it will drag on the floor even with my high heeled boots on.

Then there is a multitude of belts of varying dips and lengths, all leather, all heavily buckled and covered in rivets.

The brown leather corset is densely decorated up the sides with what looks like a lacy burn pattern and some ornamental brass zippers. The front of the corset is held together with four elaborate yet severe brass toggle closures.

Tilting my head and eyeballing the corset, I can't help but muse, "I don't think it will cover my boobs."

Corey clicks his tongue and says, "It's not supposed to *cover* them, it's supposed to *showcase* them." What his tone implies, but he refrains from saying is "Duh."

Devin jumps in quickly with, "This is called a shift, you wear it underneath. It will cover the twins." As he speaks, he holds up a wispy thin, cap sleeved, white half shirt.

"I think I would get more coverage from a pane of glass. It's so sheer Devin," I say, uncertain.

"The rest we will show you once you get these on," Devin says, as he scoots the skirt over and flops onto the bed, settling in as if for a show.

"You are going to watch?" I laugh with an ironic smirk.

"No, I'm going to *help*, you need help clasping your garter belt to the thigh highs so they are straight and you damn sure will need my help with the corset," he says smugly while crossing his legs at the ankles. He lies back with his shoulders resting on a mound of pillows.

"We need wine," Corey says, spinning on his heel to remedy the situation.

My hair is piled on top of my head and secured with a large clip to preserve the loose waves Devin's friend David put in them earlier. Hair safely preserved from the spray of the shower, I make some quick adjustments to the clip then walk toward my dresser to fish out some black lacy panties.   After stepping into them and tightening the belt on my robe, Corey returns with three upside down wine glasses held between the fingers of one broad hand and a bottle of chilled Moscato in the other.

He pours the wine with a steady hand, kissing me on the forehead as he hands me my glass. In three quick strides, he gives Devin his glass and plants a decidedly less chaste kiss on his mouth. Then he raises his glass and says, "To Jessie. May Silas come to adore you as much as we do."

"Cheers to that," I say, then swallow half of the poured offering. It slides down my throat, icy and crisp. I put the rest on my dresser, where I promptly forget about it.

"We need to start with makeup before you get dressed, so come with me," Corey says, as he disappears out my bedroom door. I follow him into the kitchen where he has a massive

143

makeup tote on the counter, and an array of clean brushes lined up on a paper towel.

"What? Are you surprised?" he asks when he sees my wide eyes. "I do makeup for photo shoots sometimes," he says almost shyly.

Really it shouldn't surprise me; Corey could chop down a tree like a lumberjack, mend the broken wing of a bird and cook a five-course gourmet meal without a second thought and without breaking a sweat. So no, I'm not surprised that he defends our country with an M-16 one minute and does make up for photo shoots the next.

When Corey is finished with my makeup, he leans in to blow on the eyelash adhesive that is still tacky on my lids. I can smell the fruity wine on his breath and see the pride in his eyes as he steps back, admiring his work.

"Ok, you can look now," he says, directing the statement toward Devin.

When Devin walks around the kitchen island, his voice hitches in his throat. "Oh Fuck Jessie. Oh my God, I just got a semi; you look fantastic!" he stammers in a very uncharacteristic way for Devin.

"Easy now," Corey laughs. "Garage the semi," he says as he beams with pride at Devin's reaction to his work.

"Baby," Devin gushes, "You did such a great job. She is breathtaking." I smile at their tenderness with each other, especially from Devin because he rarely shows his soft side. He is more like a hedgehog when it comes to relationships, mostly prickly unless he purposely puts down his quills.

I notice it is 7:25 and panic because that only leaves me thirty-five minutes to get dressed and get to 1462. "Save it for after I leave boys, I need to hurry."

Getting me dressed is a flurry of activity and excitement. True to his word, Devin makes sure my garters are straight while Corey fastens my boots then sits back on his heels, fluffing the lace at the top of my thigh-high stockings.

"To be a fly on the wall," he muses while Devin tosses me the tissue thin shift then reaches for the corset on the bed.

"I know! Right? I wish," Devin says, his excitement reaching a fever pitch, as he revels in his masterpiece Steampunk Girl.

Devin cinches me into the corset and fastens the intricate brass toggles. Then he very unceremoniously adjusts my breasts in the corset's half cups, so they sit high and proud in the tight leather.

He may as well have been shaping a lump of wet sand for all the appeal my boobs had to him. He adjusts them again, situating my nipples like the headlights of an eighteen wheeler, just below the rim of leather.

"Geez, Dev. My tits are going to arrive before I do," I challenge, trying to breathe through the constriction of my diaphragm.

Ignoring my commentary, the guys hold the skirt for me to step into. The many tiered, ruffled skirt is short enough in the front for the garters and thigh high lace to be completely visible. The back is so flouncy and free flowing that it almost looks bustled. It drags like a bridal veil behind me though no more than twelve inches or so.

Once we add the belts, swooping down around my hip at different levels, I almost squeal with delight. The outfit in its entirety, accents everything feminine about me and I can't help sashaying around the room, twitching my hips as I walk. The guys are excited too, I can tell they are thrumming with enthusiasm.

The corset is super tight, so I have to accustom myself to taking quick, shallow breaths twice as often as regular breaths.

Devin helps me into a short black jacket. It has stiff, folded ruffles in the same dark fabric of the jacket that rides high on the back of my neck, forming two semi-circles that recede at the base of my ribs to the short back of the jacket. The shoulders are squarely creased with box pleats, and the sleeves become increasingly more fitted all the way to my forearms, where they fit tight like a wetsuit. Big, military looking clasps and buckles span the back of the jacket across my shoulder blades.

"Now, for my favorite part," Corey says as he helps me slip on a gorgeous, white lace, fingerless glove with a gaudy but fabulous broach at the base of my wrist. He sighs, cocking his head to the side in the manner of a mother realizing her little girl is all grown up.

Devin unclips my hair, feathering it behind me and finger combing the long heavy sections. He lifts some hair at the crown of my head and starts back-combing it with the finesse of a water buffalo.

"Take it easy, that's attached," I protest.

He shakes his head saying, "We are out of time, and I don't want you flogged for being late." He gulps back the rest of his wine then gently collects my hair, dragging it forward over my right shoulder and fastening it with a leather strap. Even with the waves, my hair reaches to just below my breast.

With barely a pause, he begins fastening the small leather top hat with the post-apocalyptic goggles securely to my head

146

with copper colored hairpins. With all the backcombing Devin did, the hat sits forward on my head at an angle and off center.

"Shake your head a bit," Devin instructs. When I do, he adds, "Yeah, that's not going anywhere." He slides in a few more hairpins just to be sure.

"Corey, would you please go get the car? It's already after eight." He speaks through a mouthful of bobby pins and doesn't take his eyes off my hat as he works. When he finishes, he's evidently happy with the immobility of the hat and the flowing auburn waves of my hair.

He pulls me into my bathroom, closing the door so I can look in the full-length mirror behind it.

"Holy crap, I look awesome," is all I can say. My makeup is heavy, but my skin looks flawless, like a porcelain doll. My eyes are gorgeous with heavy, dark makeup and shimmering copper eye shadow. My eyes are topped with long, intense false eyelashes that make me feel like butterflies have landed on my lids.

I take in the whole outfit with tears springing to my eyes. I have never in my life felt this glamorous, and it makes my throat hitch and eyes prickle.

"Is this a good time to tell you, you owe me $270?" Devin asks lightheartedly.

I cough up a laugh then say, "It's worth every penny."

I can't take my eyes off the mirror; every aspect of the outfit is so perfect, so gorgeous. I look like a Victorian bad ass, and I can't wait for Silas to see me.

CHAPTER FIFTEEN
Ball

I stand at the huge iron door on the alley side of the building. My breaths are quick and succinct due to the corset's primal death grip. I'm nervous to slide the card and go in, and my shallow breathing makes it near impossible to calm myself.

It's already well after eight o'clock, but still, I stand here paralyzed. On the ride over, I could barely contain myself. I was so excited to see Silas, and now, now all I have to do is slide the card...and go in. That's it. Slide the card...take a step. So, with shaking hands, I force myself to do it.

I step into a short hallway; inside the music is thumping, enveloping me like a heavy, wet cloak. The atmosphere is dim but crackles with energy that snaps and sparks at will. The music is haunting. It's almost like slow, forlorn, techno music. It causes the entire club to pulse with the noise of a thunderous, despairing heartbeat.

I cautiously step deeper into the entrance and am met at once by a huge man. He is dressed in all black with a monocle clamped to his shiny bald head. His teeth are chipped, so he gives the impression by his look as well as his demeanor, that he eats glass for breakfast. He steps in front of me in a challenging manner, crossing his arms across his barrel chest and eying me up and down.

To my utter surprise, he reaches out his hand and grabs my throat. His thumb and fingers are digging into the sides of my neck, but he's not actually restricting my already labored breathing.

"No collar I see," he glowers, as he tips his beady head forward in an intimidating fashion.

I hold my ground, glaring at him with rapidly growing anger. Absolutely no one is allowed to touch anyone, in any manner here without prior consent. Yet here he is, with his hand on my throat.

"Get your fucking hands off of me! I'm not even five steps in the club yet you stupid oaf."

He drops his hand, "I beg your pardon, perhaps I'll see you later." He says this menacingly slow, through a clenched jaw and eyes gorging me with contempt.

Seeking the safety of the crowd, I make my way down the hallway that stands as the threshold of the club. As I round the corner, 1462 opens into a massive room of revelers. I smile, recalling Devin and Corey telling me it's just a big, uninhibited costume party that people get VERY into.

As I look around, so many things catch my attention. First and foremost are the aerial performers, they have long, silken, scarf-like devices hanging from the hulking wooden beams of the ceiling two floors up. There are eight of them divided amongst the room.

The performers are wearing gold jeweled thongs, the men have bare chests, the women, shimmering pasties. The one piece unifying all the performers is a black strap around their heads and the vivid red ball gags in their mouths.

Besides the aerial performers, there are two stages, one empty at the moment and one with an impressive looking band. The kick drum displays a picture of a Zeppelin with the name "Diesel Punk" scrawled across it.

The singer looks like Bettie Page with a bionic arm and long black pencil skirt. Her pursed, blood red lips are crooning into the vintage, cage style microphone. Her band mates all look like futuristic Victorian men, wearing vests with pocket chains or waistcoats.

Of the horn section, one man wears a fedora, one a flight helmet with goggles, and the others wear various bowler and top hats. The smallest of the group is squirrelly looking and stands behind the bass guitar. He wears a thick Ascot and round, purple eyeglasses.

On one hand, they look very aristocratic, but on the other hand, they look dirty and sinister, all covered in gadgets and wicked contraptions. They are strangely compelling though, and the music is captivating. The next song shifts to more of a dark, foreboding swing music and I can feel it in my teeth.

Around me, more than a few of the revelers are dancing a gritty Charleston along with the morose swing music. I look on in awe as one man flips his dance partner over his back, never missing a beat as they resume, both partners back on the floor.

The impressive horn section of the band, despite their menacing appearance, sway their instruments back in forth in unison as if they really are a swing band. The synchronized movement adds a whimsical nature, perhaps to temper their ferocity.

I turn my attention to the cages suspended from the ceiling; they hang around the perimeter of the immense room, so the base of the cage is roughly at eye level. I'm guessing there are fifteen or twenty of them, each containing a person.

The one closest to me holds a naked man, bound by a rope with loops and tight knots securing him in a hog-tie manner, as well as gagging him. I shudder while backing up and hope Silas' predilections are of a different nature.

The next closest cage holds a naked woman on her back; her legs are up against the side of the cage in the shape of a V, while her ankles are shackled to the bars above her. A small group of men stands before her cage, perhaps discussing the merits of her vagina, as it is mere feet from their faces. I'm gaping at them with unabashed curiosity, as they begin to caress and stroke her nakedness. My mouth drops open as I watch one bring his face straight to her core. *Oh, Holy Shit.*

I feel a gentle tap on my arm and spin around, embarrassed by my focus on the caged woman and her taunting suitors. In front of me is a shirtless man, with his own thick goggles hanging from his neck. "Mistress, may I be of service to you?" he asks, all the while keeping his gaze on my feet.

Realizing he takes me for a Domme, all I can squeeze out is, "Uh...no thanks." He bows his head further and backs away, dejected.

Almost immediately another man approaches, not nearly as meek and pliable. He has heavily plated shoulder pads, buckles crisscrossing his chest, long dreadlocks and a sharply pointed, inky goatee. His eyes are emerald green, but they soften his appearance, not at all.

"You playing tonight Cherie?" he asks with a French lilt.

"Not yet, I mean...maybe later." It comes out in an embarrassing stammer, and I'm the one to back away. I bump awkwardly into a muscular blonde. He's handsome save for the Hannibal Lecter style leather and metal face guard.

He leans in to speak into my ear, so I can hear him over the music, or so he can place a hand on my hip while he talks.

"That was awesome, super smooth," he teases, pulling back from my ear and smiling. Though his smile is only evidenced by his laughing eyes because the savage mask veils his mouth. I can smell his minty gum through the macabre metal bars. "Is this your first time?" he asks over the music, leaning in again.

"Is it that obvious?" I ask. It figures, I might as well carry a flashing neon sign.

"Well, yes. I just watched you shoot down a sub and a Dom. I think you have people confused about you."

"Really? And you're not confused?"

"Not at all," he says with a smirk.

"I could have you tied up and flogged for being so direct," I wager while squaring my jaw, hoping to sound even a little legitimate.

That would be fine with me, although normally I'm not into that." He smiles again. "Would you like me to show you around the club?"

"No, this right here is already sensory overload," I answer.

"Have you seen any of the private rooms?" he asks, no doubt trying to get a read on my personal kinks. "My current favorite is the Peep Show room, I'm not really into bondage and submission, but I really love the other aspects of 1462."

"What are the other aspects of 1462?" I ask, ignoring his first question, not wanting to discuss my familiarity with the Scottish room.

He leads me away from the ever expanding crowd around the stage, raising his mask to his head like discarded sunglasses. "Damn, where to start… First of all, there are theme rooms for every possible kink you can think of, Military, Medical, Geisha, Western, Cops, Zombies...and they are not just lame theme rooms, they are like Hollywood sets."

153

"Ahhhh," Is all I can say because my own experience in Declan's room had been so incredibly authentic. I assume the other rooms must be just as accurate in their portrayals.

"Then there are rooms of mirrors, rooms for body wrapping...like mummification in Saran wrap, there is a slave auction room--it's huge, you could hold conventions in there." (deep breath) "Human furniture room, there is even a room of fucking machines, although I have only heard about that one, I've never seen it." He is almost shouting in my ear now, with the ever growing chaos.

"What's your pleasure?" I ask, wondering if he has firsthand knowledge of all the rooms he just spewed out. I'm guessing his lengthy litany speaks to a certain familiarity.

He smiles a broad smile and leans into my ear, even closer than before. "Whatever yours is."

I laugh heartily, struck by his boldness. I realize too late that my question, meant purely out of curiosity, was taken as an equally bold encouragement. I'm disappointed by my own naiveté. What an amateur move, I still don't totally grasp how sexualized even normal conversations are in here.

I open my mouth to explain but stop dead when I notice Silas.

He is standing next to the bar about twenty feet away. Even from this distance, I can see a muscle in his jaw tick. How long had he been watching? The conversation had been mostly innocent but the laughing, and our proximity due to the noise could be very misunderstood.

Gauging by the heated look in his eyes as he makes his way over, I'm guessing he misunderstands. The truth is, I had been grateful to talk to someone who didn't want to lick my boots or shackle me to the wall. I was certainly happy to not be alone in the packed club, feeling intensely vulnerable. So I don't feel *too* badly when Silas marches up, stating plainly, "We need to get you a collar," as he leans in and lightly kisses my cheek. Then he offers his hand to the man next to me saying, "Carson, good to see you, buddy."

"You too Silas, I was just explaining to our friend here, the many different options available to her as a valuable member of 1462." Carson offers as he straightens up, adjusting his mask back over his face and re-effecting his menacing, nameless persona.

"Yes, I see that," Silas says deliberately. "Jessie is still new to the club. I've yet to put her through the paces." He says this evenly, yet I still feel like he is marking his territory like an attentive Schnauzer.

Carson extends his hand to me and says through the metal bars covering his mouth, "Jessie is it? It was wonderful to meet you. Perhaps we will run into each other again." When he speaks, he gives me a knowing wink and nods to Silas.

Uneasy, I can't help but feel like I've missed something in the exchange.

Mercifully the band stops playing, announcing a short break as Carson disappears into the crowd. The band music is replaced by a keening tune that fills the air. The aerial performers drop from the ceiling, unrolling in unison from their cherry red scarfs.

There is a collective gasp from the crowd while we're held in rapt attention. The agile performers drop nearly to the floor. Then, they wind themselves back up with theatrical precision and acrobatic feats of tremendous skill.

Despite the distraction, my attention turns to Silas. He is dangerously handsome, wearing a double breasted military style waistcoat with tails. The waistcoat is unbuttoned, revealing both his strong, smooth chest and his remarkably chiseled abs. The heavily buckled belt is slung low on his dark trousers. The belt looks like the inner workings of a clock, but my eyes linger on the sexy ridge at his hips. His left forearm is wrapped in a wide brown leather cuff, almost like an archer's armband, except this one has cogs and spikes on it. His boots are old, beat up combat boots, left loosely tied. The boots compliment the perfect European cut to his well-fitting pants. He is wearing wire-framed aviator glasses and, as usual, his light brown hair is perfectly disheveled. His stance in front of me is that of a Versace model, not a BDSM club owner.

When I see how sexy he looks, my body has a visceral reaction. A backdraft of heat flashes over me, singeing every fiber, every pore with a deep, abiding, *craving* for him.

He seems to be taking in my outfit as well; his eyes linger on my garters then slowly make their way to my face.

"I wasn't sure you would come," he says, while his eyes drift to my corset. He closes his eyes in a long, slow blink then opens them piercingly on mine.

"And miss all this?" I say playfully, then add, "Sir" through batting eyelashes. I take a half step toward him. I can see the same muscle twitch in his jaw again, but otherwise, he makes no response. It's as if the angel and devil on his shoulders are at war.

I'm feeling emboldened in this atmosphere, with the costumes, the music…him. The tightness in my corset alone causes a clamping down on the butterflies, caught in their airtight jar.

Another half step forward, "Are you afraid of me?" I ask demurely, purposely goading him.

"You're playing with fire Jessie," he says, with an almost imperceptible flare of his nostrils. "You should be afraid of me," he finishes, as if in warning.

"I'm not afraid." Another half step toward him. Now I'm only a breath away from his body, it's taut as a bowstring.

"If we are going to do this, you have to stop trying to top," he says through clenched teeth while hardly moving his lips. "To do this right, you have to surrender to me and trust that I will take care of you," he explains, as though to a bratty child.

"I do trust you," I say, meeting his indignant gaze then quickly averting my eyes, lowering them to the sexy shelves of his hips.

"Then act like it, or I will have you gagged," he says in a growl that makes my shallow breaths come faster, my lungs already barely able to convert the oxygen.

"Yes Sir," I say, but cursedly, I'm smirking at the same time. I keep my eyes on his hips. My role of submissive will be short lived if I can't get control of my petulant lips. I ratchet down the bubble of nervous laughter in my throat and pinch my lips together, effectively removing the smirk, or at least masking it, sort of.

"Are you done?" he asks impertinently.

Not trusting my mouth, I simply nod my acquiescence. He takes my hand and leads me briskly across the dance floor, bobbing and weaving through the crowd to an elevator at the back of the cavernous room. He walks swiftly, and I have to scamper along to keep up. My heels feel like stilts as they tap a quick percussion behind him.

We step into the elevator, and when another couple tries to follow, Silas cuts them short with a glance, and they both step back. The elevator doors close and just as I'm about to ask Silas why he is angry, he rounds on me, backing me into a corner of the swanky, mirrored elevator. His feral demeanor brooks no argument.

157

"I expect you to do exactly as you are told. Do you understand?" He bites this out while clamping his big hands on my waist then lowering his lips to mine without touching them.

"Yes," I whisper, closing my eyes, waiting for his lips to make contact. I can feel his warm breath on my face. He is so close, so imposing. He is testing me, will I kiss him or will I be a good little sub?

The elevator dings, and he backs away but not much. His darkened eyes are seething. "Come," is all he says, as he extends his hand to me.

I enter the room on Silas' heels, his commanding frame obscuring the space for a moment. I am expecting a dungeon of sorts, so I'm surprised when he guides me into the room. It's much smaller than the Scottish castle play area I'm so acquainted with.

The room smells of deep woodsy pine, with scented candles flickering throughout. Despite the candles, the main source of lighting in the room is a huge antique chandelier hanging from a wooden plank ceiling. There must be thirty bulbs on the massive structure, but each light is so dim, the effect is moody and ambient, brooding and masculine.

The walls are exposed brick, crumbling in places, and with a chipping plaster overlay in others. The loft style windows take up the entire far wall. They're filmy and obscured, so they give no indication of the city life that bustles on the fringes, just beyond the hazy glass. Throughout the crumbling brick and mortar, there are O-rings bolted to the walls with a myriad of fasteners.

There is a bulky pulley system with coils of rope hanging in front of the windows. In the far corner, there hangs a bar. It's reminiscent of a circus trapeze but gives no illusion of gaiety and laughing children. The cuffs hanging loosely from the sides bring a different image to mind than that of the Ringling Brothers.

There is no furniture; however off to the side of the room is what looks like a giant sandwich board. It's a standing 'A' frame with some expertly placed horizontal planks, some missing, some padded. There is a small lip at the bottom that must serve as a footrest and near the top, a circular cutout for the face; however, this is no massage table. A shiver trickles through me.

Silas stands looking at me, as I take in the room. If he notices me shiver, he gives no indication of it. He just waits patiently for me to finish absorbing the room with all of its many contraptions.

I meet his eyes for an instant before I remember my role and quickly avert them to his well-tailored slacks and his relaxed stance.

"Shall we begin?" he asks.

Afraid to meet his eyes or speak, lest he interprets it as too assertive, I can only nod and keep my eyes trained on his scuffed combat boots.

"Jessie, I need to know that you want this. That you are ready for it." He says this with cocky assertion veiling the uncertainty of his question.

"Yes, I'm ready," I answer with my eyes down. I can feel my chest heaving as my breaths start to come faster. I crave his touch so much; at this point, I don't care how he gives it to me. I want him to take charge and show me the confident man, the skilled lover.

I have come to know the tender, gentlemanly side of him. Like when he took care of me, bathing me carefully and opening doors for me on our date, his boyhood stories--all of that was perfectly charming, but now I'm ready. Ready for the aggressive side of him, the thought of which makes me smile in spite of myself.

He pauses a moment longer and then as if coming to a decision, he snaps back into Dom mode with the suddenness of a slapped face. "Come," he says, as he guides me toward a plush, furry white rug in the center of the room. "Kneel, spread your legs and clasp your hands behind your back." He directs me to do this with all the gentleness of a Drill Sargent.

I do as he commands, with my long flowing skirt trailing behind me and my knees sunk deep into the pristine white faux fur rug.

"Now sit back on your heels, keep your eyes down," he commands.

As I sit back on my heels, I'm grateful for the Steampunk get up; it's perfect for this position. The thigh highs trimmed with lace and the straps of the garter against my bare skin, the short ruffled front of the skirt, barely concealing the tops of my spread thighs. As subjugating as this position is, I feel enormously powerful, almost in control of Silas and his desire for me. Almost.

While sliding the jacket off my shoulders and dropping it to the floor he says, "First, I'm going to remedy the collar situation, because make no mistake, You. Are. Mine." This he grinds out. His words however, bring another ill-timed smile to my lips. I have to drop my gaze further so as not to incite a mutiny.

He steps away, then returns to stand at my back. A moment later, he lowers a wide leather collar in front of my eyes. He methodically catches my chin with the top edge of the collar, tugging it up before he begins fastening the leather at the back of my neck. The collar is very wide and stiffly darted; it covers my whole neck and part of my collar bones. It forces my chin up high like some crazy Elizabethan collar.

"This is called a posture collar," Silas purrs in my ear, the tickle of his breath causes my nipples to prick to attention. He lifts my arms up from where they rest at the base of my back, with hands clasped against the ruffles of my skirt.

He slides a cold swath of vinyl up between my arms and back, then begins to wrap my arms in a cocoon of chilly plastic. The hair at the base of my neck prickles beneath the leather collar in response to the coolness of the plastic.

Expertly and systematically Silas begins to lace up the wrap, starting at my wrists and making his way up to my triceps, then cinching it tightly like the arm corset it is. By the time he finishes, my arms are tightly bound behind my back, my shoulder joints ready to spring free from the sockets.

"The tightness in your shoulders will ease, just relax into it," he says, admiring his work while he circles around my bound frame. My breasts are thrust forward from the arm binding and held high from the corset; Silas' eyes are locked on them.

"I can see your nipples, you must be enjoying this," he says as a statement, not a question.

I close my eyes and attempt a nod, loving the effect I am having on him.

"Spread your legs wider," he commands.

I spread them as wide as I can while opening my eyes slowly, hazarding a look at his face. He has discarded his glasses and belt, but the rest of his Steampunk outfit is still provocatively intact.

His salacious look dwells on my spread thighs. I'm still wearing panties and even the scandalously short skirt offers some refinement to the dirty, raw pose. Silas' look darkens as he clenches and unclenches his fists, staring for long deliberate minutes.

His dingy boots stand in stark contrast to the feather soft, pure white rug; it illustrates perfectly the contradiction within Silas. He is soft and hard, kind and ruthless, gentle...rough. Unclenching his fists finally, he steps forward placing his hands on the sides of my shoulders.

"Stand."

He braces me between his strong hands and helps me to stand up, his forearm cuff briefly snagging on the light fabric at the side of my breast. He's standing close, hands still on my shoulders.

I have to readjust my stance to keep from wobbling on my legs as blood surges back into them. Once he is sure I'm stable, he drops one hand and reaches between my legs, his knuckles brushing against my bare inner thighs.

Unable to lower my head because of the posture collar, I'm forced to look into his face. The eye contact doesn't seem to bother him as he looks right back, into my soul it seems.

He nimbly fingers the lace of my panties, drawing a finger under the lace at my crotch to rest against my warm, silky skin.

My eyes drift closed, as my body warms to his erotic touch. He gives a severe yank, pulling me into him hips first. I feel the thong of the panties bite savagely into the crack of my ass before they relent and give way altogether.

He steadies me again, and while looking unapologetically at me, he says, "One of these days you will learn that panties simply get in the way, and you will stop wearing them. I'll be relieving you of the corset too but not just yet," he simmers, his velvety voice is hot with desire. "Tell me, are you partial to this top?" he asks as he closes his hand around the lightly sewn neckline.

Before I can even respond, he reaches up with his other hand and rips the shift open like a piece of discarded newspaper. He makes quick work, tearing at the cap sleeves until the entirety of the garment falls to the floor, leaving my breasts showcased above the stiff corset, a declaration and an exhibit all at once.

My breasts jiggle at his show of force but the collar prevents any sideways or downward movement of my head, so I have little choice but to meet his gaze or close my eyes. I look at him, I see his weakness for me, and a surge of strength flows through me.

My wrenched back arms are starting to loosen but being gripped so tightly by the arm wrap, and the corset has me feeling both safe and vulnerable at the same time. I'm held securely in a thoughtful embrace, yet open and waiting for the vultures to descend.

Silas places his open palm between my breasts on my sternum; I can feel the heat of his skin. He is looking into my eyes as though he is contemplating, searching for a clue in their mossy depths.

I look back, unable to do anything else. His eyes, the color of the deepest ocean, somehow look more intense, crueler maybe.

In contrast, my eyes implore my body's ache; deep as a gaping cavern. I feel desperate for his touch, his kiss.

The waiting is almost impossible to bear. It has me tarrying like a chained inmate…with an inaccessible, itchy rash. My exposed skin prickles with a cool heat around his warm palm, waiting.

I close my eyes in exasperation, and he finally removes his hand. "I have one rule, and it is absolute." He leans in, in a completely serious manner. "You are not to orgasm without my permission. If you fail this one task, you will be punished."

My eyes drift open as a traitorous smile creeps to my lips. I replace it quickly with a more appropriate submissive mask, but it's a moment too late.

Silas notices, his eyes flash with anger? Frustration? Maybe even resignation--but he is definitely unhappy with my contentious response.

"Clearly you have a lot to learn," he says in an ominous warning, completely devoid of playfulness. His teeth are clenched tight.

He steps away from me, and I know to stay put, afraid to wake the sleeping giant. I hear him rustling behind me briefly before he returns to stand before me with a wicked grin on his face and a dangerous glint in his eyes.

He holds up what looks like a wide silver hair clip with dangling jewels, and his grin broadens. Again he drops his hand, reaching under my ruffled skirt and finding the tender skin between my legs. He begins to lightly explore my soft petals.

"Good girl, you're already very wet for me," he murmurs approvingly.

Reaching down with his other hand, he deftly finds my clit and inner labia. He pinches them between his fingers and slides the clip on. The clip firmly grips my sensitive bud between the intimate flesh around it.

The dangling jewels brush against my inner thighs and tickle the bare skin relentlessly. I freeze with the sensation. The clip produces a throbbing in my clitoris that mimics a heartbeat. Coupled with the feather-light tickle of the jewels, the clip could produce an orgasm all on its own.

If I squeeze my kegel muscles, the intensity of the sensation ratchets up tenfold. *Oh God. Don't squeeze.*

Happy with himself but still looking mischievous, Silas pulls some rubber tipped nipple clamps out of his inside jacket pocket. They are connected by wires to a small black box. When he teasingly presses a button on the box, I can hear a pulsing vibration as he drops them back into the inside pocket.

"Now it's time to adorn your beautiful nipples," he says. He places his hands on my breasts, slowly dragging his thumbs back and forth across my already hard nipples. After a moment of tender ministrations, he pinches and rolls them harshly between his thumbs and pointer fingers.

I gasp with the suddenness of it, then he withdraws the nipple clamps. He squeezes the ends of the pinch clips, opening them wide then slowly lowering them down simultaneously on both nipples. When he lets go of the ends, the clips close and pinch snugly, the vibration rhythmically strumming. The clips are not so tight as to be painful but they are insistent and unyielding just the same.

With my nipples vibrating in quick pulses and my clitoris pinched, it takes incredibly focused effort to fend off the arousal.

Silas knows my struggle and takes great pleasure in his erotic torture. "Kneel down, sit back on your ankles and spread your knees nice and wide," he instructs.

I do as he says, although a bit clumsily due to the tight arm corset. I find the posture an immediate relief because the tickling of the jewels against my thighs has stopped.

I feel an almost automatic need, a primal urge to squeeze my kegel muscles. It's almost like the intuitive subconscious that tells your heart to beat, or your lungs to expand. When I do squeeze, it pushes me closer and closer toward my forbidden climax. I learn quickly to keep the orgasm at bay by fighting the urge to squeeze.

The vibrating throb of my nipples travels to my clit as efficiently as nerves carry electrical impulses to the brain. The sensation is maddening but doable as long as I don't *squeeze*.

I'm held on the precipice of insanity while Silas walks to the hanging ropes and the pulley system in front of the massive windows.

He pays virtually no attention to me as I'm left in gluttonous limbo. It's a horrendous reminder that yes, Silas is in fact in charge.

The clamps on my nipples do not bite into my skin, but rather hug them snuggly. They tug my breasts like buoyant pendulums, weighted down by the small black battery pack that hangs between the toggle fasteners of my corset. Alternately still and then humming. Still then humming. Still........hummmmming.

The clip between my legs is increasingly distressing because the stimulation continues to build with every pulse beat. Every surge of blood through my veins reminds me of my pinched little button, ready to detonate at any moment. Ten, Nine, Eight…

Having satisfied himself with the ropes and pulley, Silas makes his way casually back over to me. He leans his head to the side appraisingly. He smiles and needlessly states, "That's quite a lot of stimulation."

I'm sweating from the inside out, as I fight the ridiculous urge to squeeze, so Silas seems satisfied with himself.

"You have done very well. Now stand."

He helps me to my feet, where my heels snag on the plush carpet, causing me to teeter in my bound and crazed state.

"Which would you like me to remove first?" he asks.

"The clip," I spit out, nearly choking on the words.

"No." Tisk, tisk, tisk. "That's not at all how you address me here." Then, as if to admonish me he says, "I believe I will start with the arms." Stepping behind me, boots straddling my voluminous skirt he begins unlacing the arm corset.

As my arms and shoulders loosen, the focus shifts from my screaming sex to the sweet relief of unbinding my arms. The relief washes over me like a cool brook. Once completely unbound, my arms feel foreign to my body and somehow awkward, hanging loosely at my sides.

"Now Darling, which would you have me remove next?" he asks, as though speaking to a child.

"Please, Sir," I stammer, "The clip."

"Ah yes, a proper response from a submissive." He reaches down, his eyes burning holes through mine. He flicks his fingers against the jewels, causing them to flutter against my thighs and swaying enough to tug at the clip.

I gasp as he explores my pulsing skin, brushing against my engorged clit before deftly sliding the clip off.

I nearly crumple to the floor with relief as blood rushes to the area in a torrent. Though grateful to be free of the clip, the ensuing surge of endorphins only heightens the lingering sensation. I clench my jaw and squeeze my eyes shut, fighting through the onslaught of sensation.

When he reaches for, then disengages the nipple clamps, the same surge of blood and endorphins causes my spine to dissolve. I slump forward a bit before Silas steadies me. He holds me until I feel sufficiently stable and can stand with his help.

My mindset has altered so significantly, I feel as though I am underwater, with every sound dulled and every movement in slow motion. Even my blinking eyes are methodically slow; time seems to have slogged to a crawl.

"You are doing beautifully," he murmurs. He unlaces the posture collar and eases it from my throat. My chin, tasting freedom merely lowers, as if too exhausted to be prideful.

Silas studies the fasteners of my corset then begins to tediously free my ribcage. The relief of being unbound is

167

exquisite. When he pulls away the leather corset, sweat trickles down my heated skin then dissolves into the cream-colored ruffles of my skirt. My skin, now rapidly cooling in its freedom, brings my hazy mind back into a dull focus.

"Tell me, have you ever heard of predicament bondage?" he asks, while unhooking my heavy belt and then letting it drop to the floor with a muffled clatter.

"No Sir," I respond quietly, not needing to remind myself of the sub status that has descended on me like a film.

He continues undressing me, finding the zipper at my hip and lowering it one tooth at a time. He lets the skirt drop, to pool at my feet in a fit of ruffles. Taking my hand, he helps me to step out of the nest of fabric.

"Follow me." He directs, as he steps off the carpet onto the darkly stained concrete floor.

I follow him wearing nothing but boots, thigh highs, and a garter belt. My hat seems silly and out of place now that I have been stripped to such basics. Even my panties are gone, having been torn away.

"Back on your knees while I take the hairpins out and remove your hat." I sink to the hard floor, sit back on my heels and clasp my hands behind my back. Only then do I notice the deep ache residing in my shoulders.

He stands looking at me, head cocked and waiting. As understanding dawns on me, I spread my knees wide, opening myself to his wicked gaze.

After a long moment lost between my legs, he steps forward and begins to work on the plentiful bobby pins in my hair.

The cold, hard floor seeps into my knees and the laced section of my feet, as they are pressed heavily against its surface.

Standing between my spread knees, Silas frees the hat then drops it unceremoniously to the floor. Then he unties the strip of leather holding my loose side ponytail.

Were my head not lowered and eyes averted, I would have been able to make out the stitching in his pants. He is so close I can smell the fabric of his trousers, clean and warm.

He piles my long hair into a lumpy ponytail near the top of my head. Then he ties it tightly with the strip of leather before standing back to admire the view. Even with my eyes averted, I can feel his gaze locked on my spread legs, my pert breasts, my complete exhibition.

"I could keep you like this all night. Your body so open to me, so tight and wet, but I have many things for you to experience before I allow you release. Come."

He begins to uncoil the rope. Then he places it behind my neck and down my breasts, to pool at the tips of my boots. He then ties the two sides together into three knots, one at the base of my clavicle, one between my breasts and one about two inches above my belly button.

Slowly circling behind me, I can hear him tear what sounds like plastic wrap. He reaches between my knees then winds a barrier of cling wrap around the dangling ropes. He brings both pieces back, across my sex and up the crack of my ass. Then he loops the two ends under the rope at the back of my neck.

The rope is snug between my folds and cheeks, not tight, just a light pressure against my clit as I ride the plastic clad rope.

Silas brings the ends around my sides, one under each arm then feeds them through the loophole made between two of the knots. Then back around to my back, crisscrossing them and bringing them forward to repeat the process through the next loophole.

When he is finished, I'm honeycombed by the rope with each breast protruding through a concise, knotted polygon. The rope between my legs tightens every time Silas slides his fingers under the rope to make sure it isn't too tight but loosens once he withdraws his fingers.

The exertion of securing me in the ropes heats his skin so I can smell the warmth of it. He takes off his jacket, then stands before me bare chested, rippled with well-defined muscles and his pants hanging low on his hips. He is so sexy, so rough...so manly.

I bite my bottom lip just imagining his smooth skin against mine. I picture our mingled sweat, his chest sliding against my breasts like satin while he glides in and out of me.

Unhappy with my wandering thoughts and my lip biting, he grabs the rope at my belly, tugging me forward and causing the rope to mash into my clitoris.

"I wouldn't do that if I were you. You're already driving me mad just seeing you bound in my ropes."

I don't respond so he pulls tighter, sending electricity flashing to my clit.

"Yes Sir," I finally reply, and he releases the rope.

"And now for the predicament," he says, while raking a hand through his hair. He arranges the rope on the pulley, fastening it around my ponytail, pulling tightly and forcing my head up; my neck stretching in an effort to ease the tug.

I feel the crotch rope tightening against my clit as he raises the rope harness so my toes can no longer touch, missing the floor by millimeters.

Immediately the predicament becomes clear, if I'm to ease the rope's pressure against my clit by leaning back a fraction, my hair pulls tighter.

I'm caught in a pleasure-pain cycle. Leaning against the crotch rope, the exquisite pressure against my button will surely lead to the forbidden orgasm. However, the wrenching of my hair is right on the edge of my pain threshold.

Silas steps back and crosses his arms across his chest, no doubt satisfied with himself and waiting to see how my ordeal will play out.

After an agonizingly long time and through quite a bit of trial and error, I become quite adept at switching between the two extremes. I ride the pleasure until it builds almost too far. Then I rock back, settling into the ruthless yank of my hair until the pain becomes too much. Then I lean into the embrace of pleasure once again.

"Tell me, how do you like being a submissive at my club?" he asks with an innocent grin.

"Ahhhhhh," I moan, almost waiting too long to rock back this time.

"Do you think Carson would be as good to you?" he asks.

"What, who?" I ask, dazed.

"Carson, the man you were flirting with so shamelessly earlier tonight," he prompts.

Not sure how I should respond, I say nothing. It feels like a trap, and it reminds me of the curious exchange that took place between the two when I felt like I had missed something. *Carson. Right.*

"Well," he says as he lowers me down, "Let's find out, shall we?"

Just as my feet are hitting the floor, my legs wobbly after the lengthy ordeal, Silas taps a quick text into his phone.

"No," is all I can get out, but is it, 'No I wasn't flirting,' or 'No he wouldn't be as good,' or 'No let's not find out'--I'm not at all sure, and my reasoning abilities have been greatly reduced, having to fight off the threatening orgasm for so long.

"Don't worry, he is going to play, but he can't have you--I won't allow that," he says, as if to make it that much easier to swallow.

Almost silently, with nothing but a click of the door to announce his arrival, Carson enters the room. As he strides towards us, he raises his Hannibal Lecter mask, pulling it over his head and saying, "Oh good, costumes are optional I see." He waggles his eyebrows at my bound nakedness.

Flooded with embarrassment and feeling all at once the tightness of the ropes crisscrossing my body, I start to fidget, feeling the blush crawl up my cheeks. I turn to Silas, silently pleading with him, and my back to Carson. Silas' face is unreadable.

Carson closes the distance and asks, "Jessie, is this Ok with you?" He gently places his hands on my waist, and his unexpected touch makes me gasp.

"You're perfect," Carson whispers as he unties my hair and lets it fall down my back. "Let me look at you," he says into my hair, hardly above a whisper.

I raise my eyes to Silas, silently questioning, but his stoic nod tells me all I need to know. Awash with embarrassment, I turn naked toward the man I have only just met and nod my acceptance.

Having only known Carson briefly and not particularly *choosing* to be naked in front of him, I feel suddenly insecure. I'm timid of my erect nipples and bound body. I'm shy and bashful, so I don't meet his eyes.

Carson looks at me for a minute before reaching out and loosening the knot at my belly. He slowly works on the other knots until he is able to unlace the binding rope from between my legs, leaving it hanging loosely. The only part of the rope honeycomb remaining is the part that frames my breasts. He undoes this part last, grazing my pert nipples as he loosens the rope, then pulls it away altogether and drops it to the floor.

His hands feather across my breasts, he's enraptured as he plays with them. He lifts them as if testing their weight.

"Your tits are amazing. I had thought so earlier, but now I can see that I was right." He says this as he jostles them around, enjoying their bouncing movement. "Perfect size, firm, perky…" he says. Then he pinches my nipples and tugs me forward, like a horse with a bit in its mouth.

I step toward him, so he releases, "Good girl, now go get on the Berkley Horse," he directs.

"The what?" I ask, confused.

Carson's look darkens as he reaches to his hip, unhooking a leather tipped riding crop.

"An impertinent tongue will get you lashed. Do you care to amend your question?" he asks, not bothering to disguise his threat.

"What is a Berkley Horse? Sir," I ask, with heavy sarcasm on the 'Sir.' The slap to the inside of my thigh is instant. I flinch as the sting turns into a thousand pin pricks. Silas is across the room with his back to me, busy with something else.

"Careful," Carson warns, as he guides me to the A-frame device that had reminded me of a tall sandwich board earlier. "Up you go," he directs as he guides me to step up onto the foot platform. He leans me back, placing my back against the angling board. He needs to slide the headrest closed but had I been facing the board, the opening would have been for my face.

Silas makes his way over to us carrying a small bucket and a tall white pillar candle. Carson cuffs my arms at my sides with a thick, black leather strap on each side. The two men work together as easily as if it were second nature, or as if they had done it before a thousand times.

Silas pulls a blindfold from his back pocket and slips it over my head as Carson busies himself with the spreader bar he is currently fastening my ankles to. As my legs are wrenched recklessly apart, I can feel Carson's breath on my spread body, and I know he is intimately close.

I'm naked except for my stockings, garter belt and boots and I'm spread wide open for what feels like a convention hall full of people due to my unrelenting modesty. Because of the blindfold, my world has gone dark, but I know the men are close, I can feel their eyes on me, searching for hidden wonders through the valley of my soul. My heaving chest represents nothing more than two ripe playthings to dally with. My spread body is merely a vat of opportunity waiting to be exploited.

I feel the soft leather of the crop drag from my neck down to my belly, the soft caress causing my nipples to pinch tighter. Next, I feel it go from the top of my thigh-high up the front of my leg to my hip, across my belly, and down my other thigh. Then it slides from the inside of my taut, stretched thigh and continues up across my sex then down the inside of my other thigh.

I'm beginning to relish the stroke of the soft leather, but suddenly and without warning, or even a pause, it slaps against my unguarded clit.

My shrouded eyes roll back with the sensation. It's so fierce yet so delicious, with the pain ebbing into exquisite pleasure as blood surges to my affronted flesh. My body betrays my mind by further dampening for the two men.

The unspoken threat of another slap to my clitoris makes me attempt to clench my body closed to shield my delicate parts, but the spreader bar is unrelenting. The reflex to try to clamp shut something that's being forced open is remarkable.

As another caress playfully tickles, then ruthlessly slaps my revealed clit I groan. In pleasure or pain, I'm not even sure.

I'm sweating now, as my wrists struggle against the damp leather straps. I can feel the moisture between the leather pads of the Berkley Horse and my skin, it's hot and sticky. I can smell wet leather and pheromones, and it's intoxicating and revolting at the same time.

"That's right. Sometimes it's hard to tell the difference between pleasure and pain," Silas offers. "Now that your body has been so highly sensitized, we will be testing you. Angel or devil, you decide."

"And if you're wrong..." Carson warns, "you will be punished." The wicked glint to his voice is undeniable.

Again the soft leather crop drags between my breasts, followed by hot wax.

"Ahhh," I wince.

"Hot or cold?" Carson challenges.

"Hot," I bite out as the wax cools, the edges peeling up as I squirm.

SLAP! On my inner thigh, hard and painful, I can almost feel the welt growing, angry and red.

"Hot Sir," I amend.

Again a dollop of wax falls, this time on my hip. "Hot or cold?" Purrs Silas.

"Hot Sir."

Then again right below my left breast. I suck in air and answer before I'm asked. "Hot Sir."

SLAP! Again, same spot, now tender as a bruised peach.

175

"No Darling, that was cold," Carson says.

Another dollop trickles down around my bottom rib. This time I am sure it's wax by the cooling wax trail it leaves behind.

"Hot Sir."

"Very good," Silas coos.

Wax again, this time at the base of my sternum. "Fuck! Hot Sir."

SLAP! Same place, now there is a deep ache in that spot, I don't want to be wrong again.

"That wasn't polite and it was cold," Carson says.

By now the endorphins are surging through my body. The slushy ice feels every bit as hot as the melted wax, I can only tell the difference if it slides off my body or curls around it. I've also learned the wax is slower as it cools and the slush faster as it melts.

After dozens of attempts, I'm wrung out. By now the tops of my thighs are streaked with crumbling wax trails that feel stiff against my sensitive skin, and the slaps of the crop are now focused solely on my bared clit.

When the last dollop falls squarely on my nipple, I cry out, "Cold Sir."

I have started to tremble, but it's not from cold, it's entirely from need. My body, kept at the edge of orgasm since I entered this room and flooded with endorphins repeatedly, is starting to crack and slowly fall apart. I am desperate for Silas to touch me in a meaningful way, I need a release or my body will implode.

I moan and beg, "Silas please, I can't take it anymore…please."

With that, Silas tugs off my blindfold, looking at me like he is questioning my sanity.

176

Carson begins to un-cuff my wrists, but leaves my legs wrenched open by the spreader bar. He steps back, pulling his shirt over his head with one hand and a swift gesture.

Next, Carson steps out of his pants, his erection bobbing like a mid-channel buoy. He quickly rolls a condom down the length of his shaft, then smiles at me. His brown eyes are twinkling with delight. He surprises me by leaning me forward and slipping in behind me, naked and hard.

Now we are both leaning against the Berkley Horse, or more correctly, Carson against the Berkley Horse, and me against him, tip to toe.

His hard on is pressing into my back like a thick post of rebar, hot and insistent as he whispers in my ear, "You're going to ride my cock while Silas fucks your sweet pussy." As he says this he widens his stance, effectively lowering his body and positioning his latexed dick between my ass cheeks, like a hot dog in a bun.

I can feel his short cropped pubic hair prickling against my ass crack as he slowly begins to slide me up and down his shaft.

"Silas, let's go. I'm not going to last," he calls to Silas.

For his part, Silas is frozen before me, his massive erection bulging in his pants.

"Silas," I beg, still quaking with need, "Please."

He snaps out of his daze and begins fumbling with his pants. His body looks as tense as mine, ready to snap or spring free like a Jack-in-the-Box. He drops his pants, his heavy erection swaying as he steps forward with a condom packet.

He rolls on the condom as if it's made of brittle toothpicks--slow and unsure.

When he finally steps forward, he leans into me, palms against the Berkley Horse. His penis thumps against my vagina, soft and smooth yet heavy and untrusting, almost hesitant.

Carson reaches around to fondle my breasts and pluck my nipples, gradually lowering one hand to my spread sex. "She is soaking wet. What are you waiting for? Do it!" Carson roars, as he begins rubbing my clit and sliding me up and down his shaft.

"Silas, I need you," I whisper, hardly able to wait another second.

Silas looks down at me with abject horror on his face. He begins to back up, slowly at first while bending down to pick up his pants, then rushing out of the room, with the door slamming behind him.

Tears pool in my eyes then spill down my cheeks, hot and dejected as the realization settles around me. Silas left, and he's not coming back.

"Don't worry Baby, I'll take care of you," Carson soothes, as he resumes rubbing my clit.

"No…Stop…" I whimper, and when he doesn't, I find my quavering voice and whisper, "Rumpelstiltskin" in a voice so small I hardly register it.

Carson stops immediately, recognizing the club safeword. "It's Ok Jessie, I'll stop. I'll do whatever you need right now." He is kind and attentive, nurturing almost.

"Unhook my legs," I whisper, nearly crying.

"OK, Shhhhh," he murmurs, as he slides out from behind me. Once free, he grabs Silas' discarded jacket and helps me put it on before he begins to unhook my ankles.

I'm crying full on now, unable to stem the flow pouring down my cheeks. "What the fuck was that?" I ask.

"I have no idea," Carson says, wrapping his arms around me and pulling me forward off the Berkley Horse into his arms. He holds me tight while I cry.

"I know I'm a poor substitute, but I'd really like to take care of you, Jessie." The fact that he is still completely naked doesn't seem weird at all and his offer is not skeevy in the least. "That was intense and...and abrupt, and I don't want you to be alone right now."

"I don't care, I want to go home," I say, lunging from his embrace.

"Jessie please."

"No. How do I get out of here?" I ask while stepping back into my skirt then hastily grabbing the other various scraps of my clothing.

"Jessie please," he begs, "Whatever you need."

"Ok then, give me your phone and find my purse," I say, challenging him between sniffles.

He grabs his pants, stepping into them but leaving them unzipped. He pulls his phone from the pocket and hands it to me.

I hastily punch in the number and after a lengthy pause, say, "Hi, I need you." It is all I can get out before my voice breaks.

Carson gathers the rest of my stuff saying, "Jessie--"

I stop him before he can get any further, "Stop. How do I get out of here?"

With a resigned sigh, he turns and pulls the door open for me.

1462 South Broadway

CHAPTER SIXTEEN
Sub drop

I roll over, stuffing my face into the pillow in an attempt to escape the relentless beating of the sun's rays through the sloppily closed curtains. My head is pounding with the intensity of a Mariachi band. My headache brings stomach acid to the back of my throat, a simmering, burning mix of napalm and regret.

Suddenly, without much warning, I need to bolt from my bed. I tumble into the bathroom, clumsily tripping over shoes and clothes, my room looking like a yard sale after last night. I need to crawl the last few feet to the toilet before vomiting, for the most part in the bowl.

Retching and heaving with my eyes bulging out of my skull, it feels as though my head is trying to turn itself inside out. After the first couple of fruitful hurls, I grab the sides of the toilet bowl to dry heave in vain. As I sputter and gag on the revolution in my gut.

Once the retching stops, I lay my cheek against the cool toilet seat. I ignore the droplets of toilet water splashed haphazardly around until the riotous migraine forces my eyes to cross. Then I slide rather clumsily to the floor.

I curl up, squeezing my temples between my bent arms. I'm shivering in a speedy tempo compared to the slow, deep throb of my head.

A knock on my bedroom door registers somewhere in my subconscious, but I make no move to get up or speak.

Devin carefully makes his way through the minefield of my room then stands at the bathroom door.

"Honey, come here." He is reaching out to me, but I shake my head and find a cool untouched spot for my cheek on the tile. My shivering has stopped, but my headache rages on.

Devin lowers himself to me, rubbing my back and murmuring sweetly, but his kindness only makes me dissolve into a new bout of silent tears.

He lies down and curls himself around me, his front to my knotted back. He continues holding me until he is sure I'm done crying, my reservoir dry.

When Devin and Corey picked me up last night, they hadn't asked any questions, just neatly swooped in and carted me home. It wasn't until Devin helped me into bed that he let his rage show.

"Jessie, this is not ok, you realize that right? This is not over; I'll take it from here," he had seethed.

Unable to say much through my quaking lower lip, I had just nodded, knowing full well that I would not let Devin handle anything. If Devin were to handle it, Silas would probably end up with an envelope of Anthrax.

Corey had gone home shortly after picking me up, and Devin brought me some hot tea. He'd kissed my forehead and said, "We don't have to talk about it right now, but you best believe we will be talking about this tomorrow."

"Ok, goodnight," I had forced through my lips, trying to sound indifferent but hardly able to get the words out.

He'd left my room, the tea had grown cold, and still, I laid there, staring at the wall unable to land on an emotion.

I had opened myself to Silas, trusting him implicitly. I bared my soul and was abandoned with nary a look back. He had given no consideration for my physical or emotional well-being whatsoever.

Was I sad? Angry? Humiliated? The truth was, I was all of these, but they seemed too oppressive, too insurmountable. So I had settled on feeling void, devoid of feelings, like space, emptiness…and eventually I'd fallen into a fitful sleep.

After a while on the bathroom floor, Devin touches my cheek and whispers, "Honey, I think you have a fever." He sits up on an elbow, rolls me onto my back and feels my forehead while smoothing the sweaty, matted hair off my cheek.

"Up's a daisy, let's get you into bed," he says as he hoists me up.

Devin gets me tucked under the covers and pulls my hair into an erratic bun on top of my head. He twists the hair tie with the hands of a barbarian and rattles the cage of my brain, inciting further insubordination within.

Hunching back into my pillows and squeezing my eyes shut, I croak, "Aspirin" with a muffled pleading that begs urgency.

He brings the Aspirin promptly, helping me sit up to swallow them along with some tepid water. As he lays me back against the down pillows, I can still feel the chalky trail of the pills down my throat, but I'm suddenly too tired to bother with another sip of water.

The next thing I know, Devin is tickling my nose with a cluster of my hair, rousing me from a deep, cavernous sleep.

"What? I'm exhausted, go away," I mumble, turning away, disgusted by the dry sticky feel of my mouth.

"You have been asleep for eleven hours. I brought you some chicken noodle soup and crackers," he says amiably.

I sit up scowling at him as my eyes adjust to even the dim light streaming in through the living room.

"I'm not hungry."

"Maybe not, but you have to eat," he says while fluffing the pillows behind me.

"I'll eat later," I say, sinking back into the newly fluffed pillows and the cocoon of my comforter.

"Eat a few bites and drink something then I'll leave you alone for a bit."

I sit up, shakily reaching for the ice water. I take a long sip. The coldness hammers against my teeth and makes them feel too big for my mouth. I start to pull the covers back up, but Devin tugs them away.

Anxious for him to leave, I hurriedly slurp up a couple of the proffered spoonfuls of soup placed at the clamp of my lips.

"Jessie, you are experiencing sub-drop," he says. He sets the bowl on the nightstand by last night's long cold tea. The tea has already evaporated enough to leave a brown ring around the inside of the mug, just above the oil slick on the surface of the liquid.

"We can talk later Devin, now go, I'm tired." But as soon as he leaves I have to lurch out of bed and deposit more bile and a bit of broth expeditiously into the toilet.

The next time Devin comes in, he brings a Gatorade and my cell phone. I still feel nauseated, but thankfully the headache is gone. I sit up and thank him, then ask, "What?" as he stands there, uncomfortably shifting his weight.

"Silas has been calling and texting," he says regrettably.

"Oh," is all I can muster.

"Do you want me to respond to him for you?"

"No," I say too quickly, then, "Actually yes, tell him to fuck off."

Devin smiles, "Now that's the spirit. But remember, the last impression you leave him with is the one he is going to remember."

"Oh, like the one of me naked, pressed up against another man with his dick between my ass cheeks and a spreader bar between my ankles?" I lash out, but realize I'm most horrified at myself. I'm supremely hurt, and astonishingly embarrassed, especially once I give voice to the whole charade.

Devin looks down at his hands while shaking his head, not knowing what to say for once. It's the first he has heard about that night. He begins softly, "Jessie, the thing about the kink scene is that it's based on trust. If there is no trust, or if that trust is broken, it doesn't work. Look at you. I've heard of sub-drop, but I've never witnessed it…until now."

"Stop," I interrupt. "It's just a little flu. Don't turn it into something as obsequious as the dreaded *sub-drop*."

Shaking his head in defeat, or because he isn't going to argue such a transparent fact, he says flatly, "Please tell me you are done with him."

"Isn't it obvious? He most assuredly is done with me," I say, while pulling the comforter to my shoulders and flopping over with my back to Devin.

185

"He is begging you to let him explain. Please God, don't be the battered wife who goes through hell then accepts contrition and elaborate apologies. He has shown you his true self and believe me; a leopard can't change his spots."

"I'm tired Devin," I mutter, feeling like our line of conversation is pointless, and that Silas' contrition would never actually come.

He gets up with a sigh, saying over his shoulder, "I'll make you some toast."

Many hours later when I finally emerge from the grim den of despair my room has become, my legs feel crotchety and frail. My body feels like it's made of wet paper, my mouth, of sawdust.

I pull open the fridge, grabbing a Gatorade and bowl of cut up fruit, when I have to pause and steady myself against the lightheadedness that swirls around and bumps into me.

Shuffling on bare feet to the couch, I slump down. Feeling alternately sad and angry over the last couple of days, I have finally decided on a feeling, it's crushing disappointment. My romanticized version of Silas is gone, the handsome, witty, sexy and successful man, all coupled with his knowledge of a woman's body and the fact he could make my body sing like no one else. Gone.

My former lovers have all been so dull and unskilled in comparison. Always choosing the same boring routine and approach to sex; never exciting, just mediocre, mundane...sometimes a chore and always, always vanilla.

Popping a piece of ripe peach into my mouth, all I can feel is a deep, unabiding and pervasive emptiness. I stare at the bowl of fruit on my lap for a while before I set it on the coffee table, no longer interested.

I slump over, with my neck at an awkward angle against the arm of the couch. Bringing my knees up to my chest, I gaze at the black screen of the TV for a few minutes, or maybe hours, before tears prickle at the back of my eyes again and I have to squeeze them shut.

I must have fallen asleep on the couch, amongst empty Gatorade bottles and broken fairy tale dreams, because the next thing I'm aware of is Devin standing in front of me.

"Ahem," he clears his throat, waking me from my dreamless fog.

"I see you found the fruit I cut up for you," he says, gesturing to the mostly uneaten, dried up fruit in the discarded bowl. Dropping his keys on the coffee table he asks, "Are you feeling better?"

"I suppose, I'm just drained, and I have to travel for work this week."

"Well I brought you some Pho from Wild Basil, that should help." He sets the brown take out bag next to his keys. He is wearing a typical Devin look, tank top, loose, garage band style shorts, and flip-flops. He disappears into the kitchen then emerges with two large bowls. He sags into the couch next to me, close like a pesky little brother, then ladles broth and vegetables into the bowls.

I push my greasy, matted hair behind my shoulders. I had abandoned Devin's attempt at a bun after a few hours of not feeling able to fully close my eyes. Two days of sleeping and sweating on the thick mass of hair, along with an occasional dash to the bathroom have left my hair in wild, limp clumps and my skin sallow.

The Pho revitalizes me, but I am still in no mood to discuss Friday evening, so eventually Devin stops persisting, asking instead, "So, where are you headed for work?"

"To Montana, to secure some land for drilling up near the Bakken shale formation."

"Well," he says, while wiping the noodle splatter from his chin with a paper napkin. "Have fun with that."

My job makes no sense to Devin, and his eyes glaze over at the mere mention of work stuff, but he is secretly proud of me for having such a powerful position. I have even caught him bragging about me to his friends.

"It won't be fun, but it will be good to get away, clear my head of Silas," I say, as I reach for the remote.

CHAPTER SEVENTEEN
Options

"Well, that went about as well as can be expected," says Salinger, my Land Technician. He slides into the driver's seat of our rental car, then reaches for his sunglass case. "Now, do you want to tell me what the hell is going on with you?"

"What do you mean?" I ask, playing dumb and looking him square in his hazel eyes. His brown hair is perfectly parted down the side and combed neatly, in a nerdy physics teacher kind of way. He is my right-hand man, and due to the eternal hours we spend together working and traveling, he is also a good friend.

"You were so aggressive with those landowners. What happened to the sweet, abiding, likable Jessie Hayes?" he asks, hesitating to engage the ignition.

"I wasn't aggressive, I was assertive, and sometimes it's called for," I say, by way of explanation while vigorously pulling my hair into a ponytail. "Just get me your report, and I will handle my end," I add, flagrantly ignoring his implication that something is wrong.

We drive a few miles in silence before Salinger looks at me and says, "So, this mushroom walks into a bar."

I roll my eyes but smile in spite of myself.

He continues, "But when he orders a drink the bartender says, 'I'm sorry, we don't serve your kind.' So the mushroom says, 'Why not? I'm a fungi.'" He finishes with a broad, white-toothed smile, the same smile that causes women to stammer and forget what they were talking about when he flashes it at them.

"Oh dang, we still have an hour to drive before we get to the hotel. Is this what I have in store?" I ask as my mood lightens incrementally.

"No, absolutely not, that little gem is all I've got. I don't want to set the expectations too high you know," he chuckles then adjusts the stereo while one wrist is still slung over the steering wheel.

I've never known Salinger to wear anything but long sleeved shirts, neatly pressed of course and nice slacks. So his music choices always surprise me, they are very heavy for someone so perfectly dressed and styled.

I settle back to watch the rather dull miles upon miles of farmland whiz by. I have been busy enough to not think about Silas much these last few days. However, now on the long drive, with all the work negotiations behind me, he creeps in like a bitter miasma.

I haven't been this upset by a guy in ages; maybe ever. I'm usually the one to pull the trigger and end the relationship. Maybe I'm too picky, or maybe men are overall disappointing, but usually, when a relationship ended, I was relieved instead of devastated. Granted Silas and I were hardly in a relationship, more of a whisper of one, but the future had seemed promising before it came to a screeching halt.

Salinger pulls off the highway long before our hotel exit, driving instead to a little dive bar with big, unlit neon, block letters identifying the near shanty simply as "BAR."

I look at him questioningly, but he just un-clicks his seatbelt and exchanges his sunglasses for his thick rimmed regular glasses in the hard case.

I follow him across the gravel parking lot, swatting at the flies buzzing around my head, and wondering if perhaps they speak ill of the bar's standing with the health department.

We enter the dim, seedy establishment and are assailed by the eager bartender, who's wiping the bar with a sour smelling rag. In fact, the whole place smells sour, like a carnival tent that had been put away wet then set up a year later.

"Evening, what will it be?" says the limp, skinny man with a pointy face and small beady eyes.

"A pitcher of beer and an order of wings, the hotter the better," Salinger says over his shoulder as he walks to the pool table and begins racking the balls.

I'm still pondering the bartender's use of 'evening' when it's barely three o'clock, and the fact that Salinger actually ordered food from such a dismal place, when he shouts, "Come on Jessie, you break."

I walk slowly over to the pool table as Salinger asks, "Are you afraid?" He sweeps his arm, indicating the game.

"Yes, of many things here, but not of your game," I say with a smile.

The mousy bartender sets down the pitcher of beer and two frosty mugs on a small table, leveled by a book of matches stuffed under one pipe leg. Then he scurries away without a word.

191

I start pouring the beer as Salinger announces, "I think our bartender is a tweaker." His bland delivery of the very apropos comment makes me laugh out loud. Sweet, Salinger even knowing the term "Tweaker" is funny to me in itself, but his accuracy is dead on and describes the man's demeanor perfectly.

After two pitchers of beer and three games of pool--two for Salinger, one narrowly won by me, I am feeling much better. Salinger has me laughing almost constantly, and I find I am having a genuinely good time.

The wings, although taking an eternity to arrive, are surprisingly welcome when they do. They are crispy and dripping with some sort of blazing inferno sauce if the nose searing smell is any indication.

Giddy and buzzed, we clamor into a booth with strips of duct tape holding the burgundy vinyl together in more places than not.

Nervous about the heat of the wings, I first go for a carrot stick, letting Salinger sample the wings first.

He eats a wing, wipes his mouth with a napkin from the dispenser and takes a swig of beer before he says, "Do you know there are over 300 million people in the United States?"

I laugh at his randomness and say, "Really?" as I reach for a chicken wing.

"Yeah and if you take away the 150 million that are female, then the probably 50 million that are too young, and the 80 million that are too old, you have, what? 20 million left? Then let's say 60% are taken. Of the ones left, at least half are not good matches. So, by my calculations, that leaves you with around four million good men still left in the sea." He finishes speaking with raised eyebrows, then takes another swig of beer, holding his saucy fingers away from the frosty mug.

I smile, looking away from his pointed glance, "Thank you, Salinger."

He wipes his hands on a napkin then reaches out, taking mine and says, "I mean it, you are the smartest, funniest, and most beautiful woman I know, and any man that makes you sad is a fucking idiot."

I blush, although Salinger is a great friend and co-worker; he also has an incredible amount of sex appeal. I have always kept him at a romantic distance because we work together, but I'm not completely impervious to his sexy lure. My heart begins to pump faster as I fidget beneath his gaze.

He lets go of my hand and jumps up saying, "I'll give you one more chance to even the score." Then he gives me a sexy grin as he chalks the tip of his pool cue.

"Have I ever told you what a terrible short term memory I have?" he asks, with his eyes twinkling as I approach the pool table.

I know where he is going with this. "Salinger, we work together," I say, unable to suppress a smile at his playfulness.

He walks around behind me, puts his hands on my hips and slides up against me, his voice low in my ear, "Short term is just shot. It's the cross I bear from my deployment in Iraq."

I close my eyes, it would be so easy. I turn to face him, but before I can speak, he cradles the back of my neck in his hand and pulls me into his kiss. It's warm and comfortable, and for a few minutes, I lose myself kissing him back. The haze of heartache and beer makes it easy to forget that we work together and that I am hung up on another man.

He lifts me onto the pool table in a sitting position and steps between my legs, kissing me tenderly. His kisses are impassioned, full of lust and... reverence.

Kissing Salinger feels good, he feels good, so I carry on, just happy to feel something again, anything but pain and disappointment. Before too long though, realization slaps me in the face.

"Salinger stop."

He pulls away; slowly shaking his head but doesn't miss a beat when he points to the far end of the pool table and says, "Five ball, corner pocket."

Back at the hotel, I step out of the shower and wrap myself in a towel. In another life, a relationship with Salinger would be phenomenal, but I rely on him at work so a sexual relationship would only complicate matters. I have never really thought of him as anything other than a friend and co-worker because up until last year, he was married. Even after his wife's affair and the disintegration of his marriage, I never consciously thought of him as a viable option because of work.

Shaking my head against the pondering, I realize one hot night with Salinger would only lead to many awkward months or years at work, and the sad fact is, I'm not over Silas.

Thinking of Silas, I cross the room to my cell phone to check my voicemail...hating that I still care. I have a message from Devin, he says that Silas sent flowers and a card saying "I'm sorry" but he had them sent back, *return to sender*. "I hope that's Ok. He can be as sorry as he wants but that doesn't excuse his behavior," he says in his message. I sigh, then toss the phone onto the bed. *Great, Silas, clear your conscience and move on.*

I pull on a tank top and some beat up jeans, content to zone out in front of the TV for the rest of the evening. I towel dry my hair then brush my teeth, trying to get the taste of rejection out of my mouth. As I'm spitting into the sink, I hear a knock on my door.

"Hey Salinger, what's up?" I say, swinging the door wide open.

"Let's go get some late dinner," he says, standing in his own ratty jeans and a long sleeved T-shirt.

"I'm not hungry," I say, somewhat unconvincingly.

"Come on, there is an elephant in the room, and we need to address it," he says plainly.

"I don't want to address it," I say.

"Fine then, we won't, but I won't let you avoid me either. Let's go."

I'm happy about his light demeanor, so I say, "Just let me put on some mascara and lip gloss first."

"Ok, and for the love of God, put on a bra," he says.

Realizing my nipples are almost piercing my tank top I spin around and go to retrieve said bra.

At dinner, we don't discuss the kiss and the conversation is not weird at all, so I relax and gratefully sweep it under the rug with all the other crap I'm choosing not to deal with. The easy banter takes my mind off Silas and by the time we finish, it's well after ten o'clock.

Once back in my hotel room I peel off my jeans and with a few contortionist moves, shimmy out of my bra. I leave on the tank and panties and climb into bed.

After I stare at the ceiling for a while, I start to wonder, why, after a heavy dinner of pasta and shrimp, I feel so empty.

1462 South Broadway

CHAPTER EIGHTEEN
Endorphins

The last few weeks have blurred together. In my disappointment, I have kept very busy at work and exercised maniacally at the gym. My workouts have been intense, because I'm eager for the false happiness the endorphins afford me. With no further contact from Silas, I've been sliding grumpily through the stages of grief, landing me not yet at acceptance but begrudgingly stuck in the depression stage.

Devin and Corey have done their best, dragging me to movies or coffee or on hikes but so far they've been unsuccessful at pulling me from my funk. Devin teases that I have never been rejected before, so it is fitting that it be amplified, "To even the score with the rest of the world's heartbreak."

I'd rolled my eyes when he said it, but I didn't feel the need to correct him, or justify my feelings, so I'd just left it at the eye roll.

I finished up at work early today and went to the gym much earlier than usual. Unfortunately for me, the charge on my iPod Shuffle was low, so half my workout was spent listening to

CNN on the gym's mounted TV's. Too bad political banter doesn't have the same effect as angry music to inspire my workouts.

Driving home from the gym, I manage to time it perfectly with the ring of the school bell. Children explode like confetti from the elementary school on the corner, and traffic slows to a mandatory crawl.

I'm essentially surrounded by school buses and flashing caution lights as an entire lane of traffic peels off into the "kiss n go" lane of the schools' rainbow drive. Maybe it's only a kiss n go lane in the morning, what would you even call it in the afternoon for pick up? The grab n dash lane? Or is that too child abductor sounding?

My thoughts are interrupted as a crossing guard half-heartedly holds up a hand for me to stop, with the actual stop sign held in his other hand. He must be pretty confident I actually will, in fact, stop because he doesn't even glance up at me as he leads the brood of laughing kids across the street like a mother duck with her ducklings.

Once the kids are safely across, he turns his sign to "Slow" and waves me forward. As I meet his eyes I realize, with sweaty, post-gym horror, that underneath the neon orange reflector vest and crossing guard cap--*helping little kids across the street after school,* is Silas.

He turns the sign back to "Stop" and hurries to my driver's side window. "Jessie, hi," he says, somehow out of breath.

With my window open and my arm hanging out, I can hardly pretend I don't see him standing there. So I say, "Uh...hi, I guess."

"He puts a hand on the car saying, "Please, give me a chance to explain. Please."

"There is nothing to explain, you don't need to let me down easy--it's fine, I'm a big girl." I glance in the rearview mirror at the agitated drivers behind me.

"Let me make you dinner--I need to explain."

"Silas really--"

"Jessie seriously, I need to explain," he interrupts, looking at me with pleading eyes.

Cars are now honking behind me, and another group of kids are waiting for him on the school's sidewalk, but he isn't budging, his hand is still firmly on my car.

"I'll think about it," I say, putting the car in gear and easing forward. My heart is thumping in the back of my mouth, my tongue, thick like gravy. Why do I always run into him at my sweaty, gross, worst? I'll have to start showering at the gym.

Pulling into the parking garage of my condo building, my phone chimes with a text. I park in my designated spot, grab my gym bag and hustle into the building. Once in the elevator, I read the text. "6:00 my place, 7100 Grant St. Unit 18A, garage code is 6332*." The message makes me smile. Maybe I am being weak and pathetic, but I actually want to hear what he has to say. I need to hear it, if for no other reason than for me to finally understand what he was thinking, and to have a bit of closure.

Thankfully Devin's old Ford Bronco was not in his parking spot. With any luck, I won't have to explain myself to his cold, hard, judgmental stare.

I want to look nice but not like I'm trying too hard-- casual but indifferent, light and unaffected. So I settle on an ordinary, simple, olive green sun dress that is made less ordinary by the halter style, with a deep V neckline, and my bare upper back. Some modest wedge sandals and light makeup complete the look I'm going for, tempting but disinterested.

Having showered off the punishing gym experience, I let my hair air dry with a salt spray product that leaves my hair in tousled waves, like I spent the day at the beach. Devin calls it my, "well-fucked hair." I like it because it looks like I didn't bother with it, but it still looks sexy.

At this point, I'm ready but don't have to leave for another 20 minutes. I'm so afraid Devin will come home and find out where I'm going that I grab my purse and bolt out the door, leaving the faint flowery smell of liberally applied body lotion in my wake.

I decide to stop at a market a few blocks from my apartment for fear of being early and appearing too eager. As I wander the aisles trying to burn time, I start to wonder if I should bring something. Perhaps wine or maybe dessert? After agonizing over the decision, I decide wine would be too presumptuous and dessert too familiar. So after spending way too much time fretting over it, I leave the store empty handed.

Sliding back into my car I tap Silas' address into my GPS. I can't help but wonder if I am making a huge mistake. Am I jumping to attention just because he snaps his fingers? Am I excusing his behavior just by going over there? Do I look pathetic, like I'm crawling back? Finally, I decide, no, he sent flowers, he called and texted continually, he wants to make me dinner at his house. No, he can't just be an asshole; it has to be something more complex than that. But he *has* practically run screaming from me twice. *What the hell am I doing?*

Stepping off the elevator, I realize there are only two units on the 18th floor, A and B. As I approach unit A the door flings open and a woman and child just about plow me over in their haste. "Oh my goodness! I'm so sorry. Come, Ruby, let's get moving." The woman is agitated, only stopping long enough to adjust her purse on her shoulder and grab the little girl's hand. She drags her deftly behind as the little one steals glances back at me.

I stand rooted to the ground, still stunned by the passing tsunami when I hear the little girl call out, "Hi Jess-ieee." Her voice is drawn out, and she uses a teasing tone in her voice. I spin around to see her grinning and waving at me before she is yanked onto the elevator, the doors closing behind her.

A thousand things go through my head, vaporizing any jitters I had harbored only minutes ago. My primary thought now is, *Silas has a child.*

I compose myself as well as can be expected and knock on the door, still spinning from the heavy realization.

Silas opens the door with his hair still damp from the shower. He is wearing a gray T-shirt and jeans. He stands in front of me, a smile lifting the corners of his eyes. He seems nervous to touch me but steps forward to pull me into a hug as we stand at the threshold of his condo. "Thank you for coming," he says into my hair, and my chilly demeanor warms marginally.

"I just," I stammer with my thumb pointing over my shoulder.

"Ran into Analise and Ruby?" he finishes, raising his eyebrows at me.

"Yes, literally and figuratively," I say, still a bit stunned.

"Come in, please," he motions me inside. His condo is expansive, open like a loft but so well appointed as to still be cozy. The entire far wall consists of huge, glass, pocket doors, opening out onto a sprawling terrace. The city view is breathtaking with the sun just beginning to disappear behind the tall buildings.

He leads me out to the terrace where a large rattan sectional borders a gas fire pit, lit with aqua blue crystals. "Really, thanks for coming."

CHAPTER NINETEEN
Atonement

I walk to the edge of the terrace where a glass half-wall borders the expansive space. I find that I am uncharacteristically taken with the beautiful view and the surprisingly peaceful quiet surrounding me, it's only fractured by a soft breeze.

Silas approaches quietly and hands me a glass of wine. I accept gratefully, then turn back to the sun disappearing behind the downtown cityscape.

Leaning on the half-wall with his elbow, Silas says softly, "I couldn't just...*take* you like that." His face is pained but steadfast.

I say nothing, but turn to him as his words sink in. I meet his pleading blue eyes; they are as clear and sharp as cut glass in the light of the sunset.

"You didn't like it?" I ask, sounding more plaintive than I would like.

"That's not it at all," he says imploringly while taking my hand with his free one. "It was raw and provocative and intensely erotic. Don't get me wrong, there is a time for that...but, that's not how I want to, to... I just couldn't...couldn't take," he is

203

stammering, blindly seeking just the right words. "I didn't want it to be like that for you, for us...the first time."

Realizing the implications of his rather awkwardly delivered statement, my throat clamps shut against my sharp inhale. He referred to our first time as if there would be others, he also didn't want to have me... aggressively, or with someone else.

Morally outraged at myself for letting weeks of anguish slip by under my own martyrdom, I find I have no response to his confession.

I take a sip of wine, staring out into the middle distance. I'm searching for the exact right words to properly sum up my unbalanced feelings. I open my mouth to speak but slap it closed instead. Silas looks expectantly into my troubled eyes.

After a stiff moment and another sip of wine, I take a breath and say, "Let me get this straight," I pause while Silas steps closer with a sullen nod and wounded eyes. "You...have a daughter?" I ask, feeling completely unable to address his explanation but suddenly feeling the impact of the little girl.

Silas lets out his held breath and says, "I'm so sorry." He sets our wine glasses down and takes both of my hands. I'm not sure if he means he is sorry for running out on me or for not having mentioned his daughter.

I can't seem to rely on an emotion about either possibility, so instead, I stare blankly at my hands, still held loosely in Silas'. I am ill-equipped to ration out and compartmentalize the many feelings swirling in my head. At once I feel elated *and* despondent, clarity *and* confusion. My bewilderment is consuming, so it is with blessed relief that Silas speaks, "Come, sit." He leads me by the hand to the rattan sectional. He retrieves our wine glasses then sits down next to me.

"Her name is Ruby, she is six," he says while I nod slowly. "I never thought I would have kids, my lifestyle never felt conducive to children, but most of all I never thought I would settle down. I've had incredible success in business, which has afforded me a very selfish existence. If I wanted something, I bought it. Outside of business, I've never had to work for anything. Tickets landed in my lap for sporting events, the best tables at restaurants, women if and when I wanted them, and discarded neatly when I no longer did." He has the grace to look somewhat disgusted with himself as he clears his throat and goes on.

"Selfish--unbelievably selfish. I was always careful with women because I didn't want kids. I thought they would complicate my life, and I couldn't even conceive of being tied to one woman forever through a child." He is solemnly shaking his head, looking at his feet. "I was such an asshole. I'm ashamed of the man I was, arrogant and unflinching, I was an unguided missile."

I nod.

He continues, "One day that all changed and I didn't know it then, but it was the best day of my life." Now he makes eye contact with me, his story on its way to redemption. "A woman named Amber walked into my real estate office with a little girl. She handed her to me and said, 'Her name is Ruby, and she's yours.' I stood up nervously, holding on to this kid--I had never even held a child before. I remember being afraid I wasn't doing it right. I had tried to give her back to Amber while demanding an explanation. I didn't want her to be mine, but I knew in my gut she was--she looked just like me when I was a kid."

"What happened after that?" I ask, my eyes wide with interest.

205

"Amber dropped a manila envelope on my desk and a pink paisley diaper bag at my feet. Then she just walked out."

"How old was she? Ruby, not Amber," I ask.

"Fourteen months, I remember feeling super hot all of a sudden and having to sit down." He laughs, then continues, "I was holding Ruby under her arms and out in front of me like she was covered in arsenic or something." He shakes his head at the memory, softening with nostalgia then goes on. "When my arms got tired of holding her up like that, I sat her on the edge of my desk, still gripping her under the arms. I was so stunned, I didn't have the first clue what to do or who to call, so I just stared at her. It was so much like looking in a mirror it was crazy. She was wearing these cute little jelly sandals, and I remember marveling at how small they were. Anyway, I sat there like a deer in the headlights for God knows how long, then she grabbed my face with one chubby little hand. She lifted my chin up, while she pointed to the fluorescent light above me, and said, 'lights…hot' with a slobbery mouth and a cute little lisp. With that, my frozen heart started to thaw."

"Oh, how sweet, the misogynist becomes a father," I say sarcastically through a smile.

He smiles at my response. "When my receptionist returned from lunch, she came in my office with a stack of files and saw me leafing through a contract with this little girl on my lap. Ruby was grabbing at the papers but otherwise sitting contentedly. My receptionist stood there with her mouth hanging open. I remember asking her, 'What do I do?' She was a saint, within the hour she had my lawyer, a pack n play, and a string of nannies to interview in my office," he says, still chuckling at the memory.

I slide off my sandals and tuck my feet up under my body. I settle in with my side leaning into the back of the cushioned sectional and my arm across the top of it. "You really were thrown to the wolves weren't you?"

"Then and a thousand times since. I never guessed I would be reading, 'What to Expect in the Toddler Years' instead of the New York Times, but I muddled through. Ruby's nanny Analise, has this look that says, *Are you sure you didn't just fall off the turnip truck?* And I have come to know that look all too well," he laughs as he pours me more wine.

"So, do you share custody?"

"No, actually Amber signed over her parenting rights that day. That was the paperwork in the manila envelope. My lawyer told me to have it approved by the court system, which I still haven't done, but Amber walked out that day and hasn't so much as inquired about Ruby, not a phone call, not a birthday card, nothing."

"So, insta-daddy."

"I know, Right? But that moment was the turning point in my life. I never knew you could love someone so much."

"When did you realize you loved her?"

"It's crazy because I know the exact moment. I knew I *could* love her when she pointed at the lights, warning me they were hot. Here is this little mini-me that I somehow need to figure out how to care for, and she is worried about *my* safety. Anyway, I knew I loved her pretty quickly into the new arrangement. I thought she should have a crib, but Analise insisted she needed a big girl bed. So consequently, she was able to get out of bed whenever her independent, little self, felt like it. I remember the first night when she got in bed with me. She stood at the edge of my bed with her arms raised and demanded, 'Up!' So I lifted her up. She snuggled up against me, gave my cheek a wet kiss, then fell soundly asleep. I watched her sleep, her angelic little face and pouty lips. It was then that I realized I loved her. I remember I just watched her sleep for hours. I stroked her hair and apologized for her crappy mother, then promised I would take care of her forever."

"That's so sweet."

"Yeah, until you try to convince a headstrong three-year-old that it's time to sleep in her own bed when she is used to sleeping with you," he laughs.

"How do you do it? Run the club I mean, with the crazy hours and the commercial real estate career?"

"I cook her dinner, read her books and tuck her in every night. She knows Analise is just through the lock off if she needs her. On occasion, Ruby will sleep at her place…like tonight." He winks then goes on, "The club mostly happens while she's asleep. Plus, Parker is at 1462 whenever I'm not. She is insanely eager and doesn't seem to need sleep, so I'm letting her handle the orientations and admissions more and more these days anyway. Sleep and real estate happen when Ruby is at school for the most part."

"Parker is another gatekeeper?"

"Yes, turns out, gatekeeping is a full-time job all on its own," he says, through a wide smile.

"Tell me about Ruby, what is she like?" I ask, realizing it's almost fully dark already.

He leans forward and twists a knob on the fire pit. The crystals blaze more intensely to life, flickering ethereally as the heat rises into the brisk evening. "She is sassy, wants to be a fashion designer. She is a whippersnapper, and I mean that fondly for now, but I'm under no illusions that she won't be trouble as a teenager."

"Why didn't you tell me?"

It's not that I hide the fact that I'm a father…I just don't lead with it." He says this as he settles himself closer to me, draping his arm on the back of the rattan and nestling his fingers into my hair.

"How does having a daughter affect your, um...sexual life?" I ask, then immediately feel embarrassed by the question.

"I don't bring women home if that's what you mean. I have never subjected her to a revolving door of women--"

I interrupt, not liking where the conversation is going. "So you keep the revolving door at 1462 then?"

He cracks a smile, "Not exactly Jessie, in fact, I have grown rather disenchanted with the revolving door. I have had more women than I care to discuss, but the girl who has had the biggest effect on me, is the one I didn't see coming." His hand, still resting behind me, begins toying with my beachy hair.

I lean my head into his palm and say plaintively, "Ok, I'm ready to talk about that night."

"Alright, but let's go inside, I'm supposed to be cooking you dinner," he says, rising to his feet and extending his hand to me. I take his hand, stepping over my sandals and follow him inside.

His kitchen is open and beautiful with a dark island, asphalt gray cabinets, and stark white Carrara marble countertops and backsplash. The design is classy and masculine at the same time, but the lighting designer in Devin would insist on a huge, industrial chandelier above the island instead of the row of copper pendant lights.

"Antonia's on 16th makes this amazing chicken and apple sausage; I picked some up after I saw you. I was hoping you would decide to come. Do sausage and peppers sound good for dinner?"

"It sounds delicious," I say, taking the bag of peppers and heading to the colossal apron sink, it's a sea of white.

Silas pulls out a glass cutting board and two knives as I make my way over to him, peppers and hands washed.

He starts chopping up an onion and clears his throat. "I wasn't ready. I wanted to get to know you better before taking you to the club."

"We *were* getting to know each other, and twice you ran out on me," I say, holding up two fingers to drive home my point. "Not just once, but twice." Truth be told, I sound kind of bratty.

"Right, that. Analise called me from the hospital, Ruby had an allergic reaction to some Macadamia nut encrusted fish. I panicked, I needed to get to the hospital, I was out of my mind with worry. I should have explained then, but that was not really how I wanted to tell you I have a kid," he says, his eyes glistening from the potency of the onion. He sniffles and tries to wipe his tears on the shoulder of his t-shirt.

Setting the knife down and turning to face me he says, "Jessie, I'm sorry I ran out and didn't explain. That was terribly rude of me, and I'm very sorry. I should have handled it differently, but the Steampunk Ball was right around the corner, and I thought I could explain then.

Then when I saw you with Carson, so close and so giggly, I started to worry you were more of a club girl than I thought."

"But it was so loud in there, we could hardly hear each other, and I was grateful to have someone to talk to--"

"Stop," he interrupts, placing both hands up to stop me. "You don't have to explain. I realize that now, but that feeling drove the evening down a whole different path. I had wanted to show you how strong and capable I was sexually. I pretended to be ok sharing you with Carson, but the reality is, I don't want to share you. I was so afraid if we started like that, then we would just be about the raw carnality--the fuck, but I want the intimacy with you too," he finishes, looking suddenly shy.

Setting my knife down, I look at him for what feels like the first time.

"I handled it completely wrong. The whole night snowballed downhill, and I didn't know how to turn it around. I literally decompensated and--"

"Stop, just stop," I say, as I look into his dark blue eyes and notice a starburst of yellow in their depths. I have so much to say, but the words lodge somewhere near my collarbone. So I reach both hands to the back of his head and pull him to me.

He pauses between kisses, our lips a sliver apart. "I'm so sorry," he mumbles and then closes in on me.

After a bit, he parts our mouths slightly and murmurs, "I want you so fucking bad."

I smile into his kiss and feel my heart swell. Not just because he wants me, but because I was wrong about him, totally, utterly, wrong.

"But, I want to do this right," he says, then takes a step back from me and closes his eyes for a deep inhale. "I'm *going* to do this right." Then he grabs my face, pulling me in for another impassioned kiss.

Breaking off our kiss, he murmurs into my mouth, "Would you mind grabbing the sausage from the fridge?"

When we finally carry our plates outside, the evening has grown downright chilly, but there is a warm cocoon of crackling heat that settles around the lit crystals, creating a comfortable, dreamy space. The peace settles around me like wispy snowflakes and the heaviness of the last few weeks lifts away.

The initial, bitter anxiety about the evening had chewed a hole through my stomach. However, now, in the resulting calm, I realize I am famished.

When we finish eating, Silas gathers our plates and disappears inside. I nestle into the cushy terrace furniture, feeling supremely content and finally, finally optimistic.

Silas returns with two steaming mugs of coffee and a wide grin. "I'm not taking any chances, I want to learn everything about you," he winks and hands me a mug. It smells richly of hazelnut and goes down as smooth as creamy buttermilk.

"Ummmmmmmmm," I purr. "This is perfect."

He settles next to me, closer than before with an ease that feels natural and uninhibited.

I'm sitting with my legs tucked up and facing him. With my hands cupping the warm mug I ask, "How does a six-year-old get interested in fashion design?"

He smiles a broad smile, showcasing his perfect teeth. I can feel the pride for his daughter swell in his chest; a balloon of joy and satisfaction.

"I said she is sassy right? Well, that doesn't do her justice. This is a kid that since she was very young, would not so much as go get the mail with me without a hat, a purse, her jewelry--all her accessories," he chuckles. "It must be innate to her because she doesn't get it from Analise, who is as plain and grandmotherly as they come and she certainly doesn't get it from me." He points to himself indicating that he is no fashionista.

He sets his mug down and draws his leg up so that his own knee is facing me. His arm is once again, draped along the back of the sectional, his fingers lightly twisting a lock of my hair. "Tell me what you were like as a kid?" he asks wistfully.

"Ha! I was awkward and gangly. I had spindly legs and rangy hair. I played the violin and read a lot," I laugh, "I haven't always been this self-possessed woman you see before you."

He smiles at my frank acknowledgment of my less than glamorous self. "Can you still play the violin?"

"I could probably still bust out Mary Had a Little Lamb," I say, as he laughs out loud, tossing his head back.

"I didn't care about fitting in," I say, "I think I realized very young, thanks to a few shitty kids, that different was bad, and I never would fit in."

"That's so crazy to me, because it's your uniqueness that makes you so special. You're right though, growing up, standing out is bad but as an adult, it's the blending in that is so boring. I spent a whole year in middle school wearing sweater vests because all the cool kids thought they were lame. I guess I have always purposely gone against the current, and challenged the status quo," he says.

"Such social misfits, and look, we turned out extraordinary."

He emphatically nods his agreement. "What about your siblings?"

"My brother was a year older and cast a huge shadow. He was the mighty Jonathan Hayes, lacrosse star, loved by teachers and students alike."

"He didn't look out for you? Defend you?" Silas asks incredulously, but not having a sister he needed to defend, he doesn't recognize the implications of a sibling who is a social outcast.

"A little maybe, but he had his fun too. I remember being really nervous to start middle school because Jonathan told me there was this really tough group of redheads called *The Reds* that would force me to join their ranks." I say this with a huge smile because it was so typical of my brother, who both adored and tortured me growing up.

"That's so mean," Silas quips, also smiling in spite of himself.

"He relished tormenting me. Being the recipient of recessive genes, I don't look like the rest of my family. They all have dark hair and tan easily. Then there is me, this pasty, awkward redhead. Once, when my mom left us with a babysitter, Jonathan nudged me and said, 'Now is your chance to go through mom and dad's stuff and find your adoption papers.'"

"No, he didn't!" Silas balks, laughing heartily. "That is such an older brother mentality. I bet he became very protective of you somewhere along the way though, right?"

"He did. Right about the time his friends started taking an interest in me."

"I'll bet! What about your sister?"

"Alyssa. We are very close now, but she was so much younger than Jonathan and me that she never factored into his early torment. She owns a skin care clinic, dates a fireman," I say. "What about you? You suffered your own big brother torments, but you guys are close now right? What's your brother's name again?"

"His name is Sam, and fate has a way of exacting revenge because he has twin boys now, Sawyer and James." His shoulders are rolling with stifled laughter as he takes a sip of his coffee. "He is still up to his old tricks though. Last Christmas I watched him hook the Velcro of Sawyer's shoes together while the poor kid was sitting on the couch. So when he stood up, his feet were stuck together."

"What did he do? How old are your nephews?"

"They are four--Sawyer realized right away what had happened, and knew immediately who was to blame," he chuckles. "He just said, in this deadpan voice, 'Dad, now I can't walk.'" Silas is laughing while he imitates his nephew with a whiny kid's voice.

He rests his hand on my knee. "Are you warm enough?"

I nod and lean the side of my face into the hand he has resting on the back of the couch next to me.

He leans in, kissing me soundly and says, "I'm glad you persevered your awkward childhood, it has molded you into the woman you are today."

"I'm curious, what has molded you into the man you are today?" I ask, raising my eyebrows indicating his iniquitous profession and not the proper, buttoned-up one.

"Oh that," he says, rolling his eyes. "Well, I discovered I had success with girls rather early in life, and it had nothing to do with my charming personality," he says sardonically. "It turns out, girls like hockey players. In high school, I found it so easy to have casual sex, that I never really cared about the girls. They only cared about my status as the captain of the hockey team, so I didn't even feel bad. We were using each other." (Pause) "I guess that never really having had that first love or *the one that got away*, just added to my lack of emotions regarding sex. It became more primal for me, not something loving or sweet." Pausing and reflecting, he adds, "None of this bodes well for me does it?"

"Not at all," I say brightly at his revelation.

"Anyway, I became disenchanted with feeling, like I was a notch in these girls' belts--can you believe that? I was so fucking arrogant. Anyway, after a while, I just wanted anonymous sex, I didn't want anyone to have me for their own social acclaim, and I didn't want all the drama that comes from sex with teenage girls.

So a couple of friends and I went to a *club."* He smiles as if he is finished, but I prod him on.

"And?"

"And that's how the seed was planted. The place was exactly how most people picture a BDSM club now, black leather and red vinyl. It opened my eyes both sexually and as a budding entrepreneur. I used to obsess about how I would do it differently, how mine would be high class, not dark, seedy and underground."

"That makes sense I guess. So-" I pause thoughtfully, "You're a male whore who forms no emotional attachments to women. Did I get that right?" I ask, only halfway teasing, as I put down my empty coffee mug.

"To say my daughter has changed me would be the understatement of the century. I look into her sweet face, and I already want to murder her future boyfriends. But I also see where unchecked sexuality has gotten me," he says.

"Ah, right. A few rounds of antibiotics, I suppose." I say flatly.

"Nowhere Jessie. Well it got me my daughter, for which I'm eternally grateful, but it's gotten me nowhere personally."

"But you have a lucrative career and a wildly popular club."

"Yes, but that's just business success. Yea, I can pay the bills," he says, as if that isn't a true measure success. "The reality is I want more, I want to share my life with someone. I want Ruby to have a mother, not a nanny."

Touched, I place a hand on his leg. "I just knew there was more to you than meets the eye."

"What, beyond sex and protein shakes, you mean?" He moves a wisp of my hair aside so his palm can cup the side of my face. With his thumb resting on my cheekbone he slides closer, and our lips meet for a second then again as he pulls me into him, deepening the kiss.

We kiss languidly for entire phases of the moon it seems. Yet Silas continues to hold back, keeping his hands on my face or in my hair. I ache for him to touch me with the visceral need of a predator engorged with blood lust. I break the kiss and loll my head back, exposing my full neck and pounding pulse to Silas' gifted mouth.

The heat from the fire pit infused with the mania of our desire creates a tinderbox in my soul. My craving for him has reached near impossible levels. I am no longer content with the eager kissing of two adolescents. I un-tuck my knees from the enveloping sun dress and slip onto his lap, straddling him in the reminiscent style of our first meeting, only this time it's me taking charge.

I pull him into me, not wanting to break contact with his mouth on my body. I can feel his arousal beneath me, and it floods me with covetous need.

Dropping his hands to my ass, he pulls me against him. This forward motion causes me to grind into the erection that's straining against his jeans, and summons a low groan from him. All the unfinished eroticism from 1462 floods back, and all at once, I have to feel him inside me.

"Silas," I moan into his mouth, an aching question and hurried demand.

He moves his hands to the outside of my thighs and leans his forehead into the crook of my neck. I can feel his panting breath feathering across my neck and chest.

I sit back as he slides his hands under my dress then up and down my bare thighs. Slowly, he moves them up to my hips. A slow smile lights his eyes as he raises a hand again to my cheek, dragging his thumb across my lips.

"It will be my pleasure to atone for my mistreatment of you," he murmurs through parted lips.

My breath catches in my throat as his implications become clear. He sits forward, gathering me up in the process. My legs wrap around his body as he stands, and while still kissing me, he walks inside.

He smoothly deposits me on the edge of his massive bed. It's carefully made, with crisp white bedding and sits against a wall of windows, amongst the city lights. The head of his bed is butted right up against the wall of glass leading out into the bustling world.

As he busies himself lighting a sea of candles, I marvel at the world below. Above me, hanging from the tall ceiling is a huge rusty chandelier that looks as though it came from a shipwreck at the bottom of the ocean.

Silas dims the light, then stalks towards me while pulling his t-shirt over his head in an unhurried fashion. His golden honey skin and taut, chiseled torso bring a smile to my face that mirrors the glint in his eyes.

He edges up between my knees, crawling forward while backing me down, against his downy, white bed. With one swift movement, he slides his forearm between my waist, and the bed, then hauls me up, deeper into the expanse of his bed. He kisses me slowly and sweetly.

He seems determined to set a leisurely pace, and relishes each union of our lips.

I reach around his smooth sculpted back and pull him to me, closing the gap between us.

Holding himself up on his elbows, he gazes into my face, smiling a boyish grin. The comfortable weight of him is an easy pressure as he reaches down and scoots my knee to the side. He slides my leg up to better cradle his body and to explore the bare flesh of my thigh as the sun dress falls away, pooling near my hip.

His fingers slide to the strap of my panties at my hip and begin to work them down while raising himself a bit to allow the divesting of the panties.

Dizzy with need I fumble to unbutton his jeans, only marginally loosening the strain against the denim.

In an effort to slow my fevered pace Silas draws my wrists above my head, pinning them gently against a heap of down pillows. His mouth moves from my lips to my ear where he nibbles and tugs at my earlobe, clanking the small diamond earring against his teeth. He pours into my ear a tickling exhale of breath as he whispers, "Soon Baby."

As he reaches up behind me to unfasten the dress at the back of my neck, he continues his vocal exhale into my sensitive ear, "Very soon."

My back arches with desire, straining my breasts against the loosened fabric before he tugs down the top altogether, exposing my breasts and acorn hard nipples to the flickering candle light.

With his own groan of need defying his careful pace, he drops his mouth to a rigid nipple flicking it sternly with his tongue. While one of his hands still pins my wrists above my head, he drops the other to my free breast. He tugs at my nipple, rolling it back and forth like a dial as he begins to suck carefully on the other peak, then nips the tip with his teeth.

The sensation dazes me and forces my head to strain back, pressing my face into the edge of the pillows. "OhmyGod," I moan, as the torrent unleashes between my legs.

Silas rolls me on top of him as he struggles to get the dress over my head. I reach up and deftly pull it the rest of the way off, tossing it to the floor while his hands assail my body.

He palms my breasts, pinching the nipples between his extended fingers. Then, reaching back he sweeps the mound of pillows to the floor and begins to pull me forward. He inches me up his body, so my dampness is resting against his chest. He shimmies his arms under my legs, coaxing me forward until I'm straddling his hot mouth, and nearly pressed against the chilled window that overlooks the city.

My legs begin to shake as his tongue slips small, wet circles against my clit. His deft hands reach from behind, around the tops of my thighs to spread my lips for his brilliant mouth. He focuses so skillfully on my clitoris, pressing and nudging it with his tactful tongue, that I have to lean into the chill of the window just to steady myself. My breasts are pressed against the cold glass while my arms are extended above my head, elbows bent.

Being pressed against the window naked like this feels super naughty and very exhibitionistic for me because, in a bustling city like this, anyone could be watching.

Just as my climax builds, he slows his tongue and begins to suck and flick at my inner lips, allowing a brief interlude to the intense clitoral ministrations of his tongue.   He is so masterful, every vein throbs with my accelerated pulse. I feel my whole body climbing and building toward release. He backs off again, but this time he slips a finger inside me. He begins rubbing the front wall of my vagina, against my G-spot, as he presses his tongue firmly against my clit.

My senses are so hyper-sensitized; I can smell the fresh sheets and Silas' warm skin. Our sweat and desire are mingling and flooding the room with pheromones. Throwing my head back, I can feel the beachy waves tickle the sway of my low back as my orgasm takes hold. I cry out and explode into an all-consuming release that jerks my body with the strength of a Taser firing, again and again, crashing over and over.

When the spasms still, I am resting my forehead against the window pane. There is a vibration in my teeth that answers only to the strength of my orgasm.

With my body still buzzing, Silas eases my shaky form down onto him. I'm weak, but the tenderness of his kiss as he finds my lips awakens me again to my desire for him.

I can taste myself on him, and it feels wickedly sexy knowing this tongue, these lips are so intimately acquainted with my delicate parts. With my teeth still humming, I whisper, "Silas, I need you inside me." It's a whiny groan, but I feel desperate for him.

He smiles and begins to shove down his jeans, allowing his cock to spring free of its confinement. He rolls over on top of me, nudging my legs further apart with his knee. He drops his mouth to mine and finds my nipple with his thumb.

"You taste so sweet," he whispers into my mouth, then adds, "I'm dying to get inside you, I can't wait to make love to you."

His words bring the sting of tears to my eyes. I had been so devastated thinking he didn't want me, and then all these weeks later finding out the truth, and hearing him say he can't wait *to make love to me*. He didn't say he wanted to fuck me, he took it a step further, *make love to me*. His words make me overly sentimental and profoundly emotional.

He is peering into my face as a tear slips away, leaving a wet trail across my temple. He gently wipes the tear and kisses the trail of it. Then he raises his hips a bit to edge his penis just to the threshold of my vagina.

"Jessie, I need to feel you on my cock, your silky heat all around me. Just for a second without a--"

"Yes," I breathe, pulling him to me as he eases the head of his penis into my opening. Pausing, he holds my gaze then kisses both eyes and my mouth, but he doesn't press in further.

I'm holding his face in my hands, feeling the exquisite torture of his limited penetration as I pull him in for a tender kiss. He very slowly begins rocking in and out, only halfway, still limiting his plunge.

"Jessie, you're so wet," he says, and I can hear the trembling in his voice.

"I'm wet for you Silas," I breathe.

"I'm dying, you're killing me. You're so tight," he says, voice still quivering as he stills his body.

I know he is struggling inwardly, it would be so easy to skip the rubber, but I somehow know he won't.

He keeps still except for his trembling as I clamp down on his steel hard penis. I'm trying to draw him deeper into me, I need him all the way.

He groans then pulls out, collapsing on top of me. Still shaking from his restraint, he chokes out, "I don't have any condoms."

"You don't?!" I ask, stunned.

"I don't bring women home," he says, resigned to his fate and rolling onto his back still fully erect and glistening. His forearms are crossed over his face, shielding his eyes and his discontent.

Placing my palm on his chest and leaning down to trail kisses and my flickering tongue down the length of his torso, I caress his damp skin, slowly making my way to his shaft.

He gasps when I take hold of it, lightly dragging the tip of my tongue around the head of his penis. "The way I see it, you have two choices," I pause, then take him into my mouth, bumping my lips up and down over the ridge of his head. Then I back away slightly, "One...do nothing," I say, then take him deeper into my mouth, sucking marginally harder as he writhes a bit.

"Or two...go get some," I say, before taking him deeply into my mouth, gliding up and down.

His head strains against the back of my throat, and each time I take him fully in, I swallow, causing my throat to clamp then release his tip. I increase the suction but keep my pace deliberately slow. He is moaning deeply now as he gathers my hair to the side, un-obstructing his view.

I gaze up at him with his dick in my mouth, holding his gaze and loving the effect I am having on him. I encircle his shaft with my hand, elongating the hold I have on his cock, and continue my deliberate ministrations.

His moaning intensifies, then, "Ahhh Jessie, I'm going to cum." His hands are gripping my hair, and when he cums, he pulls me off his penis.

My mouth releases his cock with a slurping pop as he spurts in shuddering waves onto my neck and his stomach.

"Why did you do that?" I ask surprised, while smiling at his spent form.

"I didn't want to cum in your mouth--it felt...disrespectful," he says between heavy breaths.

"I came in your mouth," I point out in challenge.

He grabs me and flops me onto my back with a sudden burst of energy, then devours my mouth. "And I loved every second," he says with delight, making me giggle at his playfulness.

"That was insane. I'm crazy about this talented mouth," he says, carefully biting my lower lip.

I think about his comment while our naked bodies are still pressed together. "I don't feel disrespected by you," and then add, "Well, not anymore."

He smiles, "No one will ever disrespect you again Jessie. You are mine."

"I'm yours?" I ask coyly, as I trail a finger down his spine.

"You have been mine since you walked into 1462," he says, as a matter of fact, while laying his head against my chest. "In case you hadn't noticed, nobody was allowed to penetrate you or bring you to orgasm…but me."

My heart races, that *was* him getting me off on sushi night, and that membership got revoked because that guy stuck his finger inside me…I *am* different. It's not because Silas didn't think I was ready, it's because he wanted me for himself. I smile and close my eyes in a joyful stupor.

After a sleepy moment, he begins to toy with my nipple and my eyes spring open.

"I have a quick errand to run. You rest, I'll be back soon." He gets up and tugs on his jeans while looking around for his shirt.

Once the door clicks behind Silas, I get up and head into his en suite bathroom. Its design is the same as his bedroom, stark white with rusty metal. The double vanity is white Carrara marble with two rusty metal chandelier above. Two huge mirrors hang above the sinks, framed in what looks like old, bulky railroad ties. The far wall is covered in a sheet of aged copper with a beautiful turquoise patina, and it showcases a huge stand-alone, rectangular tub. An equally massive shower stands in the corner encased in frameless glass. His bedroom and bathroom are earthy and masculine, yet beautiful in their design aesthetic.

After using, and marveling at his heated toilet seat, I notice while washing my hands that I still have cum on my neck, thick and salty. I decide to run a bath and feel only slightly guilty

224

looking through his cabinets for some scented bath salts or bubbles.

One cabinet has a plastic basket, full of bubble bath and Barbie mermaids. It makes me smile at the thought of Silas having little girls' toys in his huge, manly bathroom. The sight of the toys also makes me feel uncomfortable and inappropriately naked.

I settle on a lavender scented fizzing bath ball, dim the lights then retrieve a large candle from the bedroom as I wait for the tub to fill.

When Silas walks in with a brown paper bag tucked under his arm, he grins at the sight of me in the tub with my breasts only partially submerged. He hastily steps out of his shoes and pulls off his shirt. Reaching into the paper bag, he tosses a box of condoms toward the base of the tub, where it slides across the marble and come to a halt within easy reach, readily available.

After shucking his jeans, he says with a grin, "I'm impressed," as he takes in the flickering candle and the dim light. He disappears around the corner, and after a few minutes, I hear soft piano music drifting from unseen bathroom speakers.

When he comes back in, he asks, "Can I get you anything?"

I slowly shake my head no, and beckon him over with one curling finger that's dripping with oily water.

In three quick strides, he is at the edge of the tub, then steps into the water facing me. He sinks down, placing his legs at my sides.

Sitting forward he raises my knees, and adjusts my legs to drape across the tops of his thighs. Then he wraps his arms around the small of my back and pulls my slippery body forward into his hot, wet physique.

I can feel his hardness against my core along with the cool silkiness of his scrotum which brushes softly against me as we are clamped together. Raising myself from the bottom of the tub so I can sit more on his lap, I press his hardness between us and wrap my dripping arms around his neck.

"I was thinking about you this morning while I was making Ruby breakfast. I never would have guessed that I'd have you tonight, here in my arms," he hums, into my mouth between kisses. He is holding me tightly, his iron shaft pressing into my nub and causing my breath to accelerate.

Sitting up more and arranging my knees to the sides of his hips, I'm able to kneel above him, straddling his lap.

He pinches a nipple with his lips, and I arch my back pressing into his suckling mouth and dropping my head back with restless abandon.

Reaching between us I guide him to my opening and slowly sink down on his shaft, burying him deeply inside of me.

"Oh my God Jessie," he wheezes, his head lolling back to rest on the edge of the tub. "Oh Fuck, you feel so good."

I rise up and come down again, slowly and deeply, feeling him become part of me. Aching for more but knowing I need to stop, I lift up again, squeezing him within me as I rise higher allowing him to slip out of my warm embrace.

Hastily, he reaches for the box of condoms at the base of the tub, sloshing water all over the floor. He holds the box behind my back tearing at it while he leans in to nip at my neck. I hear the packet tear open and can feel him fumbling underwater to unroll the latex down his length.

Grabbing my ass cheeks, he begins to lower me down onto himself. I pull up, playfully shaking my head at his attempt to take control. He lifts his arms to rest them on the edge of the tub in acquiescence, splashing more water to the marble floor.

I rest my arms on his shoulders, slowly lowering myself about half way before rising. I roll my pelvis back, so his penis drags along the front wall of my vagina, moaning as his ridge grinds against my G-spot.

I continue with my slow ministrations, my nipples rasping against the emerging stubble on his face. Up and down, rocking and squeezing with each stroke.

Silas drops his hands to my waist unable to sit passively any longer as I increase my tempo a fraction. The water in the tub is churning, and my climax is building as I slide up and down, faster and tighter with his hands clamping down on my hips.

He gasps, clenching his teeth with a final grinding squeeze. He shudders against me as I begin to unravel, my own orgasm taking hold. My inner spasms are cradling him, milking him.

He holds me tightly, clutched against his warm body. My face is resting against his neck like a sleeping child, arms slung across his shoulders and hanging over the edge of the tub, dripping water. He holds me against him long after our hammering heartbeats slow and the chalky water turns tepid and fizz-less.

"You're mine," he whispers into my wet hair.

I walk into the bedroom wrapped in a fluffy towel, damp hair piled into a messy bun on top of my head. When Silas comes back from the kitchen with his own towel hanging precariously from his hips and water droplets beaded and glistening across his shoulders and chest, he hands me a glass of ice water.

"I got you something," he says.

"What kind of something?" I ask, sipping the drink.

"It's in the paper bag in the bathroom."

I walk back into the bathroom sure my ass cheeks are peeking beneath the towel and withdraw a new toothbrush from the bag. I smile at him in the mirror as he leans against the door jamb, arms crossed.

"You're staying," he announces as he walks up behind me and wraps his arms around my body, kissing my cheek. "You're staying," he whispers again, this time into my ticklish ear.

Once I finish brushing my teeth, I walk back into his room to see he has flipped back the airy comforter and is retrieving the discarded pillows from the rustic, wide planked, wood floor.

He looks at me devilishly, "Did you like knowing people could have been watching us?" he gestures with his chin toward the windows at the head of his bed. The same windows I had pressed my naked body against while his tongue had coaxed me to ecstasy.

I smile and nod as I unwrap my towel and drop it to the floor.

He follows suit, and we fall into bed giggling like school children. He reaches into his nightstand, now stocked with rubbers, and grabs a thin remote.

"Well, show's over...for tonight anyway." He presses a button and his windows fog over into an opaque frosted glass then further still until black as coal.

He presses another button, and the already dimmed chandelier light fades to black as well. We are engulfed in pitch blackness. It's the kind of darkness that is demonstrated when you go on a cave tour, and they turn the lights off to show you how dark it was for the explorers if their candles went out.

Bottom of the ocean dark, can't see your hand in front of your face dark.

Silas pulls me into him, our flushed skin fusing together as I lay my cheek against his firm chest. He smoothes wisps of hair off my cheek and raises my chin for our lips to meet.

"Goodnight Jessie."

"Goodnight Silas."

He pulls me tightly into him, as if I too will fade into the darkness.

I'm not sure how much time passes, as I lie here. It's utterly quiet and black as pitch but as rapturous as I feel, snuggled against his soft skin, with the heartache of losing him vanished, I still can't seem to fall asleep.

I re-adjust my arm and leg more comfortably over him, marveling at how well we fit together, like we were made to.

After a long time, my body contented and satisfied but my mind buzzing like a field of locusts, and sleep nowhere in sight, I open my eyes. My lashes graze Silas' chest.

He leans in, kissing my head, "You can't sleep either?"

"No," I whisper against his skin.

"I'll have to try harder to wear you out next time," he says, while rolling me to my back. I can sense his grin but still can't see a solitary thing.

"It's the coffee," I say, hushed though I needn't be.

He lowers a kiss to my shoulder as I ask, "What time do you need to be at work?" I'm running my fingernails lightly up and down his back as he ponders my question.

"Never, I'm staying here with you." He lays his cheek against my chest, the prickle of his stubble raising my nipples. "Tell me about your elicit past--you heard all about mine," he says, conversationally, as if discussing sexual escapades were par for the course.

In the dark I feel him acutely, breathing against my breasts, his smooth, muscled back, the curve of his spine leading to his firm, perfect ass. I can feel each hair on his arm as it's draped across my body and the musky smell of the pomade he put in his hair this morning. I feel like I can even feel his fingerprints as he begins to slide the flat of his palm down the top of my thigh.

"This might disappoint you, but I don't really have an elicit sexual past."

"Umhmmm," he mumbles, as his palm slides to the inside of my thigh.

"I didn't lose my virginity until I was twenty, and even then it was just to get it out of the way and be done with the whole thing."

"Was it good?" he asks, continuing to caress my thigh.

"Not at all, I remember wondering what all the fuss was about," I say into the blackness, my confessional.

"Keep going," he says lightly pressing my thigh, opening my legs a bit more and tickling with his fingertips.

"I dated him for a year. He was a complete asshole, super jealous and controlling, even demeaning sexually. I'm ashamed I put up with it."

"Then what happened?" tickle, tickle, slide.

"I caught him with another woman and broke up with him. Then he stalked me for ten months--it was a nightmare. He used to call, even months after we broke up, and demand to know whose car was in front of my house. Then he became more aggressive, lurking around my house and roommates, he started following me. He even broke in on my birthday, eight months after we broke up, he just walked into my room and announced, 'Happy Birthday Babe!'"

Silas stills his hand. "Who is this fucker?"

"He is long gone, but he left such a bad taste in my mouth I didn't date much for the rest of college. All the rest of my boyfriends have been really great guys...but a little lackluster if you know what I mean."

"Shame on them," he says while sliding my thigh much further out and dragging his fingertips up the inside of my leg. I gasp as he finds my button and begins to rub it back and forth in slow, persistent swipes as he flicks my nipple with his tongue. "Um hmm," he hums into my hard peak, "Shame on them."

He presses harder into my clit, still rubbing purposefully and asks, "Have you ever been with more than one man, at the same time?"

"No," I say breathlessly.

"A woman?" he asks, changing tactics and sliding two fingers inside me, in and out.

"No," I'm squirming, breathless.

"Anal?" Resuming his calculated movements, in and out, rubbing against my G-spot.

"Uh, yes," I pant through clenched teeth.

He stops his ministrations and says with surprise, "Yes?" Then he resumes sliding in and out.

"Yes, I hated it," I grind out. "It felt like, like...uh, going to the bathroom," I finish weakly.

"Ah yes, your unskilled lovers," he croons, lowering his mouth to mine and aggressively rubbing now.

"God, Silas. Ahhhhh," I cry out, as I fall over the precipice, quaking all over as Silas giggles in my ear.

"I love watching you cum."

231

"What? You can't see me at all," I point out, still wheezing and trying to catch my breath.

"Ok you're right, I love feeling and hearing you cum," he amends.

He rolls over, straining for the remote on the nightstand. Then light steals into the room, only a whisper, just enough for Silas to locate the strip of condoms, peel one off and open it with his teeth.

"Give it to me," I say, extending my hand in the dim light.

"Are you going to toss it out the window? Because I'm fine with that," he says, not at all joking while dutifully handing it over.

"Do you have any lube?" I ask.

He furrows his brows and asks, "Why? You are soaking wet." He looks almost hurt as he retrieves the bottle from his nightstand.

I unroll the tip of the condom and squeeze a dollop of lube into the latex. Then I wink at him, lean over and kiss the tip of his hard penis. I swipe and flutter my tongue around his smooth head, licking away the clear drop of moisture. Next, I carefully roll the lubricated condom down his shaft then demonstrate the use of the lube on the inside by sliding the tight latex up and down his length.

"Ahhhhh, that's so much better," he keens.

I back away deeper into the bed as he stalks up after me like a predator, crawling slowly, his eyes fixed. He begins kissing my belly, working his way up between my breasts and lingering at the base of my neck, igniting my whole body with goose bumps as he slides between my legs.

Hands in his hair, I pull his mouth to mine. There is a misty glow to the room now, and I can see him finally, his hair falling forward into his eyes, his jaw squared as he pulls back from our kiss to look at me for a moment.

I find it is me now, holding him tightly as if he will disappear. My hands slide to his face where his jaw moves methodically under my palms, his mouth in perfect symphonic unison with mine.

"Can you feel how hard I am for you?" he asks huskily between wet kisses. I nod, feeling his hardness throbbing against me.

He rises up reaching for his cock and guides it skillfully, finding me eager and waiting. He pushes in slowly, little by little, then back out halfway. He is very careful as if testing the lubricated condom. Then all the way in gently and all the way out, then faster, deeper and less gentle.

"Oh Jessie, I'm so deep inside you, can you feel how deep I am?" he grinds out, trying to contain himself.

"Yes, yes I can feel you…deep, oh, it's so good," I moan into his ear, clutching tightly to his back.

After a few polite glides in and out, he becomes less polite and more hungry. He reaches back, hooking my knee with the crook of his arm and pulling it forward, opening me up further, grinding in deeper, harder. He is slipping wetly in and out, over and over, pistons coming to life.

Our bodies have a certain harmony together, and I love the intensity of him, the skill. His fucking is like nothing I have ever experienced, it's primal and intrinsic and…perfect.

When I feel myself getting closer, I slide my hand under his hip, between our bodies as he slaps against me, driving me up and up. Taking hold of his balls, I grip them carefully and tug gently. The intense sensation is more than he is expecting and the tugging pressure is more than he can take.

"Ahhhhh, Ahhhhhhhh, Ah Shiitttttt!" he cries out as he unloads, pulsing deeply into me. He collapses on my body, spent and rung out like a rag, his heart thrashing into my chest. "I'm sorry," he gulps, gasping for air.

"For what?" I giggle.

"I wanted to wait for you," he heaves.

"Stop, I've never even had an orgasm from regular sex before, not until the tub, until…you."

He smiles at the thought then rolls off. "I'm done—done." He slides off the rubber, with his chest still rising and falling vigorously. Still holding the condom dangling from his fingers off the edge of the bed, he scoops me into him with his free arm.

"Jessie," he says sleepily into my hair. "I'm crazy about you."

My breath catches, and I snuggle into his neck, unable to talk for the lump lodged in my throat. I want to tell him I'm crazy about him too, that he is amazing and perfect, the man of my dreams but the words get caught. Minutes later the tears breach my lids unbidden and trickle down, pooling at, then trickling across the bridge of my nose.

He pulls me in tighter and whispers, "What's wrong Baby?"

I sniffle and choke out, "That's the sweetest thing anyone has ever said to me."

He pulls the fluffy comforter over us both, and I settle into the crook of his arm, bleary and limp.

CHAPTER TWENTY
Introductions

I wake suddenly to a loud gasp, "OH!" Analise claps one hand over her mouth, extending the other to prevent Ruby from storming in. She stammers, "Oh Goodness! I'm sorry. I expected you to be at work."

Ruby breaks the feeble barricade and pounces on the bed, throwing her arms around Silas. "Good morning Daddy!" Then she looks to me as she sits back on her heels, "Hi, Jess-ie." She says it in a playful tone, so I'm hoping she is not too damaged, finding her dad in bed with a strange woman.

Still groggy but jolted awake, I simply smile and say, "Hi Ruby, it's nice to meet you." I speak as I grip the covers tightly over my nakedness.

Silas, chuckling to himself says, "Hey Rubes, how about you go get out the waffle iron?"

She flings herself off the bed singing, "Yea! We're having waffles!"

Analise closes the door with a pointed glance over her grandmotherly glasses, silently scolding Silas and making me laugh, breaking the awkward tension.

I fall back into the pillows pulling the covers over my disheveled head.

"What? You thought she wouldn't like you?" He climbs out of bed, stepping commando into his jeans and hastily snatching the spent condom from the floor, then disappears into the bathroom to dispose of it.

I hurriedly dress as Silas peeks his head out of the bathroom, his mouth full of toothbrush and toothpaste saying, "Hey Jessie, want to meet my daughter?" He speaks in a garbled, deeply amused tone.

Spitting toothpaste into the sink, I hazard a glance in the mirror. The salt spray, the bath, the crumpled bun...the sex--all leave me looking homeless. A lion's mane of crazy disarray falls around me. I splash water on my tired face and drag my fingers under my lower eyelids, effectively swiping my smeared mascara into passable eyeliner.

I wind my ridiculous hair back up, confining the chaos into a less sloppy pile at the back of my head.

"What time is it?" I ask Silas, as he slides between me and the sink, his hands on my hips.

"It's after nine," he says, planting a kiss smack on my stunned mouth.

Ruby is a firecracker, blazing around the kitchen as we stumble into the brightness of the world around us. Analise hands Ruby a big glass bowl then quietly leaves the room-- somewhat embarrassed, I think.

"Ruby, come here and properly meet Jessie," Silas says as he scoops her up, gnawing on her belly and making her squeal with delight. He sets her down in front of me, and she soberly extends her hand, announcing, "Hi, My name is Ruby."

I take her hand, shaking it carefully and say, "I know, I've heard a lot about you. I'm Jessie."

She beams, "I know! I've heard a lot about YOU!"

"Whoa! That's enough Rubes," Silas jumps in, cutting her off and trying to preserve his dignity while handing me a mug of coffee.

I sip it slowly, peering at him above the rim, reminded of where the coffee got us last night.

He sees my look, recognizing it for what it is, and asks, "What? Would you have preferred decaf?"

I shake my head slowly, still peering over the rim as I sip. He beams at me in triumph, while I squat down to Ruby's level.

"I am very late for work but do you think you could come up with something fun for the three of us to do this weekend? You seem like a neat girl, and I would like to get to know you better."

She nods enthusiastically and spins over to Silas, "Daddy, Daddy, we could go to the Aquarium...or--" But Silas isn't really listening to her excited chirping. He is rooted to the floor, eyes on me with his hand on his heart like I just said the exact right thing to his daughter.

CHAPTER TWENTY-ONE
Salvage

When I get to the office after a hasty stop home to shower and change Salinger storms into my office incredulous. "We just lost the Harrisburg deal," he huffs, dropping into the chair opposite me at my desk. He looks at me for a moment then cocks his head in question, or in understanding about why I'm late.

I think he realizes why the sappy grin is on my face too, though he has the grace not to mention it. His penetrating look goes a long way acknowledging his awareness of the situation though.

"Salinger, let's not get hysterical, we still have the land grant coming through. It's not completely over, I still think Harrisburg will get on board, let's just give it a minute," I say, in a calming voice Salinger doesn't recognize as mine.

He looks at me through his thick rimmed, sexy professor glasses, cocks his head again and narrows his hazel eyes at me. "This doesn't bother you?"

"It happens," I say, wishing I did care more.

"Not on my watch. Pack your bags, we are going to Charleston." He stands, placing his spread palms on my desk and leaning in intently. "I mean it, you had better find your game face because we are going to salvage this." He huffs out of my office, as I sigh in resignation. Give him two minutes, and he will already have Adelaide, our receptionist booking our flights and hotel reservations.

I sit at my computer with a dopey glow swallowing me whole, despite the fallen land contract. The land is south of the Marcellus oil-play, outside of Charleston. We have been working the deal for sixteen months, but I can hardly bring myself to care about the landowner pulling out. I will revisit negotiations, of course, Salinger will see to that, but I'm just as happy to let the deal fall apart.

Salinger had been unnerved by my apathetic response, but where I put down my responsibilities to our company, he picks them up and runs with them, and he is going to drag me with him to South Carolina.

Undaunted by the collapsing deal, I half-heartedly decide to revise Salinger's power point presentation regarding off-shore drilling rigs, while my eyes glaze over. Blessedly, my phone chirps an incoming text. "Have you, or have you not been abducted? Just wondering. Love you."

Smiling, I text Devin back. "Not abducted--just falling in love." I hit send before analyzing the repercussions, they come instantaneously. "ShuttheFuckup!" and then, "You Whore." I text back a thumbs up and leave it at that. Tonight at home, I'll face the firing squad.

CHAPTER TWENTY-TWO
Dismissed

Walking into the apartment I toss my keys down on the entry table, knowing the sound will draw Devin out like a cat toward a shaking treat bag. When he doesn't emerge, I walk into the kitchen to find him balling up meatballs.

"Want some help?" I ask turning on the faucet and reaching toward the rose scented soap. The sooner I face the music and get this over with, the better. Devin is going to be pissed, and he is awfully prickly when he is mad.

"Only if you are going to tell me about this emerging love affair," he says pointedly.

"Before I start, I want to remind you that I'm a smart, educated, successful woman and I am capable of mak--"

"Stop right there. You're seeing that club owner again aren't you?"

"Devin, he's not like you think, he is sweet and--"

"He is *exactly* like I think," he says, while slapping a meatball in the frying pan then reaching for another clump of meat.

"He has a daughter…and he's a crossing guard at her school and he--"

"Jessie, you are a grown woman. You can make your own decisions."

"Thank you," I say, deflated by his acquiescence.

"But I don't have to like them." And there it is, the knife under my ribs.

"I think if you would just listen and let me finish a single sen--"

"I love you, but I don't want to hear about it."

"Dev."

"No. I'll call you when dinner is ready."

Abruptly dismissed and hotly angry, I retreat to my room to change into my running clothes.

Before I walk out, I cram earbuds deep into my ears so I can't hear Devin's passive-aggressive mumblings as I leave the condo. How dare he dismiss me like that? Like I am a child whining at his feet. He may as well have just covered his ears and started yelling, "Lalalalalala."

I turn up the music when I step out onto the sidewalk, having no patience for a warm up; I break into a punishing run.

When I get home, dripping with sweat, I'm not mad anymore. I've decided that I'm hurt, Devin should trust my judgment. I will play his game though, *humph--call me when dinner's ready*.

I'm desperate to get out of my clammy, wet sports bra so I head straight to the bathroom and turn on the shower.

Devin follows me in, plopping down on the closed toilet seat, arms crossed, jaw set for a dogfight.

"You can sit there glowering all you want, but I'm going to take a shower," I say dismissively, no longer wanting to talk to him about Silas.

He raises his chin but doesn't move. Shrugging my shoulders in a 'suit yourself' expression, I take off my shoes and socks. He doesn't move, doesn't say a word.

"Fine have it your way," I say, peeling off my sports bra and sliding down my shorts. He is studying my body but not with interest or admiration, merely noting the fact I am naked. I step into the shower, and after a minute he gets up and leaves the bathroom.

After my shower, dressed in old scrub pants and a tank top, with a towel wrapped around my head, I notice I have a text from Silas. "What abot the mounten zoo? Yor frend Ruby."

I smile and text back, "Sounds fun, can't wait. Your friend, Jessie."

Almost immediately the phone rings, it's Silas' number again, so I answer thinking it's Ruby.

"Hi, Sweetheart."

Silas chuckles, "I've never been so excited to go to the zoo."

"Me too," I say in a low, scheming voice. "I have to travel for work this week, but I'll be back by Saturday."

"Awwww, you should just quit your job," he says playfully.

"It's only a few days."

"I'll see if I can manage. Who do you travel with anyway?"

"My land technician, Salinger."

"Tell me about this Salinger."

243

"Oh, stop. I've worked with him for years," I say.

"Has he ever made a move on you?" he asks.

"Well, he did kiss me once. What, are you jealous?" I laugh.

"I don't know. Is this what that feels like? The feeling that makes me want to punch Salinger in the jaw?" he laughs after saying it. "But seriously, I'm worried about Ruby not seeing you for a few days."

"Wellll, tell her I will have my laptop with me, so we can video chat," I say coyly.

"Chat huh? That should work... for a start," he says wickedly.

I'm still smiling when I walk out and sit heavily at the table across from Devin.

"Hungry?" he asks.

"Not really," I say, meeting his gaze with something that smacks of a challenge. "You have to give him a chance," I say.

"I did, and then I spent three weeks picking up the pieces," he says, spooning up a plate of spaghetti and meatballs and sliding it across to me. "I didn't see any marks?" he says in the form of a question.

Biting into a huge meatball on the end of my fork, I say, "Because he didn't leave any." Now that I don't want to divulge any details, Devin suddenly wants to talk about it.

"Does he really have a daughter?" he asks, tisking his tongue and shaking his head infinitesimally.

"Mm hmm," I say, my mouth is full and it's a good excuse not to elaborate further.

After a while Devin says, "Ok, well, I hope for your sake I'm wrong. Should we open wine?"

CHAPTER TWENTY-THREE
Conservative

After landing in Charleston Salinger turns to me, "It's fucking hot here, I feel like I'm back in Baghdad."

He's right, it's hot. The sun is beating down on my neck and shoulders, making my skin tighten and ebb into itself. Being so fair skinned, I've never been one to overly appreciate the sun and all its esteemed glory. I bristle with growing hostility as a bead of sweat trickles down my back between my shoulder blades.

My steps have begun to feel sticky and soft as we trudge across the scorching asphalt. We finally arrive at the rental car, in the furthest lot. Salinger opens the trunk and tosses his bag in then reaches for mine.

The air conditioning in the car is meager at best, preferring to blow stale air, the kind that catches in your throat and makes you cough.

The hard set of Salinger's jaw and unwavering focus on the road makes me nervous to break the silence. I decide to fiddle with the stereo buttons instead of pressing him about his crusty mood.

After a very uncharacteristically long silence, I finally break, "Salinger, is there something you want to get off your chest?" He doesn't respond right away, so I trudge on, "Let me guess, you blame me for the Harrisburg deal?"

He looks at me with an exasperated look, "Of course not, that's been circling the shitter since we started."

"Then what?" I ask, as I shift in the seat to face him better. "What's wrong? It can't just be the heat."

Instead of answering, he fires a question right back.

"Let me ask you something. If you had to describe me in one word, what would it be?"

"Conservative," I say a bit too quickly, making his jaw drop and eyes simmer, choosing to glare at me instead of watching the road.

"Conservative?!" he asks, disgusted.

"There is nothing wrong with that. Why are you so offended?" I ask.

"Because after all these years, you don't know me at all."

"Yes I do, you're a Marine, you served three tours in Iraq, in an extreme act of stupidity your wife cheated on you, you decided you could never trust her again and tossed her out, you're fabulous at your job, all the women in our building lust after you. Oh, and you're super funny, kindhearted and awesome," I throw in as an afterthought.

"Why do you think I'm conservative? Because I fought for our country and I work in oil and gas?"

"No, of course not, it's because you are so straight-laced-- hair perfectly combed, always tucked in...in fact, I've hardly ever seen you in anything but a perfectly pressed, long-sleeved button down shirt. You just appear very, um…don't get me wrong, it's very…professional."

"Hmmph," is his only reply, but he is contemplating saying more as he continues to look at me, then back to the road.

"So it's not my liberal or conservative *values*, it's my plain, boring professional look you have a problem with?"

"First of all, I don't have a problem with you at all, I really like you, and I love working with you," I say, feeling bad for hurting his feelings. "In fact, you are one of my favorite people to be trapped in a stifling hot car with."

He scoffs again, unbuttoning his shirt sleeve at the wrist and shoving it up to his elbow. He reveals an entire arm sleeve tattoo, vibrant colors and a lifetime of experiences abruptly cutting off at the wrist. He gives me a wolfish grin, raising his other sleeve in the same way, likewise revealing his other arm, covered in tattoos.

I sink back into my seat utterly shocked. Not for the first time; I'm seeing his neatly combed hair and his thick rimmed glasses in a whole new edgy light.

Apparently satisfied with my reaction, he settles in a bit more comfortably to his own seat, tattooed arm slung casually over the steering wheel.

CHAPTER TWENTY-FOUR
Marred

We were forced to concede defeat, realizing after a four hour sit down at Samuel Harrisburg's kitchen table, that our hard-fought deal was indeed, dead in the water. We march through the hotel lobby, our spirits bent but not broken.

"What time is our flight tomorrow?" I ask.

"Not until two, I thought we might need the morning to button up this deal," he says.

"Hm, no contingencies for it taking a shit in our lap?"

"Nope, no contingencies. I hope you brought a book," Salinger says as he glances at his watch. "Since we've got nothing but time, I'm going to head out to the pier. Let's meet at seven for dinner."

"Ok," I say, a little disappointed to be abandoned by my other half and wondering what I'm supposed to do for the next few hours.

Back in my room, I sprawl out on the bed, kicking off my shoes as I dial Silas' number. When he doesn't answer I leave a message, saying I'll be back around nine, six his time and we can Skype then.

After flipping through the TV channels and finding nothing of interest, I decide to go catch up with Salinger.

I didn't pack a swimsuit, not expecting beach time, so I change into some shorts, a tank top, and some wedge sandals. I quickly braid my hair into two loose braids, grab my sunglasses and hurry off to the pier.

I find Salinger at the pier in the distance, but I don't immediately recognize him. He is wearing flip-flops, with his t-shirt tucked haphazardly into the back of his loose fitting black shorts. His tan is glistening, and his tattoos are mightily displayed. So unaccustomed am I to this new image, I hesitate before approaching him at all. He is leaning against the wooden pier on his forearms, gazing into the water.

As I approach, his back is turned to me. Almost as shocking to me as the full arm tattoos and his rippled, muscular back, is a horrendous gaping scar. It mars his back from just below his right shoulder blade, disappearing under his arm, around his rib cage.

I stand shocked and utterly speechless, frozen in place. Salinger must sense me because he turns around. I find my feet and walk to him.

Noting my trepidation, he loops an arm around my shoulders, guiding me to the pier next to him.

"It's a bit shocking at first, I know," he says, trying to help me recover.

"I didn't know. How did I not know?" I ask, feeling dizzy from all the shimmering, swirling water below.

"It's not something I like to talk about."

"Salinger," I whisper as my eyes fill with tears. This man I have known for years, held his hand through his divorce, and confided in as much as Devin or my girlfriends--really was a stranger to me. I am unable to look him in the eyes and his arm around my shoulder tells me that he can't face me either.

After a long time watching the water glisten like a field of diamonds and listening to the seagulls screech, I finally lean into him. I rest my head against his chest, his arm a comfort across my shoulders.

I want to go back years and thank him for his service, for his sacrifice, for putting himself in harm's way to protect little ingrates like me. I'm suddenly so ashamed of all the petty little injustices I had bothered him with over the years.

I want to say all this, but all I can get out is a weak, "I'm sorry."

"Come on, let's walk," he says as he turns me, guiding me through the throngs of tourists. In one day, my eyes have been opened to Salinger like my own gaping wound. I realize I've had him all wrong.

"I don't like people to know about it because then they see me as broken, or damaged. The truth is, I am broken but not by this," he says, indicating with his thumb over his shoulder at his massive scar. "I was broken by this," he says as he raises his arm from my shoulders and turns, elbow raised to show me the names tattooed on the side of his rib cage. There are seven names, seven ranks.

I close my eyes, bitterly angry at myself for thinking his biggest hurdle in life was a cheating wife. In fact, now his demeanor regarding her makes sense. Back then I thought he was being detached and too distant, but now I see that it was nothing but a speed bump for him, not a true tragedy like the loss of his fellow Marines. The loss of his wife was a choice, the loss of his friends was not.

"It was a roadside IED, and my discharge papers all rolled into one," he says, pulling his shirt from the back of his shorts and tugging it over his head, seemingly putting an end to the conversation.

"Salinger, I don't think you're broken," I say softly.

"You see? You don't know me at all," he says, with a sad expression on his beautiful face.

We stop for dinner at an outdoor crab shack, eating raw oysters on the half shell with lemon and enough horseradish to choke an elephant and bring tears to our eyes. We order crab legs by the bucketful and drink a pitcher of sweet tea between us.

By the time our waitress clears the crab shell carnage, we are stuffed, and I have tears in my eyes, this time from laughing so hard.

"Don't look now but there is a woman at the bar undressing you with her eyes," I say, laughing at my choice of words at the same time.

Paying zero heed to my directions not to look, he unabashedly turns to the beautiful blond woman. She becomes suddenly coy and looks away, re-crossing her legs slowly and deliberately.

"Looks like a mating call," I say, teasing Salinger.

"Hmm," he mumbles distractedly, then turns back to me.

"I have to address the fact you find me plain and boring," he says leaning in, forearms crossed on the table.

"I didn't say plain and boring. I said buttoned up and tucked in."

"Now you know why," he says as our waitress approaches apologetically.

"I'm very sorry, you two are obviously a couple, but this is from the woman at the bar, with her compliments." She sets the drink down in front of Salinger and hurries off, her blush running from her cheeks down her neck in molted streaks. She was clearly too horrified to be around for my response.

Instead of the angry girlfriend response she had expected, I nearly spit out my tea choking on a laugh.

"That's pretty ballsy of her, you should go thank her. I'll take care of this," I say, reaching for the check. I fumble through a few cards before finding my work expense credit card and stuff the rest back into my purse as the waitress skims by and grabs it without stopping.

"She is not who I want," Salinger says with no inflection in his voice whatsoever.

"Oh, come on. It will do you some good. Look at her boobs, you could rest your drink on them, maybe even her purse," I say as I scratch my signature on the receipt, just as stealthily dropped off, and start to gather my stuff.

Salinger stands as well, and with a resigned sigh he strides toward the bar, drink in hand.

CHAPTER TWENTY-FIVE
Virtual Sex

By the time I get back to my room, it's much later than I had told Silas. Besides taking way too long at dinner, I had somehow lost my key card and had to make an unexpected stop at the front desk for a duplicate. But now I'm finally ready, I open my computer and dial, excited to see him and anxious to get home.

He answers and his handsome face fills the screen. The stubble on his face reminds me how he felt against my inner thighs.

"Hello my little jet-setter, I'm sorry I missed you earlier."

"That's ok, you're here now," I say.

"Am I now?" he says teasingly. "Then I should get a little more comfortable," he says, leaning back into his pillows with his laptop on his lap, and revealing his bare chest.

"How did negotiations go?"

"They didn't, the deal fell through."

"I'm sorry to hear that."

"I don't want to talk about work," I say, and it comes off sounding eager instead of nervous.

"Oh, yeah? What did you have in mind?" he asks with a deep grin.

"Shouldn't you be at the club?" I ask, stalling.

"No. Parker is handling the admissions. Having her there frees me up for other endeavors," he says.

"Are you alone?"

"Um Hmm."

"Where is Ruby?"

"She's in bed, it's rather late for her."

"Oh," is all I can think to say. The mischievous grin on Silas' face makes the blood leach from my veins because I'm so nervous to engage in any type of lascivious video chat.

"I like your hair in braids, they look like pipes."

"Pipes huh? I've never heard that before--I've heard *farm girl...Pippy Longstocking...handle bars...* never pipes."

"Well I like them, they suit you."

"Tell me about your day," I hedge.

Silas draws his arm up to rest behind his head, causing his bicep to bulge and making my mouth go dry, like it's been packed with cotton. He slowly and gingerly shakes his head 'No,' with his hair disheveled and his stubble standing out like wet sand against his handsome face.

Unsure how to proceed and unable to maintain the egregious silence, thick with provocative tension a moment longer, I say the first thing that comes to mind.

"What are you wearing?" I silently chastise myself for being so cliché, but his grin broadens.

"Nothing Pipes."

My face flushing, I feel the heat rush to my cheeks like bears to honey. "Maybe you should prove it."

"I will Pipes," he is no longer smiling, "For a start." He slowly pushes his snowy white blanket down his body, revealing a glimpse of closely cropped pubic hair. He unveils nothing beyond his bare, muscled torso and a hint of what lies beneath the comforter. He lounges patiently.

Nervously I toy with one braid, feeling entirely out of my element. I take a step to the ledge and jump. I say in a low voice, "I wish I was there with you."

He nods, adjusting his laptop better on his thighs.

Nervous about my amateur video chat status, I decide to play coy. "Well since I have to sleep in this big bed all alone, I might as well get comfortable too," I taunt as I slip under my own covers, despite being fully dressed.

"Oh, but these shorts are so uncomfortable," I tease, "I'm just going to slip them off," I say as I shimmy them down my legs and produce them from under the starched hotel sheet and duvet.

He is watching me with interest as I lean forward to dim the light then settle back into a stack of pillows, laptop resting on my covered thighs.

"Take off your top," he says in an even tone.

I peak my eyebrows at him then pull my tank over my head, careful to remain obscured by the sheet.

"I want to pretend I'm in your bed," I say. "I'm lying next to you. Our bodies are clasped together, and my nipples are pressing into the side of your ribs," I draw out each word, murmuring as if it pains me to speak.

"You can feel my warm breath and my wet mouth against your neck. I'm licking and biting your warm, salty skin.

His eyes are closed, and he is waiting for me to continue.

"*Silas* .I whisper into your ear as I nibble and suck on your earlobe. I'm exhaling slowly, and my soft voice tickles your ear, making goosebumps trickle down your sexy arms."

He groans and slides his free hand under his covers.

"No Silas," I whisper, "That's for me; your cock is mine tonight." I cringe at my choice of words, but luckily Silas doesn't notice my alarm. In fact, he moans at my crude language, and his breath quickens. It emboldens me.

"That's right, you save your huge, hard cock for me."

He smiles and squirms a bit.

"I'm kissing you now, and you can feel my braids tickling your chest as they swipe over your sensitive skin, my mouth is claiming yours, hot and wet--hungry for you."

"Ummmmmmm," he sets his jaw.

"Now I'm moving down your chest with soft kisses. I stop to flick your nipple with my tongue. My braids are moving, tickling their way down your body as I drag the tip of my tongue over your salty, sweaty skin.

He lowers his hand beneath the blanket again, but this time I let him. I can see clearly the rise in the sheet. I'm also, not a little surprised at how turned on I am becoming, just seeing him squirm with the weight of my words. His taut, sexy body seemingly so close.

"You called me Pipes because you liked my braids, well now I'm swiping the end of one against the base of your cock...the soft tickle is advancing up the underside of your hardness, It caresses and pokes your satiny, delicate skin." I speak slowly, dragging out my breathy words.

"Now, you can feel my wet, eager mouth take you in, deeper and deeper, soooo deep, I'm sucking your dick--you can feel the tightness of my mouth, and you can hear the wet sucking sounds as I suuuckkk you in, and puuullll you out, in and out, harder and faster. You can feel the back of my throat with your huge, fat, cock everytime I suck you deep. Your climax is building--I'm sucking, pulling, taking you sooooo deep--"

His head cranes back and I can see his fist pumping beneath the sheet, his moans filling me with a sexy satisfaction.

"Harder... deeper...sucking you deep into my thro--"

He breathes loudly while shuddering, groaning and letting go.

His chest rises and falls for a few shaky moments before he wipes himself with the sheet. Then, the wolfish grin returns to his face.

"Damn Pipes, and I was thinking you had never done this before."

I smile, proud of my little performance and a little surprised by it too. Turns out, deep throating is a lot easier when you're just talking about it.

"Well now, it seems I have some ground to cover," he says wickedly, "And I will enjoy it very much." He re-adjusts himself then brings his laptop up to rest on his chiseled abs, his disheveled hair and delicious face now filling the screen.

"Now, about that sheet," he says with a menacing edge to his voice.

"This?" I ask as I slowly slide the sheet down, careful to keep my nipples concealed by the much commented on braids.

"Ah, now that's a beautiful sight."

"What, this?" I say, as I playfully drag the end of one braid demurely across the tip, back and forth, tickling it to a full peak.

"You're killing me with the braids. All I can think about is tugging them while I fuck you from behind," he laments.

"Ooooo, so cruel," I whine.

"Yes Pipes, I'll fuck you hard, but I'll also make love to you, gentle as a lamb. I'll treat you like a whore and like a maiden, make no mistake." The rougher, edgier side of him is a complete departure from the gentle lover I had spent the night with. The promise of his unbridled, wicked attentions catches my breath and simmers between my legs.

"I want you to move the pillows and lie down, set your laptop next to you by your hip--that's right. Now I want you to fondle your breasts, yes, now roll your nipples between your fingers and thumbs, harder."

"Ahhhhh," I moan, arching my back for good measure, knowing the pose both flattens my stomach and thrusts my breasts up. My physical ministrations definitely get me excited, but the real turn on is Silas watching, and knowing I am driving him crazy. I ratchet up my moaning and squirm a little more.

"Harder, tug them--Ooooo, that's so hot," he growls.

I can't see the computer screen, but I can tell he is focused, with rapt attention and hurried breathing.

"Now move the computer between your legs," he directs.

I slide my lower half out from under the sheet and adjust the laptop dutifully as instructed, dressed in mere panties. As I sit up adjusting the computer, I notice in the lower corner of the screen, my head is no longer in Silas' view. Taking that opportunity to torture him with a full-screen shot of my breasts, I cup them and drag my thumbs heavily back and forth across the rock hard peaks, pushing them to the side, then letting them to snap back to stern attention.

"OhmyGod," Silas grinds out, "Get on a plane so I can get my mouth on those."

Tilting the screen up, I pout my lips and shake my head slowly, while wagging a finger at his hastiness.

I settle back against a couple of pillows, with my head craning back over the top of them, out of view. I continue to tease and tug my nipples with my knees raised on either side of the laptop screen.

"Spread your legs wider--that's it," he hums.

I feel supremely naughty with the camera trained explicitly on my white lacy crotch, arched back and thrust up breasts, still straining against my fingers. The erotic nature of the act has the depths of my belly thrumming, like a thousand base drums in a tiny room. My writhing and moaning, no longer for show but now prominently center stage.

"Slide your fingers into the top of your panties," Silas says.

I comply, sliding the flat of my palm heavily across my abdomen, edging my fingertips just beneath the top of the chaste, lily white satin and lace.

"Are you wet Pipes?" he asks.

"UmmHmmmm," I groan, "So wet."

"I want you to rub small circles around your clit--yes. Do you like that?"

I moan in response, but really my hand is restricted, and the lace of the panties is pinching into my ass crack.

"Slide your panties to the side; I need to see your pussy," he commands, his words so obscene, so vulgar, yet they make my heart pound faster, and my fingers press harder. My teeth are clenched against the rising intensity.

I withdraw my fingers so I can slide my panties to the side when I feel a warm hand on the inside of my thigh and hear the click of my laptop closing.

The click doesn't really register as the closing of my laptop, but the touch shoots me up like I've been shot out of a cannon. Grasping wildly for the sheet and clinging to it like it was a metal barrier instead of a thin white sheet.

"Salinger! What the hell are you doing in here!?" I demand with white hot indigence in my voice.

"You left your card," he says while perched on the edge of the bed, holding up my room key. "I thought it was an invitation," he explains, not at all sorry.

"Salinger, Oh my God!" Embarrassment overwhelms me at the realization he has seen me splayed out, virtually naked and playing with myself. Tears fight through the shame, and I begin to cry with my face in my hands and arms pinning the sheet against my bare skin.

"Salinger, get out," I sob as a new wave of horror and embarrassment washes over me.

"Jessie, listen to me."

"No."

"Jessie, I'm in love with you," he pleads. "I thought you wanted me here, you...your card..." he trails off.

"Stop, I'm so embarrassed, just go," I whisper as his words sink in, slowly like quicksand is swallowing me.

"Please don't be embarrassed, Jessie, it's me--"

"You love me?" I ask, confused and incredulous.

"Yes, I do," he says, while gathering up the discarded duvet from the floor and wrapping it around my shoulders.

I'm still huddled into a ball, now paralyzed by his declaration.

"Plus, this," he gestures with his hand to me, "Is no worse than you do in my dreams," he smiles, trying to break the tension.

I cough up a laugh despite myself.

"Salinger, I can't...I...I," I stumble trying to find the right words. The truth is, if we didn't work together and I hadn't fallen for Silas, I could very much see myself with Salinger--the edgier, outside of work Salinger, the tattoo sleeves, the rangy, sexy Salinger, with his friends' names on his side.

It turns out the quiet, conservative guy I work with actually oozes sex. If the timing were different, I might throw caution to the wind, but I can't see beyond Silas right now, perhaps ever.

1462 makes a traditional relationship complicated, I have accepted that, but what is not complicated are my feelings for Silas. I love Salinger, I do, but I'm irrevocably in love with Silas.

"I can't be with you," my monotone voice belies my emotion.

"Is it my hair?" he says, attempting a joke.

I snort, "No."

"Listen, the way I feel about you is so, so...uh, hard to explain. I don't love you like I need to fuck you--not that I'd turn you down, mind you--but it's more than that. It's your laugh, your sarcasm, the way you stand up to people at work, the way you scrunch your eyebrows when you concentrate, or when you pull over the car for every wandering dog we see. It's, well... it's the kind of love where... I never want to be without you."

"Now *that's* officially the nicest thing I've ever heard," I say, still dumbstruck and looking at him, at his tattoos in full view, his eyes searching.

"I'm not even sure I felt this way about my ex-wife," he says, almost puzzled.

Still, at a loss for words, I watch him rise from the bed. "I'm sorry I misread your intentions, I feel like an asshole." Then, bringing some much-needed levity to the situation he adds, "Actually, I'm only sorry I didn't come in two minutes later," he winks, then heads for the door.

After Salinger leaves, I crumple into the pillows and cry. I cry for Salinger, for all he has suffered and for what might have been. I cry for him because now I know his heart and must break it. I have to look him in the eyes every day knowing my happiness with Silas brings him pain--salting his wounds on a regular basis.

I think back to something Devin had said years ago, "Men and women can never just be friends, unless one is gay of course. Because one always ends up wanting to shag the other."

I had denied it at the time, but as his words come to fruition a new plague of tears overcomes me. The crying wrings me out into the pillow that's cradling my face, the face swollen with regret for the heart I must break.

The mortification of my video chat has been trumped entirely by Salinger's sweet but untimely declaration. I have literally wasted years of my life dating the wrong men, and now in some sort of twisted cosmic joke, I have two amazing men vying for my attention.

The truth is, I could see myself very happy with either one of them. In fact, I'm not so sure I haven't been in love with Salinger for awhile now. That little bit of self-awareness is almost cruel at this stage. What the hell am I going to do now? I sob with the horrible realization that none of us will emerge from this unscathed.

The ringing of the hotel phone startles me from sleep with the abruptness of a clanging fire alarm. In my confusion, I grab the phone and answer, "Silas?"

"Miss Hayes, this is Wendy from the front desk. Do you require a late check out? I would be happy to arrange it for you because our customary check out time is ten."

I fumble for my phone, groggily swiping the screen. Seeing that it is nearly 10:30, I bolt from the bed, feeling a horrible sense of dread fill my stomach.

"Yes please!" I choke into the phone, as I practically throw it back at the cradle on the nightstand.

My fingers are shaking as I navigate my way to Silas' number and press call. It rings through to voicemail. With my heart in my throat, at the beep I begin rambling.

"Hi, it's me, I'm so sorry--I...I fell asleep, I should have called you back--I'm so sorry, it was thoughtless...uh, but I can explain--uh, sorry...call me, bye."

1462 South Broadway

CHAPTER TWENTY-SIX
Repercussions

"Devin, what should I do? We're supposed to take Ruby to the Zoo tomorrow." I plead to Devin for the help he is reluctant to give.

"You've called, you've left messages, you've texted, now leave it alone. He'll call you when he's ready," he offers. He doesn't even pretend to be supportive, as he grabs the X-box remote from its perch on his belly and reclines into a slouch.

Then unpausing his game, he adds, "He'll get over it," with a tone that makes me feel like he is tapping me on the head like a dismissed child.

Enraged by his complacency, I march over to the TV and slam the power button off. He gapes at me open mouthed, remote still held in mid-air, stunned beyond articulation.

"I get it you don't like him!" I shout, "But last time I checked, you...you--you like m....m--" My lip begins to quiver as I point an accusing finger at him. "You. I--"

He raises his hands in defeat. "Ok, you're right--you're right. I'm sorry." He gestures for me to come sit next to him on the couch.

I'm standing rigid, my hands clamped into fists at my sides. I'm fuming mad but already feel the anger starting to crumble and the tears, thus far held at bay, threatening to spill over.

"Come on. Come here," his voice is softer now, more recognizable.

"If he would only let me explain."

"Shhhhh, I know Honey, but maybe this is an opportunity for you." He loops an arm around my shoulder and pulls me into him.

"An opportunity for what?" I ask, my head tucked into his shoulder and the smell of his faint cologne, musky and warm, calming me.

"Well, for Salinger for one."

"What?" I ask, feeling disappointingly like he's missed my point entirely.

"Mmmmmm. Mmmm. Yummy. If you don't want him and he ever gets curious....--"

"Would you stop? This is about me and Silas and the fact that I have completely, irrevocably..."

"If he won't take your calls, and you really want the opportunity to explain...and trust me, you need to explain--this doesn't look good. Then just go knock on his door."

"I can't. It's complicated, but his daughter might be there," I counter sadly.

"Is that more complicated than 'Sorry, my business associate just walked in while I was getting off and now I'm naked and busy with him until 10:30 tomorrow'? Because that's what he thinks, and seriously Jessie, why wouldn't he think that?"

Burying my face in my hands I mumble, "It's just too convoluted--the truth is just too unbelievable."

"Why not go to 1462?" he offers.

"It's not like he has an office there, I'd have to--you know, GO to the club," I say, widening my eyes on the 'go.'

"Then do it. If he means that much to you, don't let your delicate sensibilities get in the way."

He squeezes me into him harder and kisses my forehead. "But just so you know…if it were me, I would be on Salinger like a spider monkey."

1462 South Broadway

CHAPTER TWENTY-SEVEN
Grovel

I'm trembling, standing at the inconspicuous alley door of 1462 S. Broadway, more nervous than at any other point entering the club. The door is a solid metal contrivance that looks like it belongs deep in a coal mine. It radiates fortitude and a fierce, wry omnipotence.

The club, locked tight as a fortress, needs only a swipe before opening its seductive doors and wrapping you in its intoxicating embrace. *Step into the chasm* it beckons, *Come forth and be restored, your autonomy bartered.*

In startling contrast to the pandemonium of the Steampunk party, 1462 has relaxed into a swanky wine bar. The nervousness churning in my stomach subsides as I realize the leashes and ball gags have been quietly tucked away, leaving a rather elegant crowd gathered in the cocktail section along the opulent bar.

There is a Baby Grand piano off to my left. The woman playing it wears a cream colored, silken gown and her skin is as dark as a plum. She is exotic looking with a broad forehead and high cheekbones. She's absolutely stunning.

Her music is classical yet baleful, and for a long moment, I'm captivated by her beauty and the absolute torment behind her song.

"Evening Jessie. What can I get for you?" A man's voice snaps me from my reverie.

Hearing my name, I spin to see the same handsome bartender from Devin's young professional's meeting. *Erik was it?*

"Hi!" I say, overly excited to see a friendly, familiar face. "It's Erik right?"

"At your service," he leans in with his elbows on the thick, gleaming bar top.

"Dirty Martini?" he asks, his voice rumbling through me like thunder through a canyon.

"Wow, you remember that?" I ask, as I slide onto a barstool, my tight, white cigarette pants infringing on the smooth transition.

"I never forget a pretty face," he says with a charming smile, "Or Silas' woman," he adds with a raise of one eyebrow.

I smile back, but his words hit my heart like a dull, rusty dagger.

"I'll take a Shiraz please," I say softly.

"Anything you want--especially in those shoes," he says, pushing himself off the bar and turning to retrieve my glass of wine.

Inwardly I'm happy he noticed my shoes, I wasn't taking any chances tonight, I needed to look irresistible to Silas. When I bought them, Devin had told me they were the kind of shoes men picture over their shoulders. I smile weakly at the memory.

Choosing the white suede, cutout stilettos was very purposeful. So was straightening my hair into a sleek, glowing effusion, flowing like a cape down my back. The deep V halter top, that was purposeful too. However, I did layer some necklaces to somewhat conceal the amount of rounded flesh announcing my arrival like a flashing neon sign.

I glance nervously around for Silas, tucked away into the loungy booths, or leaning into the ornately carved bar, or surrounded by beautiful, highly erotic women--tossing their heads back and laughing at his witty jokes.

Erik sets my wine glass in front of me then pours the deep, aromatic wine. I have no doubt it is going be too acidic for me to drink, with all the stomach acid churning in my gut. I thank him kindly then dig into my purse.

"No," he says simply, holding up both hands. To my surprise, he pours a glass for himself then raises it to mine.

"Cheers Jessie," he clinks my glass, then gives his a swirl before taking a sip.

"Are you,…playing tonight?" he asks, puzzled.

"Actually I'm looking for Silas," I admit.

Erik knits his brows together and ponders his answer for a moment before he says simply, "Silas is gone."

"Gone where?" I ask, tasting the disappointment on the back of my tongue.

"He's in Edinburgh, I thought you knew?" he says with barely concealed confusion.

"How long will he be gone?" I ask through clenched teeth, trying not to sound alarmed though my eyes film over with distress.

"Uh, indefinitely. He's looking at properties. Jessie, are you Ok?" he asks, reaching a hand out to gently squeeze my arm.

A cold sweat trickles through me, pooling in my fingertips and making them heavy and clumsy as I hop off the stool, my heels scrambling for purchase.

"Yep, I'm just fine. Thank you for the drink. It was great talking to you--um…uh, goodbye," I pinch out through the tightening clamp that is my throat.

I hurry toward the door, heels tapping briskly on the polished floor and sounding to me, like a death march.

I pitch through the door and spill out into the alley, sucking in deep lungfuls of air. The air, much like my sense of dread, stings my throat, burning and throbbing as I find myself in the noxious exhale of a bearded man.

He drops his cigarette, steps on it and with an insidious glare, swipes his card then tugs the ponderous door open. The man disappears with the soft clang of the door, like a phantom.

Forgoing all semblance of propriety, I sink to the dirty ground in my sleek white pants, crying into the crossed arms that rest on the crest of my knees.

After a while, the glare of the street light makes me realize how puffy my eyes have become as I tip my head back against the brick wall of 1462. My eyelids pillow the light that is refracted in a thousand different directions through my tears.

Reaching for my phone, I hit Silas' number. The ringing is a familiar transition to his distant voicemail. The same as it has been countless times in the last few days.

"Hi, it's Silas, leave a message." BEEP

"Are you kidding me right now?! You're out of the country? What, not taking my calls wasn't enough for you, you…you, have to leave the continent too?!" I'm angry crying now--eyes ringed with smeared mascara and venom in my voice. "You hypocrite! You fucking hypocrite! How could you not hear me out after I gave you the chance to explain your fuck up?" My nose is running now, and my voice cracks as my anger turns to anguish. "Nothing happened--Do you hear me? Nothing…

Nothing happened, you have to believe me. Please, Silas, you have to listen to me. You owe me that."

I end the call, and before thinking better of it, I throw my phone across the alley. It crashes into the opposite brick wall and lands in a broken heap, peppered with scattered pieces of brick and mortar on the cracked asphalt ground.

I sit for a few more minutes until my breathing returns to normal and I can somewhat compose my haggard self. Rising to my feet, I brush the alley debris from my pants and walk over to collect my destroyed phone. It comes as no surprise when I find I am unable to even power it on.

When I walk into my apartment, Devin is nowhere to be found--no doubt, by careful design. I toss my carried shoes into my closet and trudge to the bathroom sink to wash the twelve pounds of smeared makeup from my face.

I feel hollow after chastising myself the entire drive home for leaving such a sniveling message--and on top of that, for breaking my phone, rendering any return call impossible.

I climb into my bed feeling like a whipped dog and stare at the ceiling, thinking of everything at once and nothing at all.

Sunday morning when I finally emerge from my room after a fitful night of no sleep, I slog into the kitchen where Devin and Corey are cheerfully making blueberry pancakes.

"Hi shortcake, I've never seen you with your hair flat ironed, it's pretty," Corey says, popping blueberries into his mouth and navigating around me to the fridge.

"How did it go last night?" Devin asks, though he can read it plainly on my face.

"He wasn't there," then I add, "Can I borrow your phone?"

Closing the bedroom door quietly behind me and clutching Devin's phone to my chest, I sit nervously on the edge of my bed. With trepidation, I dial my number then my password and am rewarded with, "One. Unheard. Message." The anxiety crackles through me like static electricity as I push 1. It's him.

"Jessie, Hi," he says, bright but aloof, "Got your message and I understand your desire to explain. However I am not interested in explanations or excuses. I have Ruby to think about, not just me. Really I should thank you, because the whole situation serves as a good reminder. I need to be so careful with her, you know, to avoid breaking her heart, so, well...just thank you--for the lesson. I needed the reminder." long pause, "Goodbye Jessie."

I'm still sitting on the edge of my bed when Corey knocks quietly and pushes open my door. He sets a plate of pancakes and a glass of orange juice on my dresser then sits down next to me.

"Devin told me." He swipes a strand of my hair behind my ear.

"It's going to be ok." He wraps his arm around me and continues. "Devin doesn't know how to comfort you, it's not his way. But I can tell you really care about Silas. What you need to remember though, is it's human nature to pull away when one becomes hurt or vulnerable. It's a defense mechanism. That's all he is doing, he's trying to protect himself," Corey says in a soothing voice that belies his warrior appearance.

"He won't even let me explain," I say dejectedly.

276

"It's because he can't imagine an explanation where he doesn't get hurt. That's all sweetie. You went down in a fiery blaze of glory--he saw a man close your laptop, a man who was obviously in your hotel room. Then he spends the next, what, ten hours picturing what you are doing? I mean...there really is no other way to spin that, you know?" he says, turning my shoulders to face him better and raising my chin, so I'm looking him in the eyes.

"If it were me and Devin, I wouldn't give up so easily."

"He is out of the country," I admit.

"Then wait," he says, as if the answer is obvious.

"In Scotland...looking at properties."

"Ah. Well. Then there's that," he says with a defeated sigh.

1462 South Broadway

CHAPTER TWENTY-EIGHT
Crazy

On day ten of radio silence from Silas, I'm eating lunch at my desk when Salinger comes in. He deposits himself into the chair across from me. The drama from our trip all but swept under the rug by him, leaving me with the constant feeling of a very large elephant in the room.

"I've decided I need to do something crazy, something reckless," he says, eyes twinkling brightly through his thick rimmed glasses.

I swallow a heavy bite of chicken salad. "So, go skydiving," I suggest, "Or wait, you could just proclaim your love for someone and then pretend it never happened," I say with ever widening eyes.

"No, I've tried both of those. What else you got?" he quips.

"Get a tattoo?"

"Been there."

"Take a vacation?"

"Naw."

"1462?" It's out of my mouth before I can stop it.

"What's 1462?"

"1462 S. Broadway, it's a BDSM club."

Now his eyes widen, "You might be on to something J.B. I'll see you tomorrow," he says, rising from the chair and turning to leave.

I watch him leave while smiling at his nickname for me. He hasn't used it in a long time; it stands for Jessie Belle or Jezebel. He came up with it a few years back when he was trying to guess my middle name during a particularly long road trip.

I am grateful he has kept work as normal as possible but I can no longer look at him and not see his tattoos and scar. I can no longer listen to him and not hear those words--two bells that can't be un-rung.

I push aside my lunch, too unsettled to eat. I had called 1462 when I got to work this morning and was told Silas was due to return in four days. He'd already been gone for over two weeks.

I put my forehead down on my desk and wonder for the millionth time, how am I going to fix this.

CHAPTER TWENTY-NINE
Desperate

Sitting outside Silas' door, I feel pathetic. It's a desperate move, and the knowledge of that further unnerves me. The image that comes to mind is a bleating lamb.

I'm determined for Silas to hear me out--come what may, but he needs to listen to what I have to say. Though I don't relish the confrontation, the necessity of it sits on my chest, like an anvil.

I have been able to glean with hopeful accuracy that his flight, being one of three international flights from Edinburgh, should arrive between 1:55 and 5:20, placing him home between 4:00 and 8:00 this evening. So with dutiful resignation, I open my book.

Hours roll by, I finish my book and toss it aside annoyed I didn't bring something longer...like War and Peace.

Solitaire holds me for another hour until my newly purchased phone runs out of juice.

With an exasperated glance at my watch and a rapidly expanding bladder, I groan, it's after 10:00. My eyelids are growing heavy, and my determination is wavering, as well as the certainty of my calculations.

I shift around for the millionth time and decide to wait until 11:00 or until I have to pee too bad to stay any longer. With my decidedness comes satisfaction, so I tilt my head back against the wall to wait.

When I wake up, I'm awkwardly curled into the fetal position, with my short jean skirt twisted uncomfortably and my shoulder feeling like it had been set in a block of concrete. Initially, I'm confused, while my conscious scrambles for purchase, my eyes dart around.

Within the space of a heartbeat, I realize where I am and a second later, that I have been covered with a chenille throw blanket. I sit up fast, emerging from sleepiness like a clap of thunder.

Silas is sitting on the floor across from me; his knees are bent and supporting his arms, with one wrist clasped in the other hand. He smiles gently, bleary eyed.

"Hi," I muster, hastily smoothing rogue strands of hair out of my face.

"Hi," he says, his face drawn.

"You wouldn't hear me out," I offer, in explanation of my presence. I sound quiet, already defeated.

"I'm listening now," he blinks slowly, steeling himself as he lifts his chin and leans his head back against the wall. His eyes are raised to the ceiling as if praying for strength.

My chin starts to quiver knowing even the truth won't sound good and finding myself with so much to say but at a complete and total loss for words.

"Nothing happened," I say in a whisper.

He nods his head, fidgeting with his watch but offers no reply.

"I know what it looks like and what you think, but you're wrong."

"Do you love him?" he asks, and his voice is not at all familiar.

"Silas, I want to be with you," I say, pleading.

"You didn't answer my question," he says, his voice listless.

"I care about him, but no, I'm not in love with him," I say, my throat tight around the mostly true statement.

"I saw him Jessie, you were...open to him. And now you are going to try to convince me you didn't fuck him? He was in your room, Jessie! I'm not an idiot," he finishes, his voice raised and eyes piercing, giving away his true feelings instead of the stoic facade he has held up so far.

"He thought I left my room card at dinner as an invitation. It was *not*, I didn't even know at that point I had lost it," I speak calmly, evenly. "Can we please talk inside?"

He thinks about it for a long moment, then gives one quick nod as he rises to his feet.

Once inside, I tug off my trendy cowgirl boots and sit on his lustrous sofa, my legs balled beneath me, I watch him pad over to me with two mugs of hot tea, his linen shirt un-tucked and his feet bare.

"Is Ruby here?" I ask.

"She is. I carried her to bed. Luckily she was asleep before we got home."

"Oh," is all I can say. *Luckily she was asleep before she saw you,* is what he meant.

"Jessie, you need to understand something about me. I value trust and honesty above all else in a relationship. I have a daughter to think about, and I don't want her exposed to tenuous or flippant romances."

"Tenuous? Flippant? Is that what we have?" I say, cut off at the knees. "I didn't do anything dishonest, and I *can* be trusted." I hesitate to say more because revealing Salinger's declaration would only cast doubt. Not to mention, we still work side by side, and I can't possibly answer for, or be held accountable for Salinger's feelings for me.

"I was humiliated when he came in. I was shocked. Once he realized his assumption was wrong, he was embarrassed too." *I'm only sorry I didn't come in two minutes later.* "He left, and I cried myself to sleep. There were blackout curtains, so I overslept. That's it."

"I don't know," he says, sipping his tea and sitting forward with his forearms on his knees, as if he is afraid to sit back or get comfortable.

"I know how it sounds, but you have to believe me," I say flatly. After a long silence, I add, "Silas, please. I did nothing to betray your trust."

He sets his tea down on the beveled glass coffee table and sits back before he answers.

"Ok."

"Ok?"

"Ok, I believe you, but that may just be the jet lag. I haven't slept for nineteen hours, and that makes me particularly susceptible to your charms," he smiles weakly.

"Really? Why didn't you listen to me before?" Tears brim in my eyes as I get up and then fold myself into his lap, hugging him fiercely.

He holds me tightly tucked into him. "Trust me Pipes, there is no other version of that story I wanted to hear."

Silas leads me into his bedroom where he promptly falls onto the bed fully dressed. I finally am able to use the bathroom and relieve my distended bladder. When I return, he is face down, sound asleep.

I retrieve the throw blanket from the couch, attempt to undress him, then promptly give up--struggling against his dead weight. I climb into bed still dressed in my short jean skirt and plaid button up.

After covering us both up, I settle back on my side facing him. His arms are shoved under the pillows, his face tender in sleep. While gently scratching his back, I whisper, "Thank you for hearing me out."

He stirs enough to pull me against him, where he holds me tightly, his face resting soundly on my chest. I watch his face settle back into sleep, his strong jaw and structured cheekbones, his perfect nose so masculine, yet soft and gentle.

Watching him sleep and feeling a lump in my throat I can't seem to swallow, I eventually fall asleep. I'm holding his head to me, my fingers laced through his rumpled hair, feeling grateful to be here.

When I wake, I'm in much the opposite position I had fallen asleep in, cradled by his arm into his chest, his fingers wound through my hair. I'm not sure of the time, it's still dark out, and the city lights shine into the bedroom. I don't have the first clue how to darken his windows, so I remain where I am, feeling comfortable, like I belong.

I lay awake, afraid to acknowledge what I know about his trip, but the thought brings tears to my eyes. I give voice to the lump in my throat, "Please don't leave," I whisper into the silence, squeezing the prickle of tears between my eyelids.

Silas tightens his hold on me, announcing he too is awake. He rolls me onto my back, his elbows on either side of me. He lowers his lips to mine, kissing me sweetly.

As though he can taste the fear of him leaving on me, he slowly disengages his mouth, breathing, "I'm not going anywhere."

Grasping my shirt, he ignores the buttons and pulls it over my head, tossing it to the floor. He lowers his mouth to the base of my neck and begins pushing my jean skirt off my hips.

I shove the skirt the rest of the way down and kick it off as he stands and tugs off his own shirt, then his pants.

I'm chilled at the loss of his presence, but his hungry gaze flushes my skin.

"I just want to look at you," he says, with lust simmering in his eyes.

Giving him a coy look, I raise my arms above my head to playfully rest on the pillows. I arch my back causing my nipples to breach the tops of my half-cup, white lace bra.

His stare turns feral as his eyes lock on my breasts, but he doesn't move to close the gap.

I wonder if he realizes the white lace panties I'm wearing are the same ones from our video chat. In an attempt to jog his memory, I raise my knees and spread my legs, so I'm open to him, save for the familiar panties. As a further reminder, I slip a hand just under the lace and begin a slow circular, teasing motion.

No longer satisfied to watch, he grabs my ankles, and in one fluid motion, yanks me to the end of the bed. Kneeling on the floor between my spread legs, he settles himself with my thighs draped over his shoulders.

Using his teeth, he tugs the lace to the side. Feeling the nip of his teeth, I gasp and then moan as his hot mouth takes me.

"God, you taste so good," he keens, while his masterful tongue flutters against my clitoris, infusing me with a voracious need. His tongue, flickering tirelessly, slowly increases the pressure on my clit, causing me to clutch handfuls of the comforter and moan loudly as his focus intensifies. The dedication is almost too much, as my orgasm already begins to build.

"Oh Silas, you're sooooo good," I mew, craning my head back. Minutes later, my release slams into me, jouncing my body recklessly as the spasms in my vagina roll off me in a torrent.

Pulling me deeper into him, his tongue dances against my orgasm, licking, tasting and losing himself in my slippery flesh.

The image of me, nearly naked and spread wide open, with his face buried so deeply into such a private region, feels raunchy and perversely erotic.

He pulls me limply the rest of the way off the bed, and I slither onto him astride his lap as he sits back on his heels.

Breathlessly I say, "You are way too fucking good at that."

He chuckles as he pulls me deeper into his embrace, kissing me with his tangy mouth. I'm limp as he draws me into him. I feel my wet, tender core press into his throbbing erection, pressing it tightly into his belly. The lace of my panties feels sharp and abrasive against my sensitive skin.

He tugs my hair back, craning my neck against his wet mouth as I grind into his shaft, eager for the feel of it.

"I want you so bad," I whisper to the ceiling, my head still wrenched back. I raise myself up above his weighty hardness and slide my panties again to the side.

"Not like this," he says, squaring his shoulders.

"What, don't you like me on top?" I ask playfully, bringing my peeking-out nipples to his face and rubbing my slick vagina against his shaft.

"Not tonight Pipes," he says, leaning up from his knees. With his hands on my hips, he helps me to rise then stands himself. "Tonight, I'm in charge," he says in a deeply commanding voice while shaking the circulation back into his legs.

He lays me back on the bed, sliding his hands down my back, between skin and sheets. With a twist of his fingers, my bra releases. Then with gentle hands he slides the shoulder straps down, peeling the lace from my breasts.

Lowering his head, I can feel his warm breath against my skin as he takes a nipple into his mouth, while simultaneously lowering his hand to slide my panties down.

I raise my hips and help to shove, then kick them off. We are completely naked against one another now. I can feel his leg hair tickle against my newly shaved, smooth skin. The combination of his raspy hair and the sucking tug on my nipple provokes my senses and excites my soul.

He releases my nipple and inches over to flick the other one with his tongue, as he slides his hands up my body then my arms, clasping our palms together above my head. The clutch of our hands feels incredibly intimate as he lowers his mouth to mine.

"I love to feel your tits against my chest, so full, your nipples so hard," he murmurs.

I smile, noticing how they stand up stiff, like the Queen's Guard after his rough flicking and sucking. I'm feeling dizzy with pheromones as he reaches between the bed and nightstand, producing a strap which he swiftly slips over my hand. He pulls it snugly around my wrist before pressing the Velcro into place. A sly smile on his lips, he deftly fastens the other wrist before I find my voice.

"Why am I not surprised you have restraints hooked to your bed," I giggle, struggling a bit to test them and finding them snug.

He drops feather soft kisses from my clavicle, down my body to my inner thigh where he makes slow circles with his tongue and nips with his teeth, all while sliding my leg to the side then binding my ankle.

"At least they're new. I told you, I don't bring women home. Well, now I do," he grins. Once he finishes with my other ankle, he turns to lock the bedroom door with a raise of his eyebrows, not wanting a repeat morning wake-up call from Ruby and Analise.

Looking at me, spread eagle on the bed with the soft glow of the city lights streaming in, he nods his head. Then decides to turn on the light, dimming it to a soft glow. With the huge rusty chandelier above me, lighting my nakedness far more than the city lights, I start to feel shy and very, very open.

I struggle against the restraints but can hardly budge, finding myself securely bound. He smiles again, "Relax, it's normal to panic a little, but you need to trust me."

The need to move, but the free will to do so, taken so succinctly away has an unsettling effect on me.

"This will help," he says, as he lowers a blindfold over my eyes.

Taking deep breaths and trying to calm down, I feel him stretch out next to me. Taking a gentle hold of my chin, he kisses me softly.

After releasing my chin, I feel the backs of his fingernails graze down my side, giving me the shivers. I gasp as the tickle shoots to my nipples like electroshock therapy.

His mouth pulls away. I can feel him propped up next to me. He drags the flat of his palm up my ribs and across my breasts, pressing as he drags across my nipples.

I groan, making him chuckle softly, "You are so responsive to my touch," he says, then flicks a nipple; hard like it was a mosquito on his arm.

Gasping at first in pain, I try to close in on myself, I pull against the restraints in a futile attempt to protect my vulnerable body. However, with the anticipation of another, I lick my bottom lip and draw it in between my teeth. The flick comes again, this time suffusing me with heat.

I feel a soft whisper-like touch starting at the arch of my foot, then fluttering up the inside of my thigh.

"Ahhh, a feather," I say with an exhale.

His response is another chuckle. When he draws the feather across my nipples, I arch my spine, lolling my head back. The tender touch is wispy, too gentle, almost timid. I'm aching for a more assertive touch. The feather tickles down my belly and ever so lightly grazes against my sex.

The touch, so light, causes me to tug against the restraints in frustration, or need, or both.

"Silas," I pant, "Harder."

He slides his hand between my legs, spread so widely by the restraints. He dips his fingers into me then utters, "You are so open to me." Before kissing me aggressively and grasping my clit between two outstretched fingers, pinching gently but firmly.

I lift my head to his rough kiss and capture his bottom lip in my teeth as he maintains his erotic squeeze of my clitoris.

He releases his hold then reaches up to cup my breast. His kisses are feverish as he slides on top of me, his penis pressed sharply against my little bundle of nerves.

"Oh, God," I grind out as I feel his smooth tip breach my opening. I can't see him through the blindfold, but I sense he is looking at me, contemplating, with my legs spread wide, open to him.

The delay tortures me, my inability to move rendering me powerless, waiting. "Please, I need you," I whine, "I'm so ready."

He pulls his tip out. I whimper at the tease, but when I feel the bed shift, I realize he is fiddling with a condom. I feel desperate and needy, my patience wearing thin.

Then I feel him above me again, his hurried breath on my face as he moves his hardness to my splayed opening again. He slides in exquisitely slow, bit by bit. I feel myself stretching with his advance. I'm taut around him as he pushes in a fraction of an inch deeper, the stretch magnifying, widening me, and forcing me open.

He slowly slides back, and then the sublime stretch again, craning me open as he fills me inch by inch. When he is pressed all the way in, I feel like the walls of my vagina have stretched, leaving the sides marbled with the fullness, like an overfilled balloon.

So slow and deep are his movements, that I can feel each time the ridge of his penis scrapes against my G-spot, driving me increasingly wild.

Surprisingly he undoes the Velcro at my wrists as he rocks back and forth. I waste no time wrapping my arms around him, tightly clutching him into me as he grinds his pelvis against my clit with his masterful rocking. Gradually he begins pumping faster. I'm clinging to him so tightly, my fingernails dig into his back trying to pull him deeper into me, the sweat tangy and slippery between us.

Suddenly he sits up, his hard cock slipping free, then I hear the *Snick* of Velcro releasing and then another, *Snick*. "Flip over Pipes, I need to get deeper in you," he says huskily, the voice of a pack-a-day smoker.

Ripping off my blindfold and rolling over, I rise to my hands and knees with Silas behind me. He wastes no time before plunging in, slowly withdrawing then plunging deeply in again.

"Lower your shoulders to the bed Baby; I want your ass in the air," he demands. The angle creates an intensely deep penetration as his penis slams into me like a battering ram, each stroke hitting my G-spot and nearly tearing through it.

He grabs my ass cheeks as he pumps deeply, faster and faster. "Oh, God...Yes!" I scream as he reaches a hand around to press against my clit.

The pressure of his fingers against my clitoris, in tandem with the deep engorging thrusts and the scraping against my G-spot makes me scream out again, "Silas! Yes! Oh Godddd... I'm cuming!"

My orgasm ripples through me, spasms clenching around Silas' shaft, milking his orgasm as he leans his head back, arching deeper into me and moaning through clenched teeth while he rides out his own exorbitant release.

We collapse onto the bed, tangled and embroiled in sweat; panting. After a minute of serene bliss, I say, "Silas, I never knew sex could be so good," I feel embarrassed to have admitted such a thing, but he only smiles.

He edges off, then turns me to him so he can caress my belly, damp with sweat. "We are very good together," he says. He draws a hand up to cup my breast and swipes his thumb across the nipple while nuzzling my neck. "Now that you know we are so good together, we should never be apart," he whispers.

I bring a hand up to hold his cheek, "Then what's this about looking at properties in Scotland?" I mean it to be a challenge but it comes out a whimper. My heart is sinking, I don't understand why he would move now, we have really only just found each other.

I stare blankly at him, my heart beginning to fracture like a frozen glacier ready to drop off into the sea.

"Och, Aye lass, I plan tae open a club. But I weel be takin ye wi me."

1462 South Broadway

AFTERWORD

"Jessie, you are a genius!" Salinger bolts through my office door without even knocking, closing it behind him and dropping succinctly into the chair opposite me.

I look at him over the stack of contracts on my desk and wait for him to continue. He is buzzing like a hive. Then I widen my tired eyes at him and prompt him with a brisk, "What?"

He boils over. "You were so right! 1462 was exactly what I needed."

Blinking slowly and exaggeratedly in surprise, I ask, "You went?!"

"Hell yeah I went! Best night of my life."

"Who let you...How did you...What did they--" I stammer, then ask, "How did you get in?"

"They fucking stripped me naked. Me and a handful of other people and marched us out to an auction block--in front of a huge crowd, naked as the day we were born! Can you believe that? The people in the crowd could touch us however they wanted to, tease us, probe us, test us--" he trails off, unsure of how much he should share with me now that my eyes are as wide as saucers, incredulous that he had indeed gone to 1462.

"Don't look so affronted Jessie, it turns out my prostate checks out just fine," he smiles at his joke, while I gulp at my forgotten coffee; old and cold, it's like thick sludge in my throat. *What have I done?*

AVAILABLE NOW!

Made in the USA
Middletown, DE
09 November 2017